EVA LAURENSON

The Mariner's Legacy

I0593175

## About the Author

Eva Laurenson was born in Berlin, Germany. After studying agricultural sciences at the Humboldt University of Berlin, she studied and worked in the field of animal breeding and quantitative genetics in the Netherlands and Scotland. After earning a PhD, she moved to Australia in 2013, where she wrote and directed screenplays and short theatre plays while continuing to work as a scientist.

In 2022, she is planning to move back to her hometown of Berlin as a fulltime writer.

www.evalaurenson.weebly.com

# Eva Laurenson

# The Mariner's Legacy

## Historical Adventure Novel

A glossary with medieval and seafaring terminology is appended on page 322.

1. Edition
Approved Paperback-Edition November 2022
Copyright © 2020 Eva Laurenson
cub & calf publishing,
Spilstr. 2, 14195 Berlin
All rights reserved
Translation: Eva Laurenson
Cover and Layout: Eva Laurenson
Editing: Michelle Hope
ISBN 978-0-6455135-5-4

For my father,

who shared his love for sailing boats and adventure stories
with me.

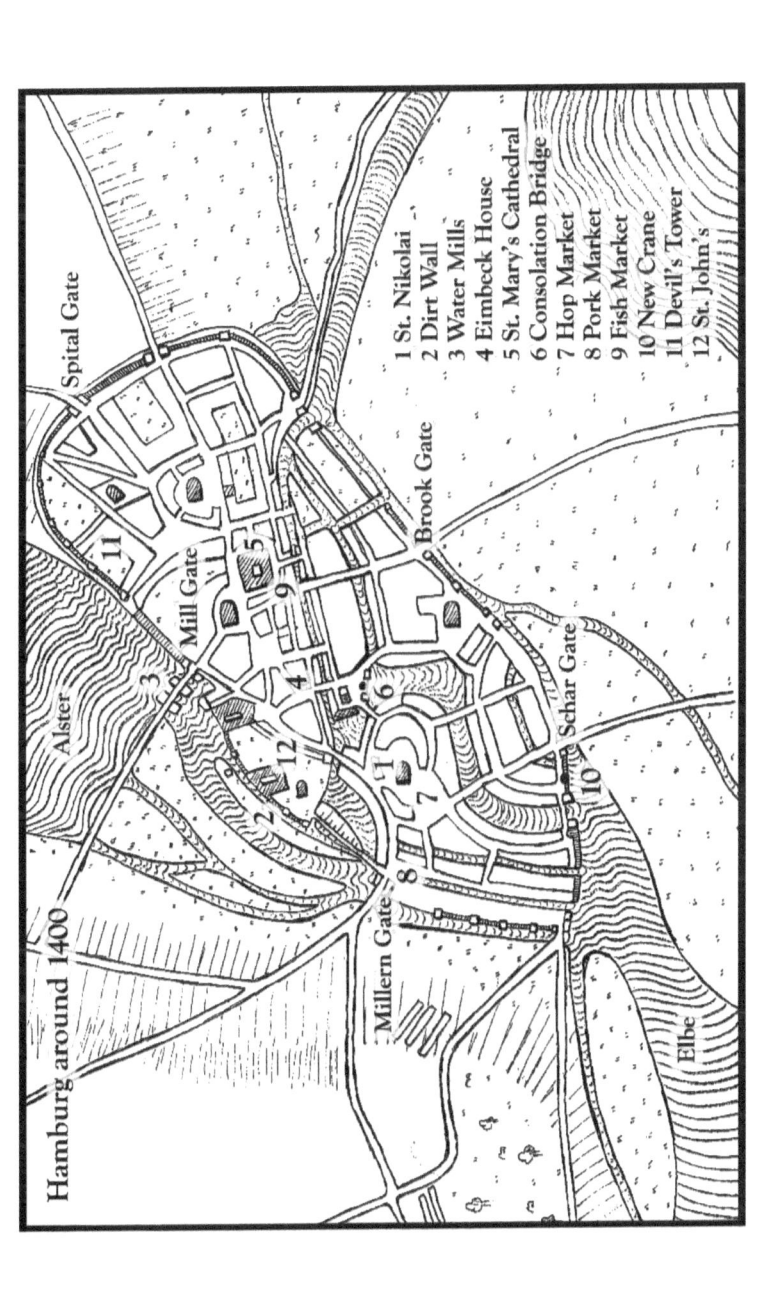

Hamburg around 1400

Spital Gate

Mill Gate

Brook Gate

Schar Gate

Alster

Millern Gate

Elbe

1 St. Nikolai
2 Dirt Wall
3 Water Mills
4 Eimbeck House
5 St. Mary's Cathedral
6 Consolation Bridge
7 Hop Market
8 Pork Market
9 Fish Market
10 New Crane
11 Devil's Tower
12 St. John's

# 1

## The Canal Watcher

"$\mathcal{G}$ met him once, seemed to be a fine fellow," Konrad Netter added to the dragging discussion, because even if it was a topic that everyone liked to talk about, the inhabitants of the small hut behind the Dirt Wall were tired from their day's work.

"So, is it true what old Kathy said? That she found a bag full of oats and a jug of milk on her doorstep? And that her neighbour saw Störtebeker sneaking through the alleys at night with two others?" asked Konrad's young son, Nikolas.

Hannes Lüders, who also lived in the hut with his wife and daughter, made his displeasure known with a whistling breath. "I don't think so. Pirates just think...about themselves, they're like robbers. Just on the sea. They don't care if you've got somethin' or not... Then they take the clothes off ye body."

Lotte, his wife, handed him a bowl of steaming tea which she had brewed from fresh herbs. Their only daughter had already retreated behind the tattered sheet giving her family some privacy in the hut.

Konrad stole a glance as Lotte gently stroked Hannes's back and placed a blanket around his narrow shoulders.

"Papa, don't ye think that was Störtebeker who old Kathy saw?" Nikolas teetered excitedly on the straw bag that was their bedstead.

"I'd trust him to do that. Even if it was quite daring. Mister Bartholomew told me today that the merchants won't tolerate it anymore and asked the Council if there was anything that could be done about it."

"But they help people, why would they want to drive them away?"

The entry of the last occupant of the hut interrupted the conversation between father and son. A draught almost extinguished the small candle on the crooked table under the window. The man, a shipbuilder who had come to Hamburg only last month, placed a stack of wood next to the firepit. He never spoke much and only gave a nod in greeting. He stoked the blaze and then retreated to his corner.

"Papa, tell a story. The one where ye caught the big fish and almost fell into the water!"

Nikolas didn't want to sleep, but his father was tired and his back hurt. Meanwhile, Hannes Lüders rose breathless and, supported by his wife, scurried behind the sheet to their sleeping place. The straw rustled and a coughing fit behind the sheet calmed Nikolas down. Then, only Lüder's whistling breath could be heard.

"Come, bedtime. I must have told ye that story a thousand times already." Konrad pulled the wool blanket up and stretched his back straight. Nikolas blew out the candle and crawled under the frayed cloth. Konrad Netter squeezed his young son tightly, his son, who had the same blond hair and blue eyes as his mother.

With a heavy heart, he thought back to how they had wanted children at the time, a whole bunch at the height of

their infatuation. Back then, when they were still living behind the dike, had a few sheep and lived from crab fishing.
But the years of hard work on the crab cutter had exhausted
Konrad's body. They had moved to the city in the hope of
finding easier work here, but fate had provided something
different for the small Netter family.

After years of childlessness, they had a son, but Margaret
Netter was given little time on earth to enjoy the late happiness. The birth had been too strenuous, and only a few days
later, Konrad had to bury his beloved wife. And then the
church wanted to take the boy to an orphanage. The capitular of St. Mary promised to give him a good education, but
Konrad resolutely resisted. He would not send his only child
to a shaveling school but would teach him everything he
knew himself. He had made this decision one evening in the
Wild Boar, where he tried to drown his pain over the death
of his wife in beer. A sailor by the name of Klaus Störtebeker, who was now one of the most feared pirates of the West
Sea, had appealed to his conscience.

It had been hard years, hard work, and hard trouble to
raise an infant without a mother or nurse. But Nikolas was
strong, and so they had spent the last seven years in this hut
without having been separated for even a single day. The boy
had not absorbed his longing for the sea from his mother's
milk, but with every story Konrad told him. For every cog
that left the port of Hamburg heavily laden and with bellied
sails, the yearning for faraway places became stronger in the
little boy.

The pleasant warmth that radiated from the small living
body next to him finally made Konrad sink into a deep,
dreamless sleep.

Nikolas, however, slid with an alert mind into a dream-world in which he took goods from the greedy moneybags with his sabre in hand. To great cheer, he steered his ship to Hamburg, where his father lifted him on his shoulders with a proudly swollen chest and led him to the Dike Street for a bowl of spicy pig's feet.

The next morning was danker and wetter than even the night had been. Dew had bound the dust of the streets, and small drops shone on the blades of grass that ventured out between cracks in houses and streets, trying to catch some warmth and light. But it promised to be a beautiful spring day. Already, the sun sent its first invigorating rays over the fields and meadows at the gates of Hamburg, where the dew slowly rose as fog.

"Now, come on. You can gawk later!" Konrad was on his way to work and had little to spare for this weather, which caused his joints to hurt. It was hard for Nikolas to break away from the view through the Millern Gate, as he believed that he could see figures sneaking away through the fog. Were they pirates? He longed to follow the shadows, but his legs obeyed his father's call.

They passed the Hop Market, which was still quiet and vestal, and by St. Nikolai. From the Hop Market, they finally turned into the Dike Street, where Mister Bartholomew's warehouse lay. Mister Bartholomew was a well-respected and wealthy patrician. As a member of the Council, he had taken on the task of controlling the trade that was conducted through the Nikolai canal. This also included guaranteeing the navigability of the canals for the barges. Seven years ago, Mister Bartholomew hired Konrad, who had been serving him well ever since as a canal watcher. Konrad was not only responsible for the Nikolai canal but also for the Alster canal up to the Small Alster and for all the little connecting waterways between.

The canals were of the utmost importance for the transport of goods between the port and the warehouses in the city, and their water was also used for washing and cooking by thousands of people. They gathered up all the rubbish from the city, which was thrown or washed in with the rain, and it was fortunate that the water was exchanged daily through the tide of the river Elbe.

But not everything was torn away from the low tide. Silt and all sorts of smelly waste were deposited, clogging and polluting the canals and the surrounding air. It was the task of the canal watcher to keep the canals free to ensure a sufficient water depth for shipping traffic.

Every day, Konrad had to descend into the water and the mud. Armed with a long rod to push the mud onward, a bucket, a rope, and a winch, he had to ensure that the canal remained usable. This was no less tedious and exhausting than working on a crab cutter, but he had no choice if he wanted to guarantee his and his son's survival. An official letter from the city allowed him access to the yards of the merchants, brewers, tanners, and, in principle, to any house built directly on a canal. The payment was meagre and his reputation in the city was only slightly above that of a beggar, but it allowed him to live in the city as a free man.

Konrad found Mister Bartholomew deeply in thought and with a wrinkle of sorrow on his forehead. He waited reverently in the door of the warehouse until the trader addressed him.

"Ah, Konrad, there you are. Come closer, come closer!" From one moment to the next, all signs of sorrow in the old

trader's face had disappeared behind an expression of be-
nevolence. "How are you doing this morning?"

"I won't complain, Mister Bartholomew."

Konrad approached, but without getting out of his slightly
bent posture. For years, it had been less due to his deference
than to his stiff limbs.

"Papa, I think I saw pirates!"

"Ah, there he is, the little whirlwind. And you say you've
seen pirates? Here in the city?" Mister Bartholomew bent
down to Nikolas, who had stormed into the store and was
now shyly clinging to his father's legs.

"Hullo, Mister Bartholomew," Nikolas greeted the old
merchant and politely shook his hand.

"Well, if you've seen them, let's hope that the bailiffs will
see them and fix these dawdlers," Mister Bartholomew continued. "Unfortunately, our lord councillors and the rest of
the Hanseatic League seem blind to the danger and even pay
these accursed Likedeelers for their raids. It is only a matter
of time before they no longer only pounce on Danish merchant ships but also befoul the whole of the West Sea!"

Nikolas had already planned to contradict him and to
vent his sympathies with the passionate words of a child's
soul, but Konrad, who sensed what was brewing in his son,
put an iron hand on the boy's shoulder. Nikolas knew, without so much as a word, that he had to keep his mouth shut.
And so he did, but he rushed out of the store and didn't
show his face for the next few hours.

Mister Bartholomew's attention, meanwhile, had focused
on a strong lad who was wearing polished clothes and
plucked at his neckerchief. Although he looked highly respectable in his garb, he did not seem comfortable in it. After
a short conversation, the two men hugged awkwardly, and as

the younger man stalked past Konrad to get outside, he recognized the striking similarity between the two.

"My son is on his way to Bruges today to polish off the last rough edges. I showed him everything I could, but the rascal has ideas in his head which will hopefully be sorted out with a change of location. Well, looks like someone else has made a bolt for it?" It was only now that Mister Bartholomew noticed that Nikolas was no longer there, but this did not keep him for long. The boy rarely stayed in one spot, be it to climb into a granary, to throw stones into the river, or to scrounge small cakes and pastries from Missus Toni that were burned around the edges.

"Now to us. Last week's storms have swept a lot of branches into the Alster, and I don't have to tell you how problematic this is." They walked through the well-sorted storage area to a wooden door in the back, which Mister Bartholomew opened. Both men looked directly at the Nikolai canal, whose water still flowed a few feet below the door.

"Do you see up there where the canal makes a bend? A branch is stuck. It must go, otherwise it will soon stink to high heaven."

"Consider it done. I can do that from the bridge there," Konrad said, and was relieved that he didn't have to wade through the knee-deep water so early in the morning.

Nikolas was still gone when Konrad started his first assignment. But he was not worried about the boy. Since Nikolas was able to walk, he was so well known and popular with all the tradesmen along the canals, and especially amongst the women, that Konrad hardly needed to worry about him when he went to work. So, Nikolas grew up amid barrels full of beer, sacks of spices, and bales of the finest fabrics from all over the world. He watched craftsmen and traders at work and was given small treats by the bakers and shopkeepers, who sighed rapturously when he looked at them with his bright-blue eyes. But he preferred to have his father tell stories about the sea when they strolled hand in hand past the canals to look for rubbish. One day, Konrad would take his son to the coast and show him the vastness of the ocean that the boy never tired of dreaming about.

In the mud that had piled up behind the branch, Konrad discovered a shiny, perfectly rounded blue shard of glass. He fished the shard out and put it in his pocket to give Nikolas later. Many times, small shiny things could be found in the filth between wasting chicken bones and rotting wood, if you only looked for them. For his son's sixth birthday, he had given Nikolas a small wooden box, which the boy kept like a treasure. For it was a treasure for him, a pirate treasure.

Usually, Nikolas watched his father from the safe shore as he laboriously poked in the mud and collected every rusty nail and metal button for him. They had also found a few halfpennies once, which were now set aside together with the shards of glass, nails, and buttons in the small wooden box for an emergency.

Today, however, Nikolas remained missing for a long time. Konrad had already worked his way up to the Small Alster. The tide was slowly coming back now, but the waterwheels in the Alster canal still rattled quickly and without ceasing. Only one of the grain mills stood still. A branch had become stuck in the mill wheel, and now the water slammed swirling and foaming against the wooden shovels without propelling them.

"There you are again," Konrad said as Nikolas appeared by his side. "I still have to pull the branch out there and then we can have lunch. The tide is coming back anyway."

"Good," Nikolas replied monosyllabically.

Konrad set aside the rod and bucket, attached one end of the rope to a shore bollard, and placed the other end in large loops around his shoulder. Then he carefully climbed down the embankment and made his way through the restless water towards the jammed mill wheel. Slippery stones on the ground made it difficult to walk, and he was almost completely soaked when he lost his balance entirely. He went underwater. His thoughts circled, and instinctively he held his breath. He tried to find a foothold, but the current pulled him away and pushed him with force against the mill wheel he had planned to free. Desperately, Konrad tried to reach the surface, but his strength left him faster than the air left his lungs.

It was only when Konrad did not show up after what felt like an eternity that Nikolas began to scream for help. A tanner, who had stepped out of his hut in time, stopped him from jumping into the water. Eventually, Nikolas ran onto the mill bridge and discovered his father underwater. He lay on his stomach and stretched his hand out, but he couldn't even reach the surface with his fingertips. With every heartbeat in his small chest, his father slipped away from him. He was so close and yet out of reach. Tears burned in Nikolas's eyes, but no sound breached his tight throat. If only he had stayed with his father, they surely would have reached the Small Alster earlier, when the water was lower. A bunch of onlookers had gathered on the shore, but no help came for the drowning man.

Konrad's strength waned. In his ears, he heard a roar that reminded him of a mighty storm on the sea. And then he saw the blurred face of his son through the water. The spring sun shone through the clouds and flooded the child's face. The roar died down, the light became brighter, and the face changed. His wife smiled at him and reached out her hand.

It took an hour before they managed to pull the body of the canal watcher out of the water. Nikolas had been led away by a friendly merchant, screaming and crying. He had not seen them pulling his father ashore, had not looked into his lifeless face, and did not yet understand that his life would never be the same.

The news of the death of the canal watcher spread like wildfire. Nikolas was sitting in the tanner's small kitchen and spooned a thin soup when the door opened and the candles flared up. Mister Bartholomew, who felt responsible for Nikolas, had sent a messenger to the St. Nikolai School, and so the craftsman brought in a young man in a cowl that Nikolas had never seen before.

# 2

## Teaching and Learning

$\mathcal{T}$he stranger was a young clergyman named Matthias, who was introduced to Nikolas as a lecturer at the St. Nikolai School. Like in a dream, Nikolas followed the man through the streets. The hammering of the smithy clanged muted in Nikolas's ears as if the sound penetrated a layer of water. The bartering of the traders rang foreign, and the swooshing of the canals had fallen silent. Instead of passing by the tanners behind St. John to get to his home on the Dirt Wall, Matthias directed them to the Hop Market. Nikolas was too preoccupied sorting through his options for burring his father and his means to bring up the money for the rent of his bedstead in the little hut to notice where they were heading. Matthias spoke kindly, but the words flew past the boy. If he had listened, he would have learned that by God's grace and, of course, thanks to the charity of the canonicus scholasticus, he would now live and learn as a scholar at the St. Nikolai School. He didn't object when he was shown a bed in a dorm room and lay down with numb limbs without touching the scarce supper or awaiting the arrival of the other occupants of the dorm.

Hours later, Nikolas awoke in an unknown room, and panic unfurled in him. He called for his father, but the voices that answered from the darkness were as alien to him as the night's shadows. A candle was lit, and a young man in a simple brown cowl came over.

"Calm down, boy. You are in the dormitory of the school to Nikolai. Your father cannot come. Sleep now," he whispered, and Nikolas recognized him as the lecturer of hours earlier.

A little reassured, he stopped crying, and when the young clergyman left, Nikolas looked around in the dark. He was not lying on a straw bag on the floor but in a wooden sleeping box. Besides his, twenty other such bedsteads stood side by side in the room, and in the moonlight, he spotted in each one a figure.

Nikolas recalled that Matthias had taken him to the St. Nikolai School, where he had passed by only that morning with his father. But he also remembered that his father had drowned in the Alster, and a sober apprehension told him that this would now become his new home. But first he had to bury his father and fetch his meagre belonging from the hut, especially his treasure chest. Sadness swamped him at this thought. Who would now go on treasure hunts with him and tell him stories about the sea? He sat on the edge of his bed and supressed his sobs. Eventually, he curled back up on his straw mattress and wrapped his arms around himself. What could he do at this nightly hour? They had surely brought his father to a nearby cloister until the funeral could be arranged. First thing tomorrow morning, he would walk to St. John to ask for help. This plan gave Nikolas some security, and without realizing it, he fell back asleep.

He had only slept for a few hours when Matthias reappeared and woke him up. He was given a brown cowl, which he pulled over his shirt, and together with the other boys and men, they went out into the night.

"Where're we goin'?" Nikolas asked the lanky boy next to him. But he only got a shake of the head in response. "I'm Nikolas, and you?" Nikolas tried again, but this time, he was grabbed by the ear and pulled aside.

He had not noticed a thin figure approaching, and now he stared terrified into a pale face. Waxy skin stretched tightly over the haggard head, making it look like a skull in the candlelight.

"The scholars are not allowed to speak until after the morning prayers," the walking-dead man hissed at him before continuing on to the church.

Hot protest rose in Nikolas; he was not a scholar, no one had asked if he wanted to be one. But as quickly as the anger had come, it left again, and he hurried to join the group in the darkness.

In the church, Nikolas looked at the other boys from his dormitory. They were all around fifteen years old, grown tall, with arms, legs, and noses that still seemed disproportionate and some with nasty pus-picks on their faces. Further forward sat the older scholars, who were trained for ecclesiastical duties. Nikolas had seen many of them on parades through the city, where they drew attention in fun disguises to collect donations and bring the word of the Bible to the people. He had always liked the processions and envied the students for the ensuing feasts. If the infinite gravity of grief and loneliness had not captured him so much, he would have been looking forward to taking part in the processions himself now.

After an hour of Mass with monotonous psalms, his grief had given way to leaden fatigue, but Nikolas was proud that he had not nodded off like so many of the other students.

They got a few hours of sleep before being woken up again for Mass. Nikolas wanted to set his plan from last night in motion and walk to St. John to take care of his father, but the pale man who had frightened Nikolas before waited for him at the gate.

"Nikolas, come here." He waved to him. Instead of the brown cowl that Nikolas and the other boys, including Matthias, wore, the pale man was dressed in a deep-black cowl with a white neckerchief. "I see you have already joined the group for church. This is laudable."

"Had nuffing else to do." Nikolas tried to hide his discomfort and his true intentions behind an uncouth answer.

The thin man examined the little boy, who apparently showed no respect. "First of all, you will address me as Master Deubel. I am the canonicus scholasticus here, and it is only out of lenity and kindness that I have welcomed you here at my school. Furthermore, Mass is of the utmost importance for the scholares sub jugo, in case it should so happen that you have something else to do."

"I think, since I kno' ye name now, it's prob'ly only right to use it. And Mass is so early, I have nuffing else to do then anyways," Nikolas pondered aloud and quickly added a "Master Deubel".

"Your language, help heavens, I will have a lot to do with you," the canonicus scholasticus exclaimed, dismayed. He looked disheartened at the bare feet of the boy. "So much could have gone in the right direction if your father had not insisted on educating you himself. Even if your mother were still alive, you couldn't expect much more than a warped street boy. What else should come from a rheumatic fisherman and a farmer's yokel?"

"My mother was no yokel!" screamed Nikolas, drumming his little fists against the wide cowl, which enveloped the master's lean body so that he hardly knew any of the blows.

It felt good to give his emotions full bent, but Master Deubel grabbed the angry boy by the wrists and dragged him to the school building, where he locked him in a small chamber.

"Other boys your age have already spent a year learning from a master or been sent to a school. I can only hope that a monastery will quickly come forward to take you in, because I see no future here for you," he thundered before locking the door from the outside.

"Let me out! I must go to St. John, bury my father!" Nikolas screamed, but no one answered.

He spent hours in the chamber without water and bread. When he stood on tiptoes, he could see through a small window into a courtyard with a gnarled pear tree on the opposite side. It was dusk when Matthias finally opened the door again. Nikolas thought that the day must be almost over, and if he hurried, he could make it to the cloister before sunset, but that was not the case.

The lecturer led him along a dark corridor illuminated only by an almost burnt-out candle at the end. Doors lined both sides. Matthias opened the last door, and bright light from several oil lamps dazzled Nikolas. In the room sat the boys from his dormitory, who, like him, were considered scholares sub jugo, as well as a few of the older pupils. To his dismay, Master Deubel sat at the desk in front of the class with an unmoved face.

"I see you have calmed down again," said the teacher.

Nikolas was pushed further into the class by the young clergyman before he closed the door behind him. He remained silent. He would have preferred to simply run away, but as this was out of the question, he just stared at the stone tiles under his feet.

"As long as there is no place in a monastery for you, you will participate in the lessons. I assume you can neither read nor write, so we'll start with basic exercises." The canonicus scholasticus took a slate and drew signs on it. "This is the letter *A* and the first letter of the Latin alphabet. In Greek, the first letter is alpha, which also means *the beginning*. The second letter is *B*." This way, the schoolmaster went through the entire Latin and Greek alphabets until he started again and, this time, asked Nikolas to tell him the name of the letter he had written on the slate. Nikolas was persistently silent. He also refused to name the second and third letters, despite recognising them. Secret giggles broke the silence while the canonicus scholasticus waited for an answer. He turned around and, like a hawk, swooped down on the troublemaker.

"Why are you laughing?" he asked the terrified scholar. When he did not get an answer, he tore the parchment from the pulpit, where the student was making a copy of John's Revelation. "The letters are all different in size," the master bristled. "Left hand on the table!"

The boy had to endure five cane strikes, while the others lowered their heads, only casting hidden glances at him. Afterwards, Master Deubel asked Nikolas to sit at the free desk next to the troublemaker.

"If you execute your lessons satisfactorily, you will be allowed to visit your father's grave tomorrow," said the master after giving the boy a penetrating look.

Wary, Nikolas looked up from his desk. Master Deubel gave him pen, ink, and parchment and told him to copy the

Latin and Greek letters from a template for the rest of the day, which Nikolas carried out diligently.

After early-morning Mass the next day, Matthias accompanied Nikolas to the graveyard, but the gravediggers were already filling the hole. They had buried his father in an unmarked pauper's grave in the shadow of the Devils Tower. Mute, Nikolas stepped towards one of the gravediggers, and after some hesitation, the man passed his shovel to him. Matthias let Nikolas proceed as well, and so he bid his father farewell, until the soil had been put back in its place above the corpse.

On the way back, Nikolas felt sobered and old. What would he do now for the rest of his life? His question was answered soon when he was ordered to continue his lessons with Master Deubel. So, the first weeks passed in Nikolas's new life, and because he often refused to answer, especially when he felt he was being treated unfairly, he was not spared the cane either. He never got praise from Master Deubel, even though he soon learned the art of reading and writing and brought the letters onto the paper with such ease and momentum that it was a pleasure to read the old texts again through his pen. As a result, Nikolas was quickly sent to other classes, where he learned ancient Greek and was introduced to the basics of philosophy and theology. These were taught by Doctor Schlegel.

Doctor Schlegel had already taught in Tours and Toulouse, and Nikolas liked him the most, as his lessons in astrology and geography were the most fascinating for the boy. The two teachers were supported by the lecturer Matthias, who had only recently completed his licentiate, which enabled him to prepare for his degree as a master.

Everyday school life and the strict daily routine with regular churchgoing left Nikolas hardly any time to hang on to his thoughts and his grief. He had also been sent to the church choir, where he had to sing every Sunday and on high holidays in St. Mary's Cathedral.

After a few months, Nikolas had finally become accustomed to life as a scholar and adapted to the unusual daily rhythm and set tasks. A message that he would be accepted in a monastery never arrived. He was less tired and had also made friends with the other scholars. If an assignment bored him, or if he completed it faster than the other students, he got lost in his dreams again. It took him several months before he allowed himself to daydream about his fantastic ideas. His favourite fantasy was still to sail the seas and be greeted with cheers in every port. But his father would no longer be there to proudly embrace him.

Summer got hot, and the younger scholars sneaked out more often in the afternoons to have water fights with the other children from the city. If they were caught, or even late to the next class or Mass, they were sent to bed hungry and had to copy psalms in their free hours. The worst punishment was to be placed in solitary confinement and to carry out their tasks without contact. But these days passed as well, and not even the meanest penalties stopped Nikolas from wandering through the city whenever possible, as he had done in the past.

When he was sent to the yard for punishment or to contemplate, he climbed into the pear tree. From there, he could see the masts of the ships at their anchorages, snack on juicy pears in autumn, and then jump like a cat over the wall when no one was looking. Most of the time, he walked down to the harbour and watched the ships slowly glide away with

the stream of the Elbe, to somewhere where there were wonderful adventures to experience.

The years went by, and Nikolas was now one of the best in
his class, surpassing even the older scholars in knowledge,
and he spoke Latin and Greek fluently. He still came into
conflict with Master Deubel regularly and had by now voluntarily spent one or two nights in the open, which had only
prompted more punishments. But so far, he had always
come back. Only Doctor Schlegel had correctly recognized
the boy's interest and capabilities, and he increasingly inflamed the boy's thirst for knowledge by giving him new readings. Although not permitted by Master Deubel, he gave
Nikolas some books from his private collection from time to
time. Nikolas enthusiastically devoured the works of Aristotle
and Eratosthenes and Ptolemy and spent entire summers
wandering along the banks of the river and reproducing the
observations of the ancient Greeks. But the more he learned,
the greater his longing to go out into the world and to escape
the constraints and duties of school became. He looked wistfully at the cogs who made their way to Bruges, London, or
Reval, and he still dreamed of the free life of a pirate.

One winter, when Nikolas had been at the St. Nikolai School
for almost six years, the Hanseatic cities met to stop the pirates on the West Sea once and for all. Mister Bartholomew
would have been pleased with this, but the old trader had
died two years earlier, and his son, returned home from
Bruges, had taken over the enterprise. A few months later,
Nikolas watched as the largest fleet he had ever seen in the
port of Hamburg assembled to put an end to Störtebeker's

Victual Brethren. Four weeks later, the ships left supported by war fleets from Lübeck and Bremen.

Nikolas later heard that the battle lasted only an hour; two ships had been seized and eighty pirates killed. Only a small group was captured; the rest had saved themselves by swimming to shore.

Not only Nikolas, but also all the other inhabitants of the city, who were sympathetic to Störtebeker, feared for the well-being of their folk hero. The few messages that leaked through were so contradictory that it could only be said with certainty that Störtebeker was not amongst those captured. Over the next weeks and months, Nikolas listened to every little rumour that gave him cause for hope. He imagined how he would meet the disguised Störtebeker and be the only one to recognize him. He would hide him until the pirate had found a new crew, and then he would set sail with him and finally be free.

But although Nikolas had sneaked after many masked figures, he got disappointed each time and found that it was mostly day labourers who wanted to visit the next brewery unrecognized by their wives and neighbours.

On one of these occasions, he even took a beating from a girl. He had once again followed a man to a small hidden taproom and ducked between beer barrels and baskets full of apples when a foot kicked him, accompanied by shouting: "A thief!" He jumped up and faced a girl, who threw a right-hander, which he only just managed to dodge. But as he ran away, an apple hit him so hard in the head that he fell forward, crashed against the next wall, and slumped to the ground.

It seemed to him like an eternity during which he lay there staring into the sky until a large, broad-shouldered man bent over him.

"What have ye done again, Mathi? Did you have to floor him right away?"

"He wanted to steal our fruit, so I just gave him what he wanted. How could I know that a rotten apple would strike him down so easily?"

"Are you alright, my boy?" the man asked.

Nikolas stood up and looked into the man's friendly face and then into the girl's as she threateningly juggled another apple in her hand.

He didn't want to have to explain what he was doing behind the baskets. So, he took to his heels, pulled his head between his shoulders in fear of another flying apple, and ran as fast as he could.

After this incident, he no longer sneaked into any alleys but confined himself to listening to the gossip at the markets and the conversations in the harbour.

# 3

## Up and Away

$\mathcal{D}$espite the victory of the Hanseatic League and a peace agreement with the East Frisian tribal princes, the Victual Brethren continued to be on the prowl. One of them was Klaus Störtebeker, who had been given a letter of marque from Count Albrecht of Holland and resumed his looting in the West Sea.

Exhilarated by the well-being of his hero and the joy of new adventures, Nikolas spent increasingly more time at the harbour with his dreams, neglecting his readings more and more.

The Hanseatic League had also learned that Störtebeker and his consorts were back at sea. So, a year after the first battle, they sent out another powerful fleet to crush the pirate gangs once and for all. This time, the fight lasted a whole day and many men on both sides lost their lives. But seventy-three Victual Brethren and their ringleader were taken into custody. The followers of Klaus Störtebeker rumoured that he had been caught alive only because a fishing net had been thrown over him and he had therefore been unable to defend himself to the last breath. Otherwise, of course, he would have chosen the honourable pirate death in battle.

The prisoners were locked in the basement dungeons of Hamburg's city hall. Nikolas passed by every day hoping to catch a glimpse of the first real pirates in his life. In his imagination, he saw himself stealing the key to the cells from the guards, passing it to the prisoners through a window, and then hijacking the largest ship in the harbour alongside Störtebeker. But the guards were so cautious that he did not even see the bars of the window behind which the delinquents were located.

The verdict did not surprise anyone, and yet a roar of outrage could be heard in the streets and alleys of Hamburg. Guilty on all counts was the sentence, and the punishment could therefore only be: death by beheading. October 20, 1401, was not only intended to put an end to Störtebeker's earthly existence but would also steer Nikolas's life in a completely different direction than Master Deubel had envisioned.

It was a cloudy grey morning, but a restlessness lay hidden under the fog that had never pervaded the city before. Nikolas sat tensely at a table noting down a letter that Master Deubel dictated to him. In the letter, the master asked to enrol one of his scholars at the Cathedral School in Cologne. Nikolas often looked out the window and heard the sloshing and tussle of hundreds of feet on the street, all of which were making their way to the same place—the small Elbe meadow and the Grasbrook, where the execution was to be held. Eventually, it became quiet in the alleys and only from time to time could Nikolas hear the quick steps of a straggler. He became increasingly nervous. It simply could not be that the man who had occupied his thoughts so much in the last few years and had given his life a meaning outside the school walls should lose his head today.

The letter was finished, and Nikolas almost signed off with *Klaus Störtebeker.* Now, he was supposed to go to the class of Doctor Schlegel, but even the lecture on astrology did not keep him on the school bench. He sneaked down the stairs and carefully opened the gate to the yard to avoid the squeaking of the door hinges. He hustled to the pear tree, which was now heavy with golden fruit, but even these did not interest him today. Quietly, he jumped down into the small lane behind the school wall and peeked carefully around the corner to the deserted Hop Market. In the shadow of the Nikolai Church, he ran nimbly across the square and took the next bridge at the New Crane over to the Schal Gate and out of the city.

The city lay like a ghost town, but they jostled on the Grasbrook. Nikolas pushed through the crowd until he couldn't get any further. When he stood on the tips of his toes, he could see the executioner and the knacker. A day earlier, a large square had been fenced off, which no one was allowed to enter. At the other end, Nikolas recognized the convicts, but he did not know which of them was Störtebeker. The indictment and the verdict had by now been read out and two wishes had been granted to the ringleader. The first was already fulfilled, and therefore the condemned stood in front of the block in their most beautiful robes, which were otherwise only worn by the high lords of the city. The mention of the second wish caused the air to vibrate with tension and whispers. Klaus Störtebeker had been granted the right to pardon all those of his brothers-in-arms, whom he could still walk past after his own beheading. The wish sounded so ludicrous that no objection had been given.

For the first and last time in his life, Nikolas was able to snatch a look at the greatest pirate he knew. Störtebeker was a tall red-haired man whose nose appeared to have been broken several times, making him look all the more daring. He was led from the ranks of his comrades to the place of execution, and when he finally knelt to surrender to his fate, he disappeared again from Nikolas's view. The executioner pulled his sword out, and a shiver and screaming ran through the spectators as the dull sound of metal on wood could be heard. A tense silence ensued in which the assembled crowd waited for the beheaded man to rise and take his very last walk.

The cloud cover burst open, and the sun dazzled Nikolas, a big man pushed himself into his line of sight, and as he wanted to edge himself further forward, Nikolas was grabbed by the ear and pulled out of the crowd. He caught one last glimpse of a finely dressed man slowly moving inside the square, but he could not see if the man still had his head or not.

"I thought I'd find you here," Master Deubel shouted in anger as he dragged him through the streets back to the school. "But I'm going to drive the pirate stories out of you once and for all. You will never go to the port again and spend hours looking at ships. I haven't travailed with you for years for this. When the answer from Cologne arrives, you will set off immediately!"

"But it was Klaus Störtebeker—" Nikolas couldn't finish the sentence as a resounding slap hit him across the face. And then he was given a hiding like he had never received before.

Sitting was a torment as he squatted with a sore bottom and bruises in front of a stack of books for the rest of the evening. Master Deubel sat opposite him and stared at him grimly.

The lines he read and copied did not penetrate Nikolas's brain. A mess of thoughts swamped everything. Had Klaus Störtebeker gotten up and passed by his mates? Were they freed? Would there ever be pirates again who shared their loot with the poor and bravely faced adventures? Eventually, the letter to the cathedral school in Cologne came back to his mind. Only then did he realize that *he* was the scholar to be sent there. Although the cathedral school was one of the most prestigious in the world and all the students scrambled to be accepted there, Nikolas only felt desperate repulsion. He would most definitely not go to Cologne and spend the rest of his life with books. He wanted to get out, get out to sea and out into the world. He wanted to experience adventures he had only ever dreamed of. He would continue the legacy of Störtebeker and become the greatest pirate on earth. He would run away and sign on to a ship.

"That's enough for today." The voice of the master jarred him out of his rebellious thoughts. "If all goes well, you will leave for Cologne in two weeks."

Nikolas stopped briefly before turning to walk outside. There it was again, this feeling of reluctance, and he decided that tonight, when everyone was asleep, he would go out to look for adventures.

Nikolas didn't have to wait long until the even breaths of his classmates in the dormitory told him that the moment that he had dreamed of for years, and that suddenly scared him so much, had come. But at the thought of a life behind church walls, his body rose almost by itself. Barefoot and shivering, he stood in the dormitory and thought about what he could take with him. But there was nothing that belonged to him or would be useful to his plan. He had never seen his little pirate chest again, which he had filled with his father. It had probably been thrown over the Dirt Wall by Lotte Lüders with all the other rubbish. If she had been wise and investigated it, she might have found the halfpennies and bought half a loaf of bread for her family. So, Nikolas only pulled his brown cowl on, laced his shoes, and tried not to think of anything more while he climbed into the pear tree one last time and disappeared into the fog that had again spread over the city.

His feet carried him determinedly to the harbour. It was only when he could hear the water hitting the quay wall that he thought that perhaps no one at the harbour was awake and ready to leave at nighttime. He would have to hide somewhere for the next few hours so as not to be picked up by the city's bailiffs.

As he pondered this, he bent around a corner and saw the glow of lanterns dancing through the fog. He ducked behind a pile of wood and crept closer. Eventually, he could see men loading a small barge. The men looked around and spoke quietly to each other, and Nikolas decided that what he saw could not be an official loading of a ship. He sneaked ahead to overhear two men who were leaning idly against a wall.

"The ship belongs to him. So, we let him be captain," one of the men said.

"For now. Time will tell what we must think of him. And then we know what to do," the other replied.

A third man with a parchment in his hand stepped into the light and passed so close by Nikolas that he could have touched his boot.

"Is this all from the storage, Derek?"

"Yes, Captain," the first man replied.

"Well, good, then make haste to get on board, and let's show the moneybags that they can separate Störtebeker's head from his body, but his spirit lives on within us."

The two men turned around and disappeared onto the barge.

Nikolas could hardly believe his luck, and without thinking, he gave up his hiding place and approached the captain, who was still standing on the shore studying his parchment. The captain looked up when he heard the steps.

"Who is there?" he asked into the fog, holding his lantern higher.

"I'm here," Nikolas replied when the captain looked in the wrong direction.

"Oh. What? You're just a little laddie. What are you doing out here at this hour?"

"I'm looking for what you're going to do."

"So! And what are we going to do, and what do you have to do with it, you little jackanapes?"

"You want to take on the legacy of Störtebeker and seize this ship." Nikolas pointed to the only vessel in the harbour where a small light was burning.

"First of all, this is my ship, so there is no talk of seizing, and the other is a mere slander. I should give you a beating for it."

These words nettled Nikolas, and he took a few more steps towards the man, so that he entered the shine of the lantern and showed his bruised face. "I've already received the beating, and you are denying yourself. I have heard your conversation and would like to sign on."

"You signing on with me? And why should I take you?"

"I can read and write, and I speak Latin and Greek," Nikolas replied.

"And what is the point of this if, as you say, we go on a looting ride?"

Nikolas didn't know an answer to that. He had never set foot on a ship or done physical work, only accumulated theoretical knowledge. But giving up and plodding back to the detested dormitory was no option.

"Even if the ship belongs to you, the court will certainly be interested in what you intend to do with it that it must be loaded in the middle of the night. A bailiff will be quickly found, even at midnight." With that, Nikolas turned around and inhaled as if he wanted to scream for help.

"Well, well, I can still use a shipboy. Get a move on and climb aboard, we'll cast off now," the captain interrupted Nikolas's plan.

With a pounding heart, Nikolas climbed the laden and swaying barge, which was to take them to the cog on the river. The two men he had listened to earlier looked at him suspiciously from under their hoods, but no one said anything to him.

It was only when they climbed on board that the captain announced that he was the new shipboy. "Make her ready for sea! At dawn, we want to reach the mouth of the Elbe."

On the command of their captain, the half dozen men disorderly set to work. During their exit manoeuvre, they almost rammed another ship, which had previously been lying quietly two ship lengths away. This would have been a hullabaloo and certainly called not only the bailiff but half of Hamburg's citizens to the scene. With his eyes wide open, Nikolas stared at the gigantic ship, which seemed to grow as they approached, and finally he tried with his bare hands to prevent the collision. But neither breaking wood nor the slightest crunch was heard. Finally, the helmsman slowly steered them into the middle of the river and let them drift away with the current without hoisting the sail.

Nikolas stood at the back of the stern and watched the dark outlines of the houses, shrouded in fog, as they slowly and silently passed by until they disappeared in the night like a faint memory.

Only the gentle sound of the wind and the quiet beating of the waves against the ship's hull could be heard in the darkness.

Nikolas had wanted to stay awake, but tiredness eventually overwhelmed him. Stiff and freezing, he woke up crouched on the aftercastle of the cog. The sun had made its way through the clouds and was reflected in the water. Far behind them, he could see the coastline, and smaller sandbanks protruding here and there from the shallower waters. But in front of them stretched nothing but the mirroring surface of the rippling sea. His heart bounced with joy and his belly tingled with excitement. At last, he was where he had always dreamed of. He stretched and looked around the ship. Since no sail was hoisted, they bobbed up and down in the mouth of the river and were pulled farther out to sea only by the low tide.

# 4

## Landlubber

$\mathcal{T}$he cog ship had already been built up with a forecastle, on which Nikolas saw the captain standing at the bow of the ship. Fore and aftercastle were equipped with pinnacles, as on a battlement, which gave the ship a chunky appearance. He estimated the cog to be about sixty feet long and fifteen feet wide. In the crow's nest sat a man with the hood pulled up, letting his legs dangle over the edge of the platform. On the aftercastle right in front of him stood a broad-shouldered man at the helm. He had a wild reddish beard, and his shaggy hair was being tousled by the wind. The giant blinked at Nikolas briefly, only to look straight back at the horizon.

"Mornin'," the helmsman muttered, pointing with his head to the forecastle and the captain.

Nikolas understood the wink and climbed down onto the deck. He passed by two men arguing over several intertwined and knotted ropes. Eventually, an old man with a weather-tanned face and only a few tufts of hair on his scalp hobbled over to them, hitting both against the back of their heads and taking the sheet ropes out of their hands.

Astonished, Nikolas walked on and climbed the forecastle, where the captain was immersed in a conversation with Derek, one of the men he had overheard last night. Nikolas waited at the side and inhaled the salty sea air deep into his lungs.

"Well, finally woken up? I ordered them to let you sleep well one last time. Working on a pirate ship is not a bed of roses." The captain eyed Nikolas from top to toe. "What's your name?"

"Nikolas."

"I'm Ben. This is my second helmsman, Derek; my first helmsman, Hein, is at the helm, as it should be."

He stepped to the edge of the forecastle and looked down to the deck, where the three men from before were now shouting violently and waving with the ends of the ropes in front of each other. Without letting the brawl irritate him, Ben continued: "Now that everyone is awake, we can move on to the most important part of the day."

Pride rose in Nikolas as he listened to the courageous tone of his captain, despite the seemingly chaotic crew. He had made it, he had hired on to a pirate ship, and Ben would lead them to fame, honour, and wealth in their future adventures. All in all, Ben did look like a highly respectable gentleman who knew what he was talking about. He wore the robes of a wealthy trader, and his rosy and still youthful face, together with a fuller middle section, suggested an upscale lifestyle.

With a few sweeping steps, Ben reached the deck, where he drummed up his crew.

"My most revered and righteous friends. Now that we are all gathered here, on the deck of the old *Gundelinde*, who has already left this river's mouth many times for my father and has happily reached it again on the way back, and on which I, as a boy in the service of my father—"

"Get to the point!" This rude heckling came from Henning, who had left his post in the crow's nest and hung halfway up the rigging. He was the second of the two men Nikolas had overheard last night.

"Well," Ben continued, somewhat distraught, "when I selected and recruited each of you by my own hand, I promised you a fortune. A fortune I don't have."

"What's that s'pposed to mean?" puffed one of the two troublemakers, who was still holding a rope and using it now as a pointing stick.

"If you remember, Pitt, I said we have to earn the fortune first."

"Well, but..." Pitt, who did not want to stop revealing his incomprehension, was a tall man who had obviously already taken part in one or two scuffles, as a fine scar penetrated his right eyebrow, and a greenish shimmer framed his left eye. Nevertheless, his appearance with ash-blond hair and mischievously blinking grey eyes was certainly not to be despised.

But before Pitt could talk himself into a rage, he was interrupted by Klaas, a stocky man with dark hair, whose lifestyle appeared to be equally rough. Klaas was waving about Pitt's nose with another rope. "Don't take it personally. If Pitt has had a beer, he even forgets his wife and children, can't hold his liquor very well, if you know what I mean."

"How many times have I told you to leave my wife out of it."

And again, the two troublemakers began brawling.

"Now, that's enough!" Hein, the helmsman, let his powerful voice thunder. Nikolas flinched, but Klaas and Pitt only broke their clutch when Hein grabbed them with his paws and dragged them apart.

"Are you out of your minds? You are here to live out your pugnacity when we raid a ship and not to be at each other's throats."

Ben, too, was no longer only irritated but downright upset by this mess. He scowled at the two bickering boars, whom Hein still had by the scruff of their necks, but his grim gaze was not very convincing due to his rosy cheeks.

"We are all here because we hope to earn a better living than at home. However, it seemed like you had a plan that would make it a little, how should I say, easier for us," Derek said.

"Yes, I have a plan and I am ready to share it with you." Ben nodded approvingly and then proudly pulled a piece of parchment out of his jerkin. As he unfolded it, everyone gathered around him excitedly and tried to catch a glimpse. There were several strokes and trembling lines next to which single words were written in a fine, curved font.

"What's this s'pposed to be?"

"No idea, but I wouldn't even hang this picture on the wall in the pantry." Klaas and Pitt were still not lost for words.

"This is a map that takes us to Störtebeker's treasure," Ben explained, fluffed like a cockerel.

"And how is the map supposed to guide us without any longitude or cardinal directions?" This time, Ben had no approving nod for Derek, and the healthy pink of his cheeks gave way to a shameful red.

"That's Rügen if my hazy eyes don't fool me. I know this coastline like the back of my hand." The old man, whose pale eyes blinked small from his wizened face, had pushed himself forward.

"And there it says it." Nikolas had climbed up at the rigging and pointed now from above to a small word, next to which a cross was painted. The old man let out a derogatory snort that sounded like *fog spirit*, although Nikolas was not quite sure if that manikin had gotten something into the wrong pipe.

"Christian and Nikolas are right. Störtebeker's treasure is hidden on the island of Rügen." Ben's self-confidence seemed restored. "And that's where our first journey will take us," he added triumphantly.

Derek and Henning exchanged looks heavy with meaning. Then, Henning climbed back up into the crow's nest, as he had heard enough, and Derek leaned back against the stairs to the afterdeck.

"Well, all hands on deck. Helmsman! Course on Rügen and may the waves be on our side!"

As enthusiastically as Ben called the departure, it was in strong contrast to the unmoved silence that followed. "What's up? Didn't you understand me? We go to Rügen."

"Captain, for my part, I was only a pilot in the Elbe estuary. I can steer a ship, but I don't know my way further than Brunsbüttel." Nikolas was surprised to hear this admission from the bearish Hein, and had his voice been frighteningly powerful before, it now shrank to a small grumble.

"Everything's fine, everything under control. We will simply follow the coast, around Denmark, and then south on the other side to Rügen. You can manage that, Hein, can't you?"

"*Tjoa joa*, one can try it," he growled to his captain.

"Well, that's the way to do it. Hein at the helm and hoist the sail."

If the first problem seemed to have been solved, the next one was already on the horizon. No one moved to hoist the sail. Klaas and Pitt still held the ropes in their hands, but they didn't seem to know what to do with them.

Gradually it dawned on Nikolas that this crew did not consist of seasoned sailors but of roughnecks and would-be pirates. And as he thought about it, he concluded that he, too, was just a would-be pirate. Not even that, he was just a shipboy on a cog that would probably keep slumbering in the Elbe estuary curtesy of the incompetence of their crew and be picked up by the local authorities before sunset.

"Christian, my good old Christian and my hope that we will soon have a well-billowed sail. Take these two and show them how to set the sail." Christian blinked at his captain from his little eyes, and Nikolas wondered how this man, bent by age, would do heavy work on a sailing ship.

But there was already a studious "Aye, aye", and with a nimbleness that Nikolas did not dare himself, the old Christian shooed Klaas and Pitt across the deck.

"Jan. Nikolas here can lend you a hand. He will step in wherever help is needed."

Only now did Nikolas discover the lanky, perhaps eighteen-year-old young man, who wore his light-brown shoulder-length hair tied to a braid and had sat quietly on some apple barrels. He jumped up from his seat; pulled up his trousers, which ended a hand width over his ankles; and stood ready for further orders. But Ben had already waved Derek over, and both disappeared in the small cabin under the aftercastle.

"I'm Jan," said the boy, to which Nikolas spontaneously replied, "I know," and then thought that Magister Deubel would have scolded him for it. But the schoolmaster was many miles away and Jan didn't seem to mind. "Come along, I'll show you what we have belowdecks. Mister Bartholomew was able to divert a lot of things."

"Mister Bartholomew?" Nikolas was surprised, because although it was a long time ago, he recognized the name of the venerable patrician family from Hamburg. From days past, the good-natured face of the trader with the clear eyes appeared in his mind, and the scent of spices and fish rose in his memory.

"Yes, Captain Ben, as he now calls himself." Jan didn't notice Nikolas's amazement and went to a hatch that led belowdecks.

"But Mister Bartholomew died years ago," Nikolas said.

"Also correct. Captain Ben is his son."

"Why didn't he become a trader?"

"Well, he was. For a short time. But he made a total hash of his father's fortune, or, rather, invested it in treasure maps. He probably gambled the rest away. This ship is the only thing that has remained and that, too, should have gone to a debtor tomorrow."

Nikolas listened, intrigued, and it seemed like fate to him, as the son of Mister Bartholomew's canal watcher, to hire onto the ship of his son, who also wanted to go to sea as a pirate. Nikolas liked Ben more and more, even if his abilities as captain did not seem to be overwhelming.

"And where did he find the crew?" asked Nikolas.

"You're a curious little lad. Every one of us has blotted our copybooks at some point." He nodded his head over to Klaas and Pitt, who tried to tie a few ropes together under the austere gaze of old Christian. "Those two have earned a reputation from Harvestehude to Hamburg as drunkards with a penchant for jokes that often end in mass affrays. Old Christian has been at sea for so long that he can hardly walk straight on land. If I understand correctly, he even sailed with Störtebeker himself. Derek and Henning keep themselves covered, but I heard a murmur that Derek is a bastard of the reeve of Ritzebüttel and had taken up money laundering without the prospect of a heritage. Someone blew the whistle on him some time ago, and I suspect he's now trying to escape his punishment. Henning is also involved in it, but nothing exactly is known. There is also a lot of talk about Hein. He is said to have used his position as a pilot to blackmail merchant ships that are not familiar with the shallows of the Elbe estuary."

"How do you know all this?"

"Oh, I've been a kitchen boy in Mister Bartholomew's counting house for yonks, and you can hear a lot there."

"And why are you on board?"

"To cook, what else?"

"No, I mean, why didn't you switch to another merchant?"

"No, I stay with Mister Bartholomew, who knows what to expect from someone else." Nikolas thought that this was a good reason, but he wasn't so sure if Jan knew what to expect as a pirate.

Jan had finally opened the hatch, and a steep staircase led down into a black hole. Belowdecks, it took a while for Nikolas's eyes to adjust to the darkness, and when Jan lit a candle, he saw boxes and barrels piled up toward the stern and bow. There was a long table and benches. A small oven was installed in the middle as a cooking place, and half a dozen hammocks had been fixed starboard between the beams. From one of the seafarer chests underneath a hammock hung the sleeve of a shirt, from another protruded the handles of swords and daggers. Jan walked around and lit more candles, which were stuck here and there on the walls in holders. The dull light that prevailed now belowdecks dipped everything into a flickering yellow glow.

"I know it looks cramped, but if you imagine that on a normal merchant ship only goods are stored belowdecks and the crew has to sleep in the open, then we live here almost like the councillors of Lübeck."

Nikolas was so excited to finally be on a ship that he would have found even a normal merchant ship just as great.

"Now I've told you everything, but I still don't know why you're here." Jan had lit the last candle and had come back to Nikolas, who still looked around curiously. "Old Christian already has his pants full and says that you were sent last night by the fog spirits to misguide us."

"What nonsense! I am a scholar of the St. Nikolai School and have nothing on my mind to do anyone wrong," Nikolas stammered, surprised by his own fright.

"Don't worry." Jan laughed. "And since you're no fog spirit, you must be hungry." While Jan filled a bowl of thin but steaming oatmeal that had stood on the stove, he explained Nikolas's new duties. "When you're done, you can feed the animals on deck. We have thirty chickens with a rooster and two goats with a buck on board. That's going to be your job every day. In the morning and in the evening, each cage with chickens gets two hands full of wheat. The goats get oats, and there should always be some hay in the rack. Can you milk?"

Nikolas shook his head with his mouth full, not even able to express his astonishment that live animals were on board. But then he thought that this was quite clever, as you could always have fresh eggs and milk on long journeys or even eat meat in an emergency.

"You'll learn that quickly. While they feed, you milk the two goats. You will also take over the cleaning of the cages. Every day, you throw all the dirt overboard. You also have to make sure that the animals always have water. Come now, I'll show you where the food is, and then you'll learn how to milk."

In addition to the oat and wheat supplies, barrels of water for the animals and light beer for the crew were stored belowdecks. Other barrels with apples and sacks full of rye were stacked on one side, and countless smoked fish and cured ham hung from the ceiling. On the other side was a huge mountain of loose beets, and further back was straw and hay piled up.

Nikolas stuffed some wheat into a bushel, some oats in his pocket, and took a big armful of hay. Packed like this, he climbed the steep steps.

Upstairs on deck, another dispute was underway between Klaas and Pitt.

"But he's claimed that the sheet is knotted to the winch," Pitt complained.

"At least I didn't try to hoist the sail on the shrouds," snapped Klaas.

"You don't even know what shrouds are," said Pitt promptly.

Old Christian sat exhausted on one of the boxes on deck and covered his head in his hands.

"Stop your antics!" Ben poked his head out of his cabin. "You both have no idea about seafaring, and therefore you will do what Christian tells you. Maybe you'll remember some of it, and you can be given a command at some point without a governess. No offence, Christian," Ben added, turning to the old sailor, who had indignantly pulled the air in between his teeth.

Nikolas watched the spectacle and still wasn't sure whether he should find it funny or exasperating. Such a crew certainly never occurred in his father's stories. He didn't notice that Derek had approached him.

"It has yet to be seen whether our captain understands much about seafaring himself," Derek whispered.

"But as captain, he needs to know something about it," Nikolas said, bewildered.

"He is a captain because the ship belongs to him. Otherwise, he is as ingenuous as a spoiled moneybag can be." They watched Ben retreat to his cabin. "As captain, he shouldn't be locking himself into his chamber all the time either, don't you think?" asked Derek.

Nikolas was grateful that the second helmsman left without waiting for an answer when Jan climbed on deck. In Derek's presence, he felt uncomfortable, and he couldn't shake the feeling that the man meant trouble.

Jan told Nikolas never to neglect feeding the animals, as it could be a matter of life and death. Nikolas didn't see it quite so narrowly, but he didn't want to hurt another creature either. So, he went over to the cages piled up on the afterdeck. The chickens stretched their heads through the bars and the goats began to bleat hungrily.

When he finished with the chickens, Jan came with a deep bowl.

"Now I will introduce you to the high art of milking," he said with a wink. He knelt next to the first goat, which was munching her oats, and milked with ease into the bowl.

"You always have to make sure that the buck is properly tied up, otherwise it can get uncomfortable."

"Why do you even have a buck on board?"

"Because goats have to get kids to give milk. Now, look. You kneel behind the goat, touch her belly, or pat her behind before you reach to the udder. Then you take hold of the teats from between the legs. With your thumb and index finger, press the teat at the base and then push the milk down as if you want to squeeze out a sausage. Like so." A fine white jet of fresh milk splashed into the bowl. "And now it's your turn."

Nikolas squatted behind the goat and gave her a pat on the back.

"Well, Jan, have you shown the little one what women want?" sounded Pitt's voice, who had watched the lesson, from the side.

He and Klaas burst into laughter. Jan's face turned beet red, and he didn't get out an answer apart from a gurgle, which amused Klaas and Pitt even more. Nikolas did not let himself be distracted by the chatter of bystanders, a trait he had developed over many years at school. The warm udder soothed his clammy hands, and he carefully enveloped the teats as Jan had shown him. But nothing happened.

"Don't pull like that, just press, otherwise you'll hurt her," Jan said, relieved that he had a reason to ignore the insults. "Maybe you try it with both hands? With one, you hold the base closed, and with the other, you push the milk out."

"But you shouldn't try this with women, otherwise she'll slap your face so hard your ears will ring," Klaas sneered loudly.

"Hey, little one, if you want advice from the greatest lover in the world, try it with your mouth," Pitt joked.

"The only tits you've ever seen were your mother's when she tried to breastfeed you! And even then, you were too stupid to know what to do with it," intervened old Christian. "Get to work, you two scallywags!"

Nikolas was surprised to hear such words from an old man, and Jan also looked at him in disbelief.

The advice to milk with both hands worked, and again, a white jet of warm milk splashed into the bowl. He looked delightedly at Jan, who nodded with a smile.

"Well, then I can leave you alone now. And remember not to pull," Jan encouraged him, "or to suckle."

Gradually Nikolas's hands became warm and supple. With the second goat, he tried it again one-handed and that worked now too.

When he was finished with the animals, Jan gave him a brush and a bucket to scrub the deck. He bound a rope to the bucket, let it down into the sea, and almost dropped it when he heard a loud swoosh above him. Nikolas looked up and saw the sail free-falling towards the deck. But old Christian had already called a command, and Klaas and Pitt threw themselves into the ropes to secure the sail. Finally, it swelled in the wind and gently the *Gundelinde* was set in motion.

# 5

## New Stories

𝒩ikolas watched the coastline travel by. Slowly they passed the lighthouse of Brunsbüttel, and he saw small fishing boats near the shore. His father must have been crab fishing somewhere here with his cutter before he was hired as a canal watcher in Hamburg. His chest tightened as he thought back to his father. How he wished to share this adventure with him, and he wondered whether he would ever have a turn to tell his story to someone else.

He breathed deeply and shook his head to cast out the glum thoughts. Then Nikolas scrubbed the deck. He had just finished with the afterdeck and wanted to continue with the main deck when he noticed a queasy feeling spreading in the pit of his stomach. He tried to distract himself and scrubbed even harder. He clenched his teeth and stared stubbornly at the grain of the wooden planks. Eventually, he thought he could feel every little surge that swiped the ship, and his brain seemed to swing back and forth in his skull. Then his intestines joined the rocking. He had made it to the middle of the deck when he couldn't hold it in any longer, but it was too late to reach for his bucket. His stomach gave way to all the back and forth and sent the half-digested oatmeal up and onto the deck.

"Has our little seaman made a mess? Next time, hang yourself over the railing," Klaas said gleefully.

"Did the baby make a burpsy," quacked Pitt.

Green in the face and weak with nausea, Nikolas looked up, but he had no time to reciprocate. He fell to the railing, shaken by more retching.

"At least he learns quickly," he heard Pitt say to Klaas before they were hurried along by Christian to memorize the meaning of standing and running rigging.

In the late afternoon, there was a hot meal. Jan had stretched the morning oatmeal with turnips and whole dried fish and cut off thick slices of bread for everyone. First the captain, the first helmsman Hein, and old Christian ate. After that, the rest of the crew had their turn.

Even at the St. Nikolai School, Nikolas had never gotten so much to eat at once. To his chagrin, the smell of the fish revived his nausea.

"You don't look like you want it," Klaas said from the side, transporting the fish into his own bowl without waiting for an answer.

"Tell us, both of you, I've heard you're good at fighting, but can you handle a weapon?" asked Christian.

"You bet, pops. Would you like to learn somethin' from us for a change? A wise choice, old man; after all, I'm the greatest fighter the world has ever seen," Pitt said.

"The greatest lover and the greatest fighter in the world. I bow to your supremacy," Christian joked. "I'm too old for that, but the rest of this crew would do well to understand something about attack and defence."

"Of course, who wants to take lessons with the greatest fighter in the world and his adjutant?" Pitt asked. No one wanted to be the first. "And you, little one," Pitt addressed

Nikolas, "you shouldn't just caress goat's buttocks, or do you want to be slashed from the belly button to the chin right at the first battle?" He used his knife to indicate a cut from Nikolas's abdomen up to his nose. The smell of fish emanating from the blade caused Nikolas to choke again, and he ran on deck to bend over the now familiar railing. After a while, old Christian came to him.

"Never look at the waves, but always fix on the horizon." He led Nikolas to the forecastle and told him to sit down. "Second rule: always take a deep and calm breath. And thirdly, try to sleep; after that, it's usually much better."

"Thank you," Nikolas muttered, pulling his legs to his body.

The sun finished her daily course and set the sea ablaze, which Nikolas seemed to warm from the inside simply by looking at it. He was already doing reasonably well again, and despite the nasty welcome of the sea, which had made him doubt his decision, the excited tingling was back in the face of the expected adventures. Also, he wanted to take Pitt up on his offer to teach him how to handle a knife or even a sword, already seeing himself nimbly jumping over blades and skilfully overpowering any opponent, despite his own small stature.

Since they probably wouldn't pillage a merchant vessel today anymore, Nikolas stayed on the forecastle until the sun had completely set and then went to sleep in one of the hammocks belowdecks. He was about to open the hatch when it flew towards him, and Pitt fell to his feet. Pitt picked himself up and tumbled to the railing but didn't make it in time. It was a disgusting sound as the supper splattered onto the freshly wiped deck, and the wind quickly spread the tartish smell of semi-digested dried fish. Klaas, who had been crouching on the other side of the deck already for a while, jumped up as well, and so both hung over the railing, puking their guts out.

Nikolas happily picked up a bucket and tapped Klaas on the shoulder. "Here, you big seaman, you can also clean up your mess yourself." Klaas twisted his face to a lopsided grin before he had to surrender to the urges of his stomach again.

Nikolas made himself comfortable in one of the hammocks. It was a strange feeling. The ship creaked and groaned under the rolling motions of the waves. Mice and rats rustled in the hay, and every now and again, he heard the steps of the guard on deck. A reverence for the sea took hold of him, for if the ship did not hold, they would all be at the mercy of the mighty floods. But as he continued to listen to the noises and nothing unusual happened, he even found it pleasant to be gently rocked to sleep.

Since Klaas and Pitt didn't fare much better the next day, Nikolas and Jan had to help with the manoeuvres on deck. Jan was once pulled overhead into the rigging when they set sail and tended to make knots in his own fingers, then into ropes. But Nikolas quickly learned which sheet rope was placed around which winch, where they led along, and which knots not to loosen without several strong men at hand, unless you wanted to sink the ship. Christian was delighted with the inquisitiveness of their youngest crew member and finally abandoned his superstition that Nikolas was a fog spirit.

Nevertheless, the sun was already high in the sky when they were finally able to take course, as not only were Klaas and Pitt out of action but Derek also seemed to avoid any physical work.

"The frog comes out of the pond, runs around the tree, and then jumps back into the pond," Nikolas explained the bowline hitch when he and Jan rested for a while. But Jan did not look at the knot that he just tightened but up to the crow's nest, where Henning had taken his seat again.

"Have you ever been up there?" asked Jan thoughtfully.

"No, this is the first ship I've been on," Nikolas said.

"As far as theory is concerned, you've got some skills, I give you that, but we can improve the execution. What do you think? The first one up?" And already, Jan was climbing up the rigging.

Nikolas didn't need to be told twice. It was wonderful, he felt so free as the wind whistled around his ears. At the top, there wasn't enough space in the lookout, and Henning did not seem to be interested in the two visitors. So, Nikolas and Jan stayed on the ropes beneath him, saw church towers looming on the coast, and watched the seagulls that followed them in the hope of food.

A calmness came over Nikolas that he had never experienced before. He pondered whether Störtebeker had felt that way in his father's stories, and for a while, they sat in the rigging without saying a word.

"Damn seagulls," Henning suddenly shouted.

One had shit him in the eye, and half blind, he forced his way past Jan and Nikolas to get down to deck. Jan finally said he had to take care of the food, and Nikolas was left alone. He could have sat there all day. Henning had not returned and no one else had bothered him.

"Slowly starboard and bear away," sounded from the afterdeck.

The wind had changed direction, and if they wanted to continue sailing in front of the wind, the sail had to be turned. Nikolas looked down and saw Klaas and Pitt swaying to the halliards to unfasten them. His heart stopped briefly as the sail beneath him slumped down.

"Don't head up, you fools. Bearing away means—the nose out of the wind!" Christian was horrified. "Hoist it at once, up with the sail, up!"

The sail slid back into its old position, and Nikolas set out to climb down. While he was still on his way, he saw the sail spin around the mast until it was in irons. At the same time, it gradually leaned to port.

"Not so far," Christian screamed desperately.

"Beam reach, the sail properly trimmed before the heeling gets too strong," Hein intervened, trying with all his strength to hold the rudder.

Klaas and Pitt ran headless from one side of the ship to the other, and Derek finally made an effort to help, but none of them understood the orders, and so the situation on board became more and more precarious.

Nikolas reached the deck and picked up the sheet rope portside, but alone he was too weak to hold it. Christian and Derek came to his aid, and together they brought the sail in the right position to the wind.

"Correctly recognized, little one," Derek said, but Nikolas suspected that he had not known what to do either.

"If these two don't buck up soon, we'll get to see the ship's kobold," grumbled the old Christian, scowling at Klaas and Pitt, who watched the sail with wide eyes, and then congratulated each other on their undeserved success.

As they all sat at dinner, the captain visited them belowdecks.

"Men, according to my calculations, we have reached the trade route from Amsterdam to Denmark. Now we wait until we see a suitable ship that we can pillage. Nikolas, the falchions, sabres, and what other weapons can be found around here must be cleaned and sharpened, ready for action." With that, Ben disappeared for the rest of the day.

Nikolas opened a seafarer chest and illuminated it with a candle. He found five curved sabre blades, ten falchions, and just as many daggers. The daggers all seemed to be in good shape, and the curved blades of the sabres were rusted but sharp. But the falchions weren't good even for cutting warm butter. He took everything out of the box and sorted it according to the type of weapon. Curious, he weighted the blades in his hand and performed little cut and stab movements.

The daggers were straight and double edged, and their shortness was an advantage in the limited space of a ship. The sabres had broad curved blades and were sharpened only on one side. Some had a basket as a handguard, others only simple handles, and they were at least twice as long as the daggers. It was incomprehensible to Nikolas where and why Ben had taken them on board. The falchions, on the other hand, were single edged with a slight bend towards the tip, almost like a large knife like a meat cleaver, and with simple crossbars as quillons.

Nikolas cleared all the blades of dust, dirt, and rust, but he couldn't come up with a way to sharpen the blades without any tools, so he simply put everything back into the chest.

Jan and old Christian found him when he closed the lid. "We've just shortened the sail so that we don't drift off too far. What a job. Could easily do with a handful of men more aboard. I don't know how we're going to deal with a strong breeze," Christian explained, exhausted. "If we had a few skilled sailors on board instead of these robbers, then even a storm wouldn't be a problem."

"Is it true that you sailed with Störtebeker?" asked Nikolas curiously, and Jan listened up upon hearing the name.

"Not directly. We were both at the Battle of Stockholm under Master Hugo, and I saw him once or twice. But we never served together on a ship."

"What did he look like, how was he?" Nikolas sat down with ants in his pants.

"He looked like any sailor. And he could drink each of us under the table. But when it came to a fight, he was like a devil, knocking down everyone in his way. That's probably why he was so successful as a pirate. As far as I know, he's always taken good care of himself. But since the court didn't want to cut a deal, he took the secret of his treasure to the grave."

Jan had filled a jug of beer and handed it around.

"I was at the execution and saw him get up after he was beheaded," Nikolas said.

"What? You saw Störtebeker pass his men without a head? The hobgoblin shall get me." Old Christian smiled, because although he believed in all sorts of things and knew a story for every occasion, he seemed to have his doubts about Nikolas's claim. "Don't worry about it. This was a good start to spinning an excellent yarn. But remember, there must also be a grain of truth in every story," Christian encouraged him.

"Can you tell us more about the Battle of Stockholm?" asked Jan.

"So, you want to hear a story from the grand master of the sailor's yarn," said the old man. "Well, let's see what I can remember. Queen Margaret of Denmark was about to conquer all of Sweden at the time, but she bit off more than she could chew with Stockholm.

"Rostock and Wismar issued letters of marque to several privateers to raid Danish ships and break the siege. At that time, I, too, was hired on one of the ships. Wasn't a young warhorse then anymore either.

"In February, which is far too early for shipping in these waters, we set off north with eight ships under the command of Master Hugo.

"Störtebeker was still a simple sailor at the time, but he made a name for himself in this battle.

"As I said, it was way too early in the year, and so it came as it had to come. Our ships were surrounded by ice before we reached Stockholm. Of course, the Danish troops thought that we were now easy prey and prepared their attack. But they had not expected the ingenuity of our commander in chief. First, he had us build a wall of tree trunks around our ships, and then we hacked large holes into the ice just before the attack, which only froze on the surface. Many of the Danes broke into the ice and drowned miserably, and we slain the rest of them on our wall. Well, that's how we won the battle, even though we were outnumbered." After Christian had finished, they sat together in silence for a while, staring into the fire of the candle.

"I'm going to have a kip now and then take over the first night watch," Christian said, and set about to suspend a hammock.

# 6

## Ship Ahoy

𝒯he days dragged on and became shorter and shorter. But since Ben had given the order to hold position until they sighted a ship, they did so, and that meant they did nothing. After his many years at the St. Nikolai School, Nikolas quickly picked up a rhythm which included feeding the animals, cleaning the deck, bookkeeping their stock, and mending smaller rags and ropes. At night, he took over guard shifts, which he carried out with the same sleepy meditation as the Mattins, and often he found himself quietly reciting the Lord's Prayer.

But without an adventure on the horizon or any form of distraction in sight, Nikolas and the rest of the crew became bored, and resentment settled on deck. It was once again a clear and frosty October morning when the captain summoned them.

"Well, men, we should rename our ship. *Gundelinde* is a bit tame for my taste."

"If it's about that, *Great Dog* wasn't any better," Christian muttered.

"I propose *Störtebeker* as a tribute to the great hero. What do you think?"

"I think we could leave it at *Gundelinde*," Pitt interjected. "Have a lot of confidence in the name."

"Oh, your wife again," moaned Klaas.

"No, my mother, if you need to know." Klaas and Pitt were about to start one of their tiffs once more.

But Ben did not let them distract him from his name giving. "Nothing against the name, my aunt was called that as well." Pitt cast a triumphant glance at Klaas. "But we are no longer a merchant ship but a pirate ship, and this requires a terrifying name," Ben said firmly.

"I don't think the name is that bad. Which trader wouldn't immediately run for it if he saw *Störtebeker* on our ship? After all, we want them to come as close to us as possible, or what tactics are we using?" asked Nikolas.

Pitt applauded Nikolas for this precise analysis. "Didn't think about that, what? Our little one had to tell you the score."

"Truly, it's best to ambush with a fast attack. But to lure a ship into a trap seems to me to be the most promising with this crew," summed up old Christian, without much care for the discussion about the name of their ship.

"Ship ahoy," sounded from the crow's nest. All controversies were forgotten. Everyone rushed to the next railing and stared out at the sea in the expectation of discovering a large merchant ship. But no ship was in sight.

"Portside, about five miles ahead," clarified Henning.

After a short commotion, they all ran to the opposite railing and finally saw a small ship on the horizon.

"So, men, you know what you have to do." As usual, Ben assumed too much of his crew. "We act as if we need help and strike when they are close enough. Raise the distress flag." Ben's rosy cheeks glowed with zeal.

They looked at each other in confusion, and after a short pause, old Christian limped off to fetch the requested flag.

"Flag hoisted," Klaas shouted a small eternity later.

And then there was nothing else to do but wait. Nikolas climbed into the rigging and tensely fixed the ship in the distance. He was so excited that he didn't even notice that the ship took an unusually long time to get closer, even though it was heading straight for them. Finally, he realized that the ship did not get any bigger, as it really only was a small fishing boat, which remained as small as it was.

"It looks like a simple fishing cutter to me," Nikolas exclaimed.

In disbelief, they continued to stare at the ship. Ben eventually staggered into his cabin and came back with a telescope. Although he saw now with his own eyes that Nikolas was right, he made no attempt to blow off the attack. "It's going to be easy prey at least."

The cutter came closer, and it seemed that the fishermen had recognized the distress flag, as they continued to steer directly towards them. Nikolas couldn't believe that they should board and rob this little boat and wondered whether there was anything worth taking. The others had already armed themselves to the teeth and seemed to have trouble pretending to be honourable traders in need.

Finally, the fishing boat had come alongside, and the fishermen had hardly asked how they could help when the grappling hooks flew across the water. Pitt was the first to swing on a rope onto the boat with jeers and almost fell into the water on the other side, so small was it.

"Hand over all your precious cargo and you will not suffer," Ben thundered.

But the fishermen, who were threatened by Klaas and Pitt with the blunt falchions, only looked at him, frightened, whilst Derek and Henning searched the boat. "There's nothing worth taking here!"

"Out with it! What do you have on board and where did you hide it?" Ben shouted in a theatrical voice a second time.

"Good Lord, we are simple fishermen, and the only thing we have is fish, which is stored in these boxes," one of the men replied.

Ben descended onto the boat to look for himself that there was nothing on board that was of any value.

"Well, if that's the case, we'll take the fish." Determined, Ben opened one of the boxes. The silvery fish wiggled bug-eyed in their prison, snapping for air.

"You can't do that," the fisherman pleaded. "If we return home without fish, we have nothing to sell and cannot feed our families."

"That's not our problem." Derek seemed to enjoy humiliating the two fishermen.

"We've got enough fish," Nikolas chipped in.

"You can always use more. We can sell some and finally have money in our pockets," Derek said, unmoved.

Nikolas looked at Ben, but either he didn't want to or couldn't abort their first looting ride, so they hoisted the fish in a net on board and let the cutter move on.

"Well, I call this a successful start to our new life," Ben said.

Disillusioned, they stood on deck and watched their haul slowly suffocate with last twitches.

"What are we doing with them now? We can't smoke them, and we don't have enough salt to cure them either." Jan considered the whole matter less against the backdrop of a successful loot than from the practical mindset of a ship's cook.

"We're going to fill them in barrels and then go to a port to sell them or cook them ourselves," Ben said.

After the slippery work had been done, Nikolas set about scrubbing the deck, as he had done so often and which was necessary this time, while Ben retreated with his first and second helmsman and old Christian to his cabin.

Nikolas later learned that Ben had admitted that they were not on a trade route but many miles away from any Hanseatic sea traffic. But before their captain made this confession, he had at least wanted to give his men the success of their first booty.

The next morning, they finally set out to reach the Danish coast. As usual, it took a long time for them until they headed into the wind without disturbances, and so they had not gone far when the clouds began to gather and a stiff breeze rose. Even before the sun set, they were in a full-blown storm. Ben screamed his commands from the afterdeck down through the howling wind. Hardly anyone heard him through the ever-louder roaring storm, and everyone was busy looking for a footing so as not to be washed overboard by the next wave. Come evenfall, they were still being tossed back and forth by huge mountains of waves that piled up to their left and right. Ben, too, clung to the stairs of the aftercastle, and only Hein stood like a tree by the rudder.

"Captain, we have to strike the sail before it rips," Hein sounded from the foamed helm.

"To hell with it, then strike the sail, men," Ben roared as a wave whipped him in the face and he swallowed a mouthful of seawater.

Nikolas, Derek, and Henning, who had for the first time become visibly uncomfortable in the crow's nest, fought their way through portside, while old Christian, Klaas, and Pitt untied the sheet ropes starboard. When the sail was finally struck, everyone looked for a safe place again to wait for the storm to end.

At dawn, the storm had passed, and they saw a lead-coloured day arrive. But it wasn't until they tried to set sail again to take advantage of what Ben thought was a favourable wind that they realised how calmly their ship lay in the still restless water.

Nikolas was belowdecks to sort the toppled load with Jan when he heard agitated shouting from above. He had just climbed the stairs with two buckets to feed the animals, which were miraculously unharmed, when he heard what had happened. They had run aground on a sandbank, and even with the help of the hoisted sail, the ship did not move one bit.

"Damned! What kind of rabble are you, can't you even avoid a sandbank on this wide sea?" Derek cursed beside himself and stomped with huge steps to the helm.

"As if we ran aground on purpose," Pitt muttered.

Derek tried in vain to move the rudder, and even his belief that it only needed his leadership did not help. They were stuck.

For the rest of the morning, they tried to get the ship off the bank with long stakes. Every now and then, and when a wave came to their aid, the ship made a jolt, but they could not tell whether they freed themselves or drifted more and more onto the shallow. After a while, they were so exhausted and hopeless that they stretched out wherever they were and did not move again for quite some time.

"Ship ahoy," Henning exclaimed from the lookout.

This time, the others rose only hesitantly, but Ben had his telescope ready and searched the horizon.

"It seems like we are lucky. It's a Danish merchant ship, and they're heading right towards us. Fly the distress flag."

"Flag hoisted," Klaas shouted. "Still," he added, as no one had taken it down yet.

It took another half an hour before they could see the Danish flag with the naked eye, and yet another half hour before they were finally within earshot.

"Ahoy! We are stuck here on a sandbank, and we are not coming forward or back. Can you help us?" Ben and his crew gathered starboard to welcome their rescuers.

"We'll come to you and drag you out. We have less draught. Get everything ready so we can get on board," a friendly smiling man shouted back, and two other men showed up behind him.

"Get the runway out," Ben ordered with delight.

A few moments later, the merchant ship came alongside, and the captain of the other ship boarded with two of his sailors.

"What a joy that you have discovered us. We got into this horrible storm last night, and it must have driven us to these shallow waters." Ben greeted the other captain with a keen handshake.

"The joy is on our part," replied the other, smiling and turning to his men, who burst into uncomfortable laughter.

Klaas and Pitt joint them hesitantly, but neither of them knew what was so funny. As suddenly as they had begun, they fell silent again.

"Go!" the merchant captain yelled.

Ten more men emerged on the other ship from hatches and behind barrels and ran over the runway or swung towards them on ropes. The crew of the *Gundelinde* realized too late that they themselves had been lured into a trap. They had no time to run away and were herded together at the point of sharp falchions. None of them had a weapon on them, so they had no choice but to surrender without a fight.

"What's all this? You are no Danish traders?" asked Ben.

"Well recognized, Captain."

"We have nothing," Ben stammered, looking sheepishly to his cabin.

"We'll see. With such a draught, there is certainly something worth taking. Search the ship and take everything we need. You and you, tie them to the mast." The pirate captain's crew followed the command swimmingly.

"Back off, you klutz!" shouted Pitt as they tried to grab him.

A targeted punch left the pirate tumbling back, but he quickly caught himself again, and, supported by his mates, they swiftly overpowered Pitt and tied him up. Ben, too, was now grabbed by the desire to fight, driven by a sense of honour and the obligation to be a role model as captain. He threw himself onto the next back that showed itself. Like on a wild bull, Ben was whirled around until he fell to the ground and a quick stroke of a sword inflicted a gaping cut on his left forearm. To Ben's good fortune, the pirate captain ordered his men not to waste their time on such shenanigans, and so he was simply left on the ground without losing his life. Tied to the mast or heavily bleeding, they experienced now firsthand how a swift pirate raid worked.

All their barrels, boxes, and sacks were loaded in a hurry, and the goats and chickens also found a new home. They only left them the raw dead fish, which were still scattered across the deck after the storm.

"Thank you for your hospitality, and I hope that we will see you again. Oh, and in a few hours, the tide will set you free." The pirate captain tapped his hat briefly before swinging over and onto his own ship to disappear with his crew.

# 7

## Land Ahoy

$\mathcal{N}$ikolas managed, with the help of a one-armed Ben, to wriggle out of his ties, and everyone else was also quickly back on their feet. Nevertheless, they had no choice but to watch their adversaries as they sailed away, for the *Gundelinde* was still stuck on the sandbank. So, they cared for their wounds, and it turned out that Klaas had excellent knowledge of nursing the injured.

"For a few years, a barber came by near the orphanage where I grew up. A colourful cart with a nag in front and the gentleman didn't exactly look well fed either. But he brought a performance, you'd be gobsmacked. I studied each of his shows to learn the magic tricks. And on the side, I also learned one or two treatment methods. He was less secretive about those than his sleight of hand... So, you shouldn't move your arm for a while until the wound closes." He tied a knot in Ben's bandage, which he had improvised from strips of fabric torn from a clean linen shirt.

Nikolas and Jan threw the scattered and smelly fish overboard, prompting swooping gulls to dive into the sea around them like arrows.

The men were all depressed and discouraged by this surprising turn in their journey, and Ben commanded them to carry weapons from now on, day and night. Astonishingly, the sabres, daggers, and falchions had been left behind. They probably still looked too shabby and were not worth the trouble even after Nikolas's efforts.

Finally, the tide came, the ship got water under the keel and began to float again. They crunched the last few feet over the sand to freedom before setting course on the shore to find a port. Derek took the helm, and Hein showed them the way between the sandbanks using a sounding lead.

Ben had put on his coat, as he felt cold. The bandage around his wound was bloodied and had dyed his whole sleeve dark red. Klaas changed the bandage, this time inserting a small wooden stick along the wound to stop the bleeding with some extra pressure, but Ben still refused to lie down in his cabin. At last, Klaas convinced him to sit down on the deck and hold up his injured arm to reduce the blood flow to the wound. The sun went down and painted the infinite sea behind them red like a trail of blood, an omen for the life they had chosen as pirates.

Nikolas couldn't sleep in his hammock and got up again after restlessly swaying in the suspensions. Warmly wrapped in a sweater that had become too small for Jan, he watched Hein letting the lead slide into the water and hauling it back up again. Between shreds of clouds, the moon illuminated the quiet and regular movements of the giant.

After a while, Nikolas broke the silence. "You measure the depth of the water, right? How exactly do you know how deep it is?"

Hein looked at him silently, and it seemed as if he was considering whether to interrupt his almost meditative activity because of the shipboy. But eventually, he smiled at Nikolas under his bushy beard.

"Come on, little one." He motioned with a head movement for Nikolas to come over as he reeled in the line with stretched-out arms. "This lead weight drops to the seabed. You can feel it hitting the ground and then you pull it back up again. You count how many fathoms you have rolled off. A fathom is roughly equivalent to the span between your outstretched arms. Well, not quite with you, but over time, you develop a sense for it." Hein had thrown the sounding lead overboard again and watched as the line disappeared in the darkness of the water.

"How many fathoms do we have here? And when do you run aground?" Nikolas peered over the railing at the black surface.

"At the moment, we have fourteen fathoms. Farther out, there are usually twenty-two, and at about five fathoms, a fully loaded ship should already be careful. Do you want to try it?"

Nikolas was surprised, as he had always assumed that Hein preferred to keep to himself. Hein smiled but said nothing and only held the lead out for him to take. Nikolas measured the weight and the wet coldness in his hand. He looked at it closely and discovered a depression at the end in which a yellowish mass stuck.

"What is that?" he asked, noting that Hein had been watching him closely.

"Lead arming. Tallow or something similar that the sand from the bottom of the sea can stick on. The seabed differs from place to place like the soil on land, and an experienced sailor can use it to determine the waters he is in."

"And why don't we do it now?"

"We don't know exactly where we are anyway. And for now, it's just a matter of reaching a port unharmed."

"But wouldn't it make sense for the future to collect soil samples everywhere and create a map that we could use to orientate us?"

"Possibly. Other seafarers have certainly already troubled themselves. Maybe our captain even has such a map, it wouldn't surprise me with all the parchment in his cabin," Hein replied pensively. "Sounds like a task for a shipboy. But for now, try it without. We still have some time."

Nikolas threw the sounding lead overboard and let the line slide through his hands as the weight quickly sank into the dark depths. After a few heartbeats, he noticed a gentle tremor, making the line between his fingers vibrate, so light, in fact, that he was not sure if the weight had really reached the bottom. The line continued to run through his hands, and he looked enquiringly at Hein.

"It takes a lot of experience to operate the sounding lead reliably, but most of the time, the first impression is also the right one. And it seems to me that you should have reeled in the line a long time ago. Don't forget, the ship moves, and the line is pulled into the water."

Nikolas recovered the line with his arms outstretched as he had seen Hein do it. He counted thirty fathoms, and they agreed that this might not be correct. Nikolas tried it once more, and so they stood side by side in the quiet night and watched as the line disappeared many times more in the water. After a while, Nikolas developed a sense for when to gather the line, and his sounding was confirmed by Hein, who measured the depth every now and then for safety. At some point, they measured only ten fathoms and Hein took over the lead. Nikolas was happy about this, as the icy wind, which was blowing lightly but steadily, had frozen him to the bone, and, tired, he went belowdecks.

He had the feeling that he had barely closed his eyes when he was awakened again.

"Get up, dopey, we have to secure the ship," the voice of Derek got through to him, who, as soon as Nikolas had opened his eyes, turned around and climbed back on deck.

Nikolas rolled stiffly out of his hammock and wiped the sleep out of his eyes. He no longer felt a rocking and wondered which port they had touched at as he followed Derek. But there was no port, not even a village. He saw only the dunes of a foreign coast.

"Where are we?" he asked Hein.

"Denmark. Probably," Hein answered in his usual barren manner, and his voice had nothing left of the kindness from last night.

Nikolas looked over the railing and found that they had run aground again, but this time on a white beach in front of a shallow dune. Unknowing of where the nearest port was, they had eventually headed to a sheltered bay.

Klaas and Pitt waded around in the retreating water, supporting the ship with beams that had been stored on deck. Jan, old Christian, and Henning were about to hammer thick pegs into the sand and to moor the ship with even thicker ropes. It took a few hours for them to secure the ship.

Since the part of the cog that was otherwise in the water was now visible, it was easy to see where the protective tar layer had been scraped off by the run-up. Some rotten planks also appeared. But most of the hull was covered with thousands of mussels, barnacles, and small crabs that had retreated into their shells in the fresh air.

"No wonder we had such a depth, with this luggage hanging on," Klaas said.

"Not only that, but the ship is getting slower and slower because of these damn critters," added old Christian.

For lunch, they had mussel stew, freshly harvested from their ship. Half of the crew then set out to explore the area.

Nikolas stayed behind with Jan and Christian and made a small fire on the beach, where they warmed themselves and listened to the stories of the old man. By evening, the rest of the crew was back.

Behind the dune, less than a mile away, lay a hamlet where Ben had his arm stitched up and acquired a small barrel of beer. He wouldn't say how he had paid for it, but everybody assumed that he had stashed away more of his inheritance than he had them believe.

Nikolas was about to sit in a hollow in the sand near the fire when he noticed a dark figure moving on the dunes. Klaas and Pitt jumped up and removed themselves from the glow of the fire with their knives drawn. Since the raid, they had even slept fully armed and apparently still hadn't noticed that their falchions were completely blunt. Nikolas, whose eyes were set to the brightness of the fire, could soon not see them anymore. Instead, he watched tensely the approaching figure, whose black outline was still visible on the dune against the cloudy sky.

Suddenly Klaas and Pitt jumped out of the shadows with terrible roars, and all three shapes plunged into the darkness. Nikolas and old Christian only heard the bodies rolling down the slope.

"Are you mad? Let me go, you dimwits," screamed Jan.

The melee stopped, and after a brief silence, a laugh penetrated the night. Klaas and Pitt returned to the fire, with Jan in their midst, who had gone to ease himself in the dunes. A little pale and frightened from the foray, he patted the sand out of his clothes.

The next morning, Nikolas set out to scrape mussels off the ship's hull, which became a daily task, and Jan cooked a soup from it again. So, they killed two birds with one stone. But it was laborious work, and with every shell he loosened, he also ripped parts of the underlying wood out of the planks. In addition, these sea creatures had unexpected sharp edges and corners, and Nikolas was soon covered with many small cuts on his hands and arms.

As St. Martin's Day approached and the Hanseatic League stopped its navigation for the winter, it made no sense to go out to sea again. Instead, they prepared everything for the cold season.

The sail was taken off, and here, too, the wear and tear became apparent under close inspection. Now they spent the fast-shortening days patching ropes and cloths. It was a hard and time-consuming job. They would not be able to repair the hull until the spring, as they lacked the tools and materials at the moment.

When the first frost came, Klaas and Pitt found work in the forge of the hamlet. Jan was taken on as a kitchen boy in a tavern, and the others also found work here and there for food and lodging. Only old Christian and Nikolas were still on the ship day and night. Every day, Nikolas tried to clean the hull a little more, but it seemed to be almost endless work.

Weeks passed and the return of the birth of Christ approached when Klaas, Pitt, and Jan were on guard duty again. Klaas and Pitt raved about the women in the village, and

Nikolas heard about things he had never thought about and that sounded extremely absurd.

"The women here are amazing, they have curves, even Irma from the Sailor's Yard couldn't keep up." They looked at Nikolas and Jan enthusiastically, both of whom knew neither the Sailor's Yard nor an Irma.

"Oh, come on, at least you, Jan, have been with Irma? For such a pretty boy like you, she'd have certainly given you a special price," Klaas said teasingly, and poor Jan once again turned red.

"I've never been with a woman," he stammered almost inaudibly.

"What did you say, you have never enjoyed the wonders of an unbridled union with a willing and irrepressible hussy? Well, then, it's time. I had fathered three children with my wife at your age," boasted Pitt.

"The first one even before the wedding, that's why it even happened, if I remember correctly?" asked Klaas.

"What happened to your wife and children?" asked Nikolas.

"What do you mean? Have you heard anything?"

Nikolas was confused. "I didn't hear anything. Just what you're telling us. Isn't she waiting for you?"

"She was the one who threw me out. Didn't want to see me anymore, and I can't blame her. But you're not entirely innocent." Pitt cast an accusing glance at Klaas. "Because of your stupid sleight of hand, I got into the biggest trouble in the first place."

"And I keep patching you up."

"If you'd do the magic tricks better, it wouldn't have been necessary."

"Don't you miss them?" Nikolas interrupted the burgeoning argument.

"Come off it. The doxies are good at dispelling any worries. And Ranghild has always been independent and assertive. She can cope without me, just as she wanted it when she barricaded the door in front of my nose."

"My father still missed Mother after her death," Nikolas whispered.

Silently, they stared into the flames of the small fire for a while.

"Tomorrow morning, you come along, and I promise you, the women here will fulfil previously unknown desires," Pitt finally said to Jan.

Jan looked unsettled, but Nikolas also noticed an excited sparkle in his eyes.

The next evening, Klaas and Pitt came back from the village singing loudly, a grin all over Jan's face. Nikolas could already imagine that it must have been something very nice to be with a woman all night. He had seen women coming and going at the St. Nikolai School at night and disappearing unnoticed into the chamber of Master Deubel. He had also seen women in certain neighbourhoods in Hamburg baring their shoulders and painting their lips red. The other boys had told him at the time what would happen when a man gave them money, but these stories sometimes seemed even crazier than what he heard from Klaas and Pitt.

In addition, Jan was obviously freshly washed, and for that alone, Nikolas would have liked to spend a night with a red-lipped, lightly clothed hussy. Jan didn't tell much, but only looked knowingly when Nikolas asked him what had happened.

# 8

## A Hamlet in Denmark

The cuts from the shells on Nikolas's hands and forearms became inflamed. When the wounds did not improve on the third day and he could hardly do any work, he decided to go to the nearby hamlet. It was difficult for him, as he had the feeling that leaving the ship would also mean giving up his life as a pirate. Still, it had to be.

He set off before nightfall and had already seen the lights of the houses from the dune, but it was still a long walk. Night came fast, and he had not taken a torch with him, which slowed him down considerably. The village consisted of a few houses and three inns which contained loud laughter and jeers. He looked through the windows of the first drinking hole and saw a motley bunch of men, some of whom he clearly recognized as sailors, and a not insignificant number of those lightly dressed and done-up women. Some brought the men jugs full of beer and wine, others sat on their laps, kissed them, and let them bury their bearded faces into their lavish cleavages, from which they reappeared with red faces and even louder laughter. Nikolas was sure that he did not want to go in there and turned to the next tavern on the other side of the village path. As he crossed the alley, the door opened, and a man half-seas over was pushed out and fell into the dirt.

"Get you gone. And don't let yourself be seen again until you have paid off your debts. We're not a poorhouse," a fat man with an apron yelled at the man on the ground.

Nikolas had retreated into the shadows of the houses as a precaution and now walked around the tavern. At the back, he peered through a window which shimmered with muted light. There was nothing in the room except a dimmed oil lamp and a simple bedstead with a naked Pitt lying on it. Pitt was staring into a corner of the room that Nikolas could not see. He turned to leave when a no less naked woman came into his sight. The woman sat down on Pitt and moved as if she wanted to knead dough with her bottom, and Pitt seemed to help greatly with his hands on her hips.

Nikolas was so immersed in the sight of this intimate union, which had always been instilled in him as a mortal sin, that he almost jumped into the window in terror when the drunkard stumbled around the corner. Nikolas took to his heels and ran back into the alley, where he fell straight into Ben's arms.

"What are you doing here?" asked Ben, holding the distraught boy by the shoulders to look him in the face.

"I wanted—I did—" Nikolas stammered. "My hands are hurt, and I wanted to get fresh water to clean them."

"Let me see," Ben told him, and Nikolas unwrapped the encrusted bandages from his left hand.

Wet white shreds of skin covered the angry cuts, and yellow pus protruded here and there.

"That doesn't look good. Come along, I know where you'll be helped." Ben turned around and led him to the last inn, where things were a little quieter than in the other two.

This establishment looked dirty and subdued in contrast to the bright colours and noise in the other houses. But here, too, were women who embraced men. At first glance, they seemed exactly like those in the other two drinking holes, but on closer inspection, they looked older, even though they probably were not, and appeared exhausted and haggard. Few men dealt with them, most of them staring down their jugs or sat in dark niches, immersed in quiet conversations.

When Ben and Nikolas entered, a tall, meagre man looked up from behind the counter where he was cleaning jugs with a dirty rag. "What do you want with the little one? He's far too young to get anything here for his age."

"He's got his hands hurt and needs something to clean his wounds," Ben said.

"And who should pay for it? You have already scrounged from us the last days, and now I am to pay for this tyke?"

"You will get your money, or at least a decent reward. I can provide you with some of my men to pay off the debt. It seems to me that you urgently need a few craftsmen in here."

"Come again? If my house doesn't suit you, then go over to those damn devils that spoil the business!"

"A few strong arms to whip this place into shape would help our business more than your lousy face," a woman interjected.

The innkeeper tightened his lips and polished his jug a little more thoroughly.

"Come here, I'll see what I can do for you." The woman led Nikolas to a chair and told him to sit down.

Ben went to the counter and ordered a beer. Since the innkeeper was still not satisfied with Ben's proposed debt compensation, but did not want to turn down the offer, he simply spit into the pitcher and cleaned it only sparsely before pouring the beer. Ben, in return, took a big sip and then wiped the foam from his upper lip with pleasure.

"Good heavens, how did that happen?" the woman asked anxiously as she took off Nikolas's bandages.

"I fell...on stones...sharp stones," he replied, as he did not know how much was already known about them in the village.

"That must have been a pretty fall. And a whole bunch of sharp stones." She examined his arms from all sides. "Beata, warm up water and bring me the liquor, but the strong one." The woman turned to one of the maids, who tried in vain to schmooze a customer. "My name is Anna," she said to Nikolas, "and this useless thing behind the counter is my husband, Willem. What's your name, my dear?"

"Nikolas."

"Nikolas, patron saint of children and sailors. And is this your father with whom you are here?"

"No, I hired on with him."

"Right, he's a shipboy on my merchant ship," said Ben, who had overheard the conversation.

"And you loaded a whole pile of stones for which you don't get any money?" she asked with a sly glance at Ben. Ben nodded as he took a deep gulp, and Anna turned back to Nikolas. She had become accustomed to not caring about the stories she heard.

"Beata, cut a few beets into the soup, too, whilst you're warming the water! The little one is completely frozen. And you look like you're going to have to be thoroughly washed," she added, inspecting Nikolas's matted hair.

Nikolas faced it all and felt better every minute. After the soup, Anna took him to another room, where there was a washing trough, and two other women joined him. It seemed as if they all had taken a great fancy to the wounded boy, who had found his way to them at such a late hour. Everyone wanted to help and mother him, enjoying such an innocent pleasure which they would probably never experience without hardship. When he was washed, they brought him fresh clothes, which were a little too big for him, but clean and warm.

"They are still from my son, Lars. He left years ago to become a priest, and I doubt he'll ever come back and demand his things. So, keep them. He's probably too embarrassed about us to show his face here again."

Comforted and comfortable, they went back to the taproom and sat down by the flickering fire. Beata brought a bottle of clear liquid and clean bandages, and another woman followed her with a comb. Anna dampened one of the strips of fabric and grabbed his right arm.

"It's going to hurt now," she said as she dabbed the moist rag onto his wounds.

A sharp pain struck Nikolas, and he involuntarily tried to pull his arm back. But Anna held him close and tenaciously cleaned his cuts. When she was done, she carefully wrapped the fresh bandages around his arms and hands, and the burning gave way to a pleasant warmth.

Even worse than the care for his wounds was the combing of his hair. The matt that had developed on his head since Hamburg was almost uncombable, but Anna and Beata tirelessly disentangled every strand. Finally, they finished, and with all the hair now lying on the floor, Nikolas thought it would have been more painless to cut it all off. Exhausted, he followed Anna into a chamber with a soft bed and thick wool blankets. Nikolas was sure that he had never been so clean in his life, and with this thought, he fell asleep instantaneously.

It was still dark when he was awakened by a thud. Someone whispered flutteringly above him, and it took him a while to realize where he was. He was lying on the hard wooden floor and had apparently fallen out of bed.

"Come on, you can lie between us, it's warmer too," Nikolas heard a woman's voice from the darkness that surrounded him.

Still a little dazed, he slipped back into the bed. But when a warm body climbed over him, he was immediately fully awake. He was about to spend the night with two women at once. Excited and yet paralyzed, he lay there until he heard a quiet snoring to his left and right, which told him that his two bed companions had fallen asleep.

Lulled by the warmth, he, too, dozed off until he awoke again, for he had noticed why he had fallen out of bed. The rocking of the ship and the hammock, which otherwise enclosed him like a cocoon, were missing, and he had unintentionally rolled out of the quiet, unmoving bed.

Nikolas remained at the inn until his hands were completely healed. He learned that they were not far from the border to the Holy Roman Empire and that there was a port located in nearby Ribe, which was also used by Hanseatic merchants. As a result, they all still spoke the German of the Hanseatic League, and the nightlife flourished so excellently in this hamlet, not least because of lonely sailors.

Curiously, Nikolas asked Anna to say something in Danish. It sounded so strange, spoken so throaty, and yet also so cordial, that it seemed to Nikolas that it must be difficult to bring out naughty expletives with appropriate emphasis. Soon he had picked up the first words, and the women had fun teaching him compliments.

The eyes of the old maids glowed when Nikolas told them "*Du cr smuk*," and Anna scolded him not to make so much "*kissemisse*" with her girls, as they should take care of the paying clients. But Anna herself was captivated by the blond boy and would have liked to keep him with her for the rest of the winter.

Storms whipped across the country, blowing snowdrifts around as Nikolas made his way back to the ship to take up his guard shift again. He already missed the warm bed and especially the two warm bodies next to him. Although he was only thirteen years old, he still did not know what exactly went on between a man and a woman. But also, because he was already thirteen years old, he knew that his body was trying to tell him something exciting.

The weeks passed and the crew had found a well-established rhythm in which they took turns between guarding their ship and warming their feet at a big fire in the village for least a few hours and nabbing something to eat. Only old Christian stayed on the ship and ate the cold dishes that were brought to him.

Nikolas staggered over the dunes and found their ship as he had left it, except for the frozen spray, which covered the whole ship in hundreds of small icicles, and made it look like glass. In the ship itself, it was quiet and only marginally warmer. Derek and Henning lay wrapped in blankets close to the small oven that Jan used to cook. They had brought in straw as bedding, which insulated them at least a little bit. Old Christian lay offside and breathed so shallowly that not even his chest showed any movement. He had been the only one who had not left the ship since they had landed here. No one had been able to persuade him to come with them; he belonged on a ship. But it was obvious that he was poorly. He was pale and trembled more than before and his face was noticeably gaunt.

No one spoke, and only from time to time one of them poked the fire. In the evening, it got even colder. Freezing, Nikolas pulled his blanket over his nose and moved closer to Christian, hoping to find some warmth.

The next morning, as Nikolas was about to go back to the village, he tried to wake up Christian to convince him to come with him. But when he touched his arms, the old man was roasting and drenched in sweat despite the iciness.

"Christian, wake up, you have to leave, you're sick and need help, do you hear me? Christian, wake up!" Nikolas shook his shoulders, and finally Christian opened his eyes. "Thank God, Christian. Come on, you can't stay here." He turned to Derek and Henning. "I need help, we have to take him to Anna, he'll die if he stays here."

Henning rose hesitantly as if he thought it was long too late to save the old man. Nevertheless, they pulled Christian up by his scrawny arms and set off. They clambered up the steep stairs to the deck and down the swinging rope ladder to the beach. The sun shone weakly through the haze, and the beach was covered with a thin layer of ice that crunched and splintered under their steps.

Finally, they stumbled into the tavern and let poor Christian sink to the ground. The few people who were still there glared at them as if they had committed a murder before their eyes.

"What happened, my dear, who is this man?" asked Anna, who came in from one of the back rooms.

"My grandfather, he is seriously ill, and I don't have anyone else to help me," Nikolas said, out of breath.

"Your grandfather is sailing with you on the ship?" asked Anna, bewildered.

Nikolas noticed that his lie had very short legs, but he had feared that otherwise Anna would not help old Christian. But here, he had misjudged her character. She didn't expect an explanation, as she had seen so many people and heard so many stories that she knew if something wasn't her business.

"What's wrong with him?" she asked instead, looking at the dirty old man lying lifeless on her floor.

"It started with a cold, and now he's hot and barely conscious," Nikolas said.

"Get him out of here, who knows what he has. Maybe even the Black Death," Willem scolded from behind the counter, which only resulted in the few guests rushing to leave the inn.

"Oh pish, stop it, you have no idea," Anna said. "Come and help me. We have a vacant chamber. Beata has left us; she truly believes this runabout is serious with her."

They lifted the still unconscious Christian from the floor and dragged him into the chamber, where they put him in a bed. Anna touched his glowing forehead and then took off his shoes and stockings and felt his legs too.

"We need a bowl of cold water, a rag, and a few warm stones. You remember where everything is?" She turned to Nikolas, who rushed out of the room to carry out her instructions.

He knew she would help Christian, just as she had helped him. When he came back into the room with the bowl and the rag, Anna was about to put fresh and dry clothes on the still body. Nikolas saw for the first time how emaciated old Christian was under his thick wool layers. The thin, parchmenty skin stretched over the ribs, and his arms and legs were thinner than a child's.

Anna covered Christian in a warm blanket and put the damp rag on his forehead.

"Where are the stones?" asked Anna, and Nikolas zoomed out the door.

In the tavern, Nikolas rolled the stones with an iron rod from the embers and onto a piece of leather, which he wrapped tightly around them. The heat of the stones penetrated even through the thick leather skin.

"Put them near his feet. We have to get the temperature out of his head and warm his legs." Anna had taken the lead, and Nikolas followed, relieved.

That night, he went twice to warm the stones, while Anna constantly moistened the rag and put it on Christian's forehead. In the early-morning hours, Nikolas fell asleep exhausted on a chair, and when he awoke again, Anna smiled at him tiredly as she felt old Christian's forehead.

"We survived the worst. He's sleeping now quietly. If you want, your grandfather can stay here for some time and regain strength, and, of course, you too," she said softly, stroking his head. Nikolas just nodded and got up to look at Christian. "He's going to get through. I'll lie down now for a while and later make a warm soup with bacon."

Nikolas was so grateful that Anna did all this without further explanation, and he admired that, despite the poorly run business, she still had so much generosity and helpfulness to take in and care for a stranger.

In the end, Christian stayed with Anna for the rest of the winter, as he recovered slowly, which did not stop him from bemoaning that he needed to get back to the ship. But it was only Nikolas who returned to complete his guard duties and who came back the following week to Anna.

Feeling indebted to her, Nikolas began to do all sorts of work around the inn. He stripped the tables and chairs so that they looked like new, then repainted the swan on the inn sign, which now hung again in bright white above the front door. In between, he peeled beets, fed the pigs, and mucked out the barn, and in the evenings, they sat together by the fire and Anna continued to teach him her mother tongue. He learned quickly and wrote each new word on pieces of parchment, which he neatly tied together to a small book. And so, the last weeks of winter passed too.

# 9

## Störtebeker's Treasure

On Candlemas, the pirate crew met on the ship for the first time in months. No one had left, and everyone was still in good spirits that life as a pirate would bring them prosperity. As the days got longer, their failed beginning seemed to fade into the darkness of the last winter. Ben had gotten wood somewhere to repair the rotten planks. Eventually, they caulked the chinks of the planking by stuffing them with straw and covering everything with a new layer of tar. It was hard work, but no one seemed to mind, for the zest for action was again itching in their fingers and the love for adventures tingled in their stomachs.

As lucky as they had been to be received so amicably in the hamlet, they had grown weary of the joys of the drinking holes. And if they had wanted to live a regular life as crafts-men, they could have had it in Hamburg. For the first time, they worked hand in hand like a real crew.

Lastly, Nikolas repainted the name 'Gundelinde' in white paint, which was left from the sign of Anna's inn.

Klaas and Pitt had sharpened the old weapons to deadly blades, and a few barrels of thin beer and some sacks of oats were stored belowdecks again. This time, they did not have the advantage of setting sail with supplies for several months, and so it was imperative that they achieved their first success as pirates quickly.

Derek and Henning had brought along two dodgy men who introduced themselves as brothers Niels and Jens Larsson, and after a brief conversation with Ben, they also boarded the vessel.

It was already the end of March when they picked up the ropes and beams, with which they had supported and secured the ship, and glided gently into the water at high tide.

A cool wind blew and allowed them to sail quickly towards the pale horizon. The next day brought fog, and Hein sounded the waters again. Nikolas took the opportunity to ask the captain for some parchment, ink, and a feather, and persuaded Hein to use lead arming. He wanted to find out exactly what information the seabed held and planned to create a map in which he would enter all the peculiarities if remarkable ones could be found. Hein agreed but lost patience at the end of the day and left the lead to Nikolas, who had shown that he had a fine sense for sounding.

The fog lasted a few days, so they didn't know exactly where they were yet again. Luckily, as the fog cleared, they identified a widely visible church tower which was marked down on one of Ben's countless maps. In fact, during their stay, Ben had bought half a dozen more maps, along with some scrolls and strange instruments.

Nikolas recorded the topography of the coastline on his map and, in addition to the landmarks, also included characteristics of the seabed like noticeable shells or the colouring of the sand.

With Niels and Jens on board, Nikolas had to do less work on the running rigging and thus had more time to complete his nautical charts—because one was soon no longer enough. He was meticulous and sounded more often than necessary.

While fine beige sands with ringworms and small mussels covered the west coast of Denmark, the sand became coarser and greyer as they sailed around the northern tip and down south on the east coast of the kingdom. The north was also unsuitable for anchoring, as the coast was flat and straight and offered little cover from the inconveniences of the weather or as hiding places. This information, too, was neatly entered in Nikolas's charts.

When they circumnavigated the northern tip of Zealand, the seabed showed itself again in bright white. Here, they finally had some success with their tactic of pretending to be a merchant ship in distress, even if they again attracted only fishermen and small coastal traders who did not expect to draw the attention of pirates.

The large high-sea merchant ships stayed on their course and did not care about them, which was perhaps better for both sides. Nikolas doubted that they could have taken on an armed and prepared crew, even though they now had two more battle-tested men with Jens and Niels on board and impeccable weapons.

It was the first evening after they had sold their loot of fish and jute bales and had set sails when they heard a joyful laugh coming out of the captain's cabin. Shortly afterwards, Ben opened the door.

"I solved the riddle," he said.

He held up the yellowed and now slightly burnt treasure map he had presented to them last year. But his crew showed no reaction and continued to look at him expectantly.

"As we have already noted, this treasure map does not indicate any points for orientation."

Derek snorted contemptuously; after all, it was he who had pointed out this deficiency.

"I have spent many sleepless nights to solve this riddle and find the treasure that so many have been looking for. Well, I tell you, they didn't have this document, or at least they didn't know its secret." Ben once again waved the parchment with glowing cheeks in front of their noses.

"And what's on this miracle sheet?" asked Jens, who didn't know about Ben's strange obsession with secret treasures.

"Well, yes, what's on it?" Ben looked at him in dismay. "I would like to draw your attention to the fact that it is written with a special ink, one that only became visible when I held it over the flame of a candle."

"*Fanden må vide,*" Jens hissed.

"The devil has nothing to do with it," Nikolas said. "You can create this effect simply with milk."

There was a brief silence during which all stared at Nikolas, who realized that knowledge would not override superstition in this instance.

Ben eventually continued with a lowered voice, briefly looking around the deserted and starlit sea as if someone could eavesdrop. "Well, well, I'm going to reveal the secret to you now.

*If you want to lift the greatest treasure, go to Cape Arkona.*
*When the virgin sits on the washing stone, the treasure is laid out.*
*But only with a slight approach can you get about.*

"And that should lead us to Störtebeker's treasure? There's not even his name in it," Jens countered again.

But now Ben's patience was at an end. "If you don't have the mind to understand the statement, that's not my problem. I'm the captain here, and I say we're on target for Rügen. Hein!"

"Aye, Captain!" replied Hein, stepping to the helm, while Ben, appalled by this open mistrust, retreated into his cabin.

It took them two days to reach the island of Rügen, and then they sailed along the coast to its northernmost point, Cape Arkona. The hitherto flat land swung up to a dazzling white cliff which seemed to reach a good three hundred feet at its highest point. At the top of the rugged cliffs stretched a dense deciduous forest which emphasized the white of the chalk rocks even more.

They sailed as close to the cliffs as the lead allowed, and all the men stared tensely at the coast, expecting to find a clue to the promised treasure. They narrowly circumnavigated a large, flat granite rock that protruded from the water not far from the coast. That had to be the washing stone. But they did not discover anything that indicated a treasure or its hiding place.

To make sure they hadn't missed anything, they sailed along the steep coast twice the next day, but again without success. The white of the rocks did not appear to have any crevices, caves, or niches and connected seamlessly into the sea.

On the second day, they let the jollyboats to sea and went ashore in a shallow bay with the tide, not far from the washing stone. Only old Christian and Jan remained on board.

They began their ascent from the south and had to fight their way through dense undergrowth. Blackberry hedges blocked their way and tore their clothes, and they had made long detours when a clearing opened in front of them with the open sea behind. They scrambled over large boulders and reached the edge of the cliffs. Deep beneath them, the sea foamed, and its bluster and bellowing were brought up to them with the wind. A little farther out to sea, they saw the *Gundelinde*, which lay quietly in the glittering water. But even up here, there was nothing to suggest that there was a treasure hidden somewhere or even that people were often treading these lands. Nevertheless, they split into two groups to re-search the site. Nikolas went with Ben, Hein, Klaas, and Pitt in the direction from which they had come, and Derek, Henning, Jens, and Niels took the opposite path.

When they reunited at dusk, none of them had discovered anything, but they were all sweaty and the scratches of the blackberry hedges itched. They set up their night camp between large boulders that shielded them from the cool sea wind and lit a fire over which they heated their provisions of dried fish.

The next day, they searched the area once more, but again without result. The general displeasure became more and more evident, and Derek finally spoke up. "I say we should go back to the ship and finally realize that this treasure is what it was from the beginning. Namely, the crazy idea of a bad captain wasting our time."

Henning, Jens, and Niels agreed with him, but the others stood by their disgruntled-looking captain. It was the first time that Derek said openly what Nikolas had heard so many times behind closed doors. And as he saw him standing with his three mates, his discomfort grew even larger. Should Derek want to take over the command, it stood now four to six, and Ben's support was dwindling. But Derek's group was still outnumbered, and so the four insurgents remained calm for now and followed Ben's further orders.

It was low tide when they pushed the jollyboats back into the water. No one said a word as they left the washing stone behind, but their disappointment was written in their faces.

When they were back on board the *Gundelinde*, Nikolas stopped at the railing for a moment to look once more at the spectacular, steep slopes. And it was then that he saw it. A small gap that opened between two rocky ledges. On their outward journey, they had come ashore with the tide, so they had not noticed the gap yesterday, as it was underwater.

"Look," he exclaimed excitedly. "There is an entrance to a cave, right over there, between the two ledges!" Nikolas pointed to the coast and now everyone saw it.

"Ha ha." Ben sounded overjoyed. "One should keep one's possibilities modest, wait for low tide, and reach the coast in small boats. Why didn't I think about it right away!"

Nikolas found it not at all surprising that he had not thought about it. A treasure map should probably not reveal its secrets to everyone.

They let the jollyboats back to the water, and this time, old Christian was also in on it. It had already gone against his grain that he was left behind the day before, when he was probably the most entitled out of all of them to discover the treasure of Störtebeker.

When the shadow of the rocks fell on them again, they realized that it would not be easy to reach the foot of the cliff, as the water rushed around countless reefs. It was a dangerous path, and the dark gap was just wide enough that they could pass through with their small rowing boats.

They had to pull in the oars and push themselves with their hands along the walls to penetrate the cliff. The gap reached a few dozen feet up and opened into a cave after several fathoms. Light fell into it from an opening far above them. The water threw dancing reflections of light at the walls, and the sploshing of the waves against the bare stone echoed back a hundred times. It was only when they lit their torches that they could observe the extent of the cave. The rear half was not covered by water and formed a natural pier. A few slippery steps, which were likely also submerged at high tide, led up to a plateau.

Iron rings embedded in the rocks clearly proved that men had been there before them. And they were shocked when they also discovered a skeleton with still discernible hair, jewellery, and clothing.

"There's the virgin, but she won't wash no more," Jens broke the silence as the dirty linen dress revealed the remains as a woman.

Many years later, they learned that, shortly before his capture, Störtebeker had kidnaped a noble damsel from Riga to use as a pawn. In Hamburg, however, no one was interested in the girl's well-being. The only clue to the hiding place was passed from one hand to another until the map landed in Ben's possession, but by then, it was too late for the girl as well as Störtebeker.

"The one who jokes about the dead will be haunted by them," old Christian hissed, and in the cave, the whisper seemed to come from the afterlife.

Jens shrugged and climbed over the skeleton to advance further into the grotto. A dark passageway so low that even Nikolas had to duck led them into another cave, which was only illuminated by the flickering glow of their torches. Every little ledge created ghostly shadows. The air was wetter and it was more difficult to breathe, but they found nothing but bare stone. This place was unpleasantly oppressive as if haunted by the dead, and so they stumbled back into the first cave.

"Look here," said Nikolas, who had walked around the large rock next to the dead woman. He pointed to the boulder, and those closest to him also recognized fine lines in the stone, almost completely overgrown with moss. Nikolas carefully scraped off the green plant layer with a knife and retraced the grooves. Ben had pushed himself forward and illuminated the place where letters were now clearly visible.

*Fine and white*
*Shells and needles*
*Surrounded by water*

"What's that supposed to mean?" Jens asked impatiently as Ben read the new message, but no one knew the answer. What seemed clear to everyone, though, was that the treasure had been taken to another place, but this place could be anywhere.

They reluctantly made their way back and faced another nasty surprise. The tide rose and the water was already engulfing the stone steps in the cave.

"Quick, we have to get out of here if we don't want to wait for the next low tide," Derek shouted to the others, and they slipped and slid to their boats.

Nikolas, Derek, Jens, Niels, and Pitt were the first to untie their boat and to disappear into the gapping exit. Nikolas saw the bright, narrow opening at the end when they came to a bottleneck and almost got stuck. It was only with difficulty that they scraped forward along the rocks. Finally outside, they made sure to put a good distance between themselves and the cliffs, and then waited for the others. But no one followed them. The gap became smaller and smaller with the rising water. Nikolas thought he heard excited voices, but he couldn't make out any words between the sound of the waves and the laughter of the seagulls.

Perhaps the others had been pushed back into the cave and now had to endure until the next low water. In any case, they could not wait any longer, as the waves increased in force with the incoming flood, and they risked being capsized and crushed against the rocks. When they were farther out at sea and out of danger, they noticed Hein and Henning emerging from the waters behind them, clinging desperately to one of their oars. Shortly thereafter, Ben, Klaas, and old Christian appeared, hanging on to the second oar. Apart from Klaas, none of them seemed to be able to swim, and they barely kept their heads above water. But they hardly managed to cope with the dangerously rising tide, which now pushed them against the rocks. Klaas grabbed old Christian by his shirt and was the only one who slowly gained distance from the rocks despite the additional load.

It took almost an hour, and the entrance to the cave was no longer visible when they had finally collected all the castaways. They hoisted Christian, who was more dead than alive, into the jollyboat, but the rest of the men could only hold on to the outside of the boat's edge, as the small vessel would not have carried them all.

The escape from the cave had exhausted them all so much that they stayed anchored and lived off their supplies for some days. Christian had lain down in a hammock with his last strength and had not gotten up since. He didn't want to talk to anyone, and when Nikolas stepped to his bedside one evening, he stopped, paralysed. Christian did not move. *He is dead,* thought Nikolas, and he stared at the peaceful but frighteningly pale face of the old man. Images from his past rose in him. He saw his father standing in a river laughing and waving at him before suddenly submerging. He saw his father being carried lifeless from that very river, and when he looked at old Christian again, he saw his father lying in the hammock for a moment.

Nikolas took a deep breath and pushed his father's face from his thoughts. To his astonishment, old Christian opened his eyes and looked at him, tired.

"I thought you were dead," Nikolas whispered.

"Close to it," Christian replied, weakly smiling.

Nikolas approached and sat down on a seafarer chest.

"You look upset. What's going on?" asked Christian.

"I was thinking of my father. He died, I was six or seven. I can't remember much of him, but he always told me stories, just like you."

"Well, we'll get along well, then, your father and me. I will tell him that he can be proud of his boy and that you will surely become the greatest mariner of all time."

"But you're not going to die?" pleaded Nikolas, which made Christian look dreary.

"My boy, it's time for me to go. I know what the others say about me, and they are right. I'm a burden on the crew, but if they think an old sea dog like me is going ashore to die, then they can go whistle for it.

"Now don't look so sad, death is part of life, and I've done everything in my life that I wanted to do and made my peace with the mistakes I made. And that is the most important thing. Always do what you long for, Nikolas, then on your last day, the farewell will be a joy.

"My dear boy, now fetch Ben, I have something to tell him."

When Nikolas returned with the distraught Ben, Christian lay there again, motionless and with his eyes closed, but this time, he immediately opened them when they stepped to his side.

"First of all, I want to thank you for taking an old geezer like me on board," he began.

"You are the best thing that has happened to us. Without you, we would have—"

"I don't have long, so listen to me," Christian interrupted Ben. "The message in the cave. It must be an island," Christian continued in a barely audible voice, motioning Ben to get closer.

"I've already thought of this, a place surrounded by water. But there are many islands, and all have white sand and mussels," Ben said.

"But it is only one of them. Störtebeker certainly did not visit this cave on Rügen alone, and he surely did not hide his own treasure there. But he often visited Helgoland by himself and without anyone knowing exactly what he was doing there or where he was going. He was always wary about others. And that's what you should be too. Your crew is not united behind you. Be cautious and think carefully about who you trust with your secrets."

At these words, Ben looked around suspiciously, and his gaze rested on Nikolas for a few seconds. "Is there anything I can do for you?" he asked Christian.

"A proper sea burial fit for an old sailor."

"Nothing else?"

Christian shook his head imperceptibly, and they left the dying man with mixed feelings.

The news spread quickly that old Christian was close to death, and all stayed on deck that night. Only the bare necessities were spoken, and everyone tried to find a place that was more comfortable than the naked planks.

The next morning, old Christian was dead. Nikolas had been trying all night to convince himself that no one could predict his own death and that the old man would soon recover and continue the journey with them. He had not gone down when Ben brought the final news and made sure to stay as far away as possible from the hatch that led belowdecks. So, he stood at the bow and threw the sounding lead ahead. He felt and he thought nothing. It was much more like he was in some way free and far removed from the things that were happening around him.

Derek and Henning made a raft. Then Klaas and Pitt got Christian's few belongings and finally his lifeless body. The preparations had lasted almost all day, and now they were waiting for the sun to go down. Christian lay on the raft, and if they had not put two coins on his eyes, it would have looked as if they had made him an unusual bed on which he was now asleep.

Nikolas knew that the dead should pay the coins to the ferryman who transferred them into the afterlife. He had stopped sounding and thought about what would happen if he took the coins away. If Christian couldn't pay the ferryman, he might have to return. But he also knew what was said if the ferryman did not get his wages. Then the souls were doomed to roam the seas forever and never find salvation. Christian himself had told him these stories, from ghost ships whose crews were cursed to cruise the seas without ever being able to go on land, and that they were commanded by the devil incarnate, who was crueller and more unpredictable than the most terrible death.

So, he only stood there motionless and watched the others. Hein had steered the *Gundelinde* far out to sea, and now they were striking the sail. Derek and Henning stood talking quietly together, and Jan frantically tried to not look at the corpse.

Ben had retreated into his cabin and was probably already making new plans to finally find the greatest treasure of all time, Nikolas thought grimly. But as the sun bowed out and promised to end the day in an unforgettable way, Ben came out of his cabin with reddened eyes and stuffed his handkerchief into his coat pocket. They all gathered around the dead sailor, and each one of them said their farewell in silence. Then they wrapped the body in a linen cloth. Now that Christian's face was also covered, the realization that he would never see him again, never hear stories from him again, leaked into Nikolas's consciousness.

They let the raft to water and pushed it a few feet away from the ship. Pitt then lit a torch and threw it onto the body. Slowly the flames spread from the torch, and where they touched the water, it hissed gently. Ben rang the ship's bell as they watched the raft drift farther and farther out to sea.

Nikolas stared into the flames as quiet tears ran down his face. He avoided looking at the others so that they did not see that he was crying. When Ben rang the bell for the third time, the crew turned away to hoist the sail, but Nikolas stood and watched until the fire on the raft was completely extinguished, and he let the grief wash over him. He said goodbye not only to Christian, but also to his parents...something he had never done before.

# 10

## Navigation

$\mathcal{N}$ikolas was stunned at how quickly everyday life returned after Christian's sea burial. In fact, it seemed as if Christian had never boarded this ship, so little had his absence been noticeable in the last weeks, but internally Nikolas did not know what to do with his feelings. The powerless grief was followed by a depressed restlessness, which was not dispelled by the daily work. He devoted every spare minute to completing his nautical charts. He recorded striking landmarks, such as large trees, dunes, mountains, or towers, and the associated typical seabed, and yet the unrest did not want to pass. Ben also seemed unusually busy, but instead of heading to Helgoland, they crossed aimlessly off the coast. Nikolas found Ben on the afterdeck handling the strange instruments he had brought on board in their first winter.

"What is that?" asked Nikolas, pointing to a wooden box on the floor. Ben turned around, blinking and rubbing his eyes. He had a long rod with a crossbar in his hand, which he held close to his face, and a clear pressure mark could be seen at the root of his nose.

"That's a compass. Got it from a trader who brought it up from the south. Said it would be used there everywhere for orientation on the open sea. But if you ask me, that sounds like the work of the devil. A little needle that always aligns north can't be right," Ben replied, turning back to the coastline with the sun high above.

Nikolas bent down and carefully opened the lid of the wooden box, which Ben had called a compass. On the lid was a beautiful inlay that reminded him of a rose, but it was the inside of the box that truly aroused his curiosity. A narrow pin, like a needle of the sailmakers, turned with the ship's movements on a small pole, but it was clear that it was aligned in a north-south direction. Under the needle was a disc with engraved symbols for north, south, west, and east, and 360 equal segments divided the circle. Nikolas realized that this classification could be used to determine the direction in which one was moving, but the needle did not point towards north, according to the disc. He turned the box until the lettering and the needle aligned. Carefully, Nikolas lifted the needle up and looked at it in detail. It was made of metal, but he could not discover the secret of why it was aiming in a particular direction. He put it back on its seat and watched it calm down and adjust its point back to north. At the St. Nikolai School, he had learned a lot about and even heard one or two secrets of the natural sciences, but this small piece of metal puzzled him. He turned back to Ben, who again held the rod to his nose and pinched one eye closed as he blinked into the sun with the other. It looked like he was aiming at the bright star with a crossbow without tendons.

"What kind of staff is this? Is that something to determine the direction too?" asked Nikolas. This time, Ben squinted slightly, and it took him a while to see clearly again.

"This is a Jacob's staff. With it, you can measure the distance to the coast by determining the angle above the horizon. I would say the tower is about half a nautical mile away."

Ben raised his thumb and took a bearing of the tower. "You only have to target a fixed star like the sun. They say that you can determine latitudes and longitudes with this as well, but I don't see what this could be good for."

"If you know the latitudes and longitudes, you could estimate your position even without the coast in sight."

"That must be a crazy son of a dog who sails so far out to sea."

"How does this staff work?" asked Nikolas.

"You measure with it the height of the sun or a star above the horizon. See here, there is a scale where you can read the angles. This allows you to make calculations. But I think it's too hard for you to understand. If you want, you can try it yourself, though." Ben put the staff aside and avoided looking at Nikolas as he climbed off the afterdeck to retreat into his cabin.

When Ben disappeared, Nikolas picked up the Jacob's staff and looked at it thoroughly. The crossbar was movable and had to be placed in a certain position to be able to read the correct angle. Nikolas put the rod on his nose, as he had seen Ben do, and aimed it at the sun. The sun dazzled him so much that he saw bright lights dancing in front of him even with his eyes closed. It couldn't work like that, as he still had to do some bearing with the crossbar. He took a closer look at the staff and pushed the crossbar back and forth, lost in thought.

Ben had been targeting the sun all the time to measure the distance to the tower. That was wrong, he should have aimed at the tower itself. Nikolas placed the rod on his nose again and pushed the crossbar back and forth until its lower and upper ends bracketed the level of the horizon and the top of the tower. Then he looked at the scale and read an angle of nine degrees.

The calculation, which, according to Ben, was too difficult for him, required some reflection, but by the end of the day, he had searched his memories of mathematics lessons and swirled images of circles and angles through his brain until he had derived a distance formula. His position was the centre of an imaginary circle, and he had to calculate the radius of the circle, which would then indicate the distance to the tower. But to check his considerations, he needed to know the height of the tower.

He was lucky. The next morning, they went ashore to scout out the merchant ships in a nearby port. But, unlike the others, he made his way to the tower.

It was another sunny and hot day, and Nikolas was sweating when he finally climbed the hill towards the tower. In his bundle were two pieces of ship's biscuit, a smoked fish, a bottle of beer, something to write on, and the sounding lead. The hill dropped away to the sea, and he stood as close to the cliff as he dared to look down into the foaming surf. Then he took the sounding line and measured thirty-four fathoms for the height of the cliffs.

The tower was built of massive stones, and Nikolas found an entrance, behind which a narrow and steep spiral staircase led upwards. He climbed the steps and looked after each half round through the small window niches that let slivers of light in, and when he stepped out onto the top of the tower into the bright sunlight again, he blinked, dazzled. He stood on an open platform, which was only bordered by a low row of stones. On five pillars, another platform was built even higher, and a ladder led up through a small hatch. As Nikolas stretched his head through the hatch, he saw several piles of weathered logs covered in mushrooms and moss, taking up the entire surface. This tower had served as a sea mark, and its beacon was supposed to warn ships off the nearby coast, but apparently the fire had not been lit for months, perhaps even years.

There was no way further up, so Nikolas descended again to the lower platform. The wind tugged at his hair, and the surf roared up from far below. Seagulls sailed in the blue sky and plunged headlong into the sea at breathtaking speed, just to come back up with fish in their beaks that they devoured on the rocks. On the horizon, the coast of another country emerged from the sea, and to his left behind a dune, he saw the western edge of a small bay where their ship lay hidden. To the south stretched wide meadows where cows grazed, and here and there were small houses with stables dotted around the flat landscape. To the east, a river had eaten itself into the plain, and as his gaze followed the feral and barely recognizable path that the others had taken, he made out a small town and the masts of the merchant ships in its port.

The tower measured nine and a half fathoms, which together with the cliff yielded forty-three and a half fathoms for the entire height. That was about two hundred and sixty-five feet, or a hundred and four steps. Now he only had to use the measured angle of the Jacob's staff and apply both in his distance formula to calculate the expanse between the coast and their ship. He determined six hundred and sixty-two steps, which amounted to a short quarter sea mile and was consistent with his estimate. He rejoiced at this discovery, and it was as if this joy finally drove out his misery.

He stood with his eyes closed and breathed deeply in and out. Hungry, he finally sat down and leaned against a pillar to unlace his bundle. He placed the clay bottle next to him in the shade and took turns taking a bite of biscuit and a bite of fish. The sun was now high in the sky, and it had become very hot despite the wind. Sleep overcame Nikolas, and he lay down on the stone floor of the platform. It didn't take long before he was fast asleep.

He dreamed of huge towers and measured the distance to his ship by walking with great steps over the water. But as he reached the ship, he remembered that he could not swim and plunged into the cold floods. He ran out of air and kicked and paddled to reach the surface, and when he finally bobbed up, he saw a burning raft floating in front of him, and on the raft sat old Christian, who reached out to him with a flaming hand. The heat of the fire was on his face, but shortly before he got burned, Nikolas woke up dripping in sweat.

The sun had wandered so far around that it was now shining right into his face. He sat up and panted. The midday heat had given way to a sweltering sultriness. The others would not come back until late in the evening, and without them, he could not return to the ship. So, he moved into the shadows and kept an eye on the bay to join them on their arrival from their scouting.

He repeated his calculations. They were correct, but what could he do with it? It might have been helpful to enter their position on a nautical chart, but if one knew the distance of only one point, one could be anywhere on the imaginary circle with that particular radius. If he had two points, he could determine their position on a map by extending the bearing to the intersection of both lines. Or one could calculate the distance to another ship if he knew the height of its mast. The next time he was in a port, he decided he would study the heights of the masts of the different types of ships.

The night came, and Nikolas was disturbed in his thoughts by the small group that walked to the bay far down the small path. The first of them carried a lantern, and the others followed this leader in the twilight.

Nikolas grabbed his belongings and stumbled down the narrow tower staircase. When he was at the bottom, he could no longer see the small group, but the moon illuminated the path down the hill. Soon he saw the friendly yellow light of the lantern dancing up and down again. He had caught up with the others quickly, and twenty minutes later, they reached the bay and their jollyboats.

"We have made allies. The men from the *Swantje* lie in a bay on the other side of the river. The day after tomorrow, a trader leaves for England, and he has the whole ship full of the finest silk cloth for the royal court. We'll wait for the moneybags at dawn and lure them into a trap, and the others will cut their way off from behind," Klaas told him with ferocious joy as they rowed back to the *Gundelinde.*

They spent most of the next day dozing in the shade on deck and maintaining their weapons. Pitt had pulled out a small flute and blew sluggish melodies. Nikolas had gone over to Hein to ask him something that had come to his mind on the tower.

"Is there a more accurate way to determine one's direction than using the sun?"

Hein looked at him awkwardly. "At night, you can get your bearings from the stars."

"And if it's cloudy at night and you don't have a coastline to orientate?"

"That would be foolish to venture so far out into the open sea. Here in the Baltic or the West Sea, sooner or later, you will always hit land, perhaps not exactly where you wanted to go. But no one has ever returned from the great water."

"Why not?"

"They fell into nowhere at the end of the world."

"The Earth is round like a ball; you'd only sail in circles."

"Oh yes? And on the other side, you're upside down, or what? I once saw a map in St. Mary's Cathedral and the Earth was flat like a disc."

"Aristotle and also Thomas Aquinas say that the Earth is a sphere."

"Never heard of them."

"The imperial orb represents the world."

"Hm," Hein muttered. "Never seen that either."

"It is depicted on some gold guilder or pieces of silver."

"And they're flat like a disc."

Nikolas gave up. "Have you ever used a compass?"

"No. I prefer to rely on my instincts than on a thing that is controlled by invisible forces."

Nikolas was not satisfied with this answer either, but there was little point in asking Hein further questions, and instead he went to the captain's cabin. He knocked and carefully opened the door when he didn't get an answer. Ben stood in the glow of two candles, bent low over a large table littered with countless nautical charts and documents.

"Ah, Nikolas, what can I do for you?" asked Ben kindly as he looked up.

Nikolas looked around the shady cabin. Opposite him, light shimmered through a series of small window hatches with open shutters. In one corner stood a well-worn armchair with an equally shabby-looking small footstool in front of it. A few boxes of food that Nikolas had never seen anywhere else on the ship stood next to the armchair. In the other corner was a narrow bed with tattered blankets. He had always thought that the captain of a ship had better facilities, but apparently Ben had put all his resources into countless maps, weapons, and food. On the walls were shelves filled to the ceiling with rolled-up parchment. In an open chest were even more daggers and falchions, and a few particularly artfully crafted pieces had been placed in brackets on a small shelf. But the huge oak table in the middle of the cabin took up most of the space, and Nikolas's gaze wandered eagerly over the countless nautical charts scattered there.

"Yes, these can keep you awake many nights," Ben said as he followed Nikolas's eyes.

Nikolas approached and studied the maps. Almost all of them showed the West Sea and the Baltic Sea, but they differed considerably from each other. Depending on what the draughtsman had valued, the southern, sometimes the eastern or northern, coast was shown with more details, while the other parts were simply roughly sketched as land or sea and often not even labelled. Even the maps depicting matching sections did not always show islands in the same place, and smaller islands were sometimes completely missing. On other maps, routes to large ports had been drawn and instructions had been entered in tiny writing describing the geography of the estuaries. These charts had obviously been made by merchants for their crossings. The map that Ben had looked at showed the section between the Elbe estuary and Denmark, with the island of Helgoland in the middle.

"You remember Christian's last words?" Nikolas nodded and Ben continued. "I think I will soon fill in the rest of the crew. The mood has improved so much since the last successful raids that they will surely agree to a renewed hunt for Störtebeker's treasure. Do you see here, this place? There is a small, sheltered bay, which can only be seen from the side of the open sea and only if one deviates from the usual trade routes." Ben pulled out another chart from under the pile. "I think Störtebeker has come ashore here, but where he went and where he hid his treasure, we can only find out once we are there."

"Does that mean we will sail back into the West Sea?"

"Yes, tomorrow. I will tell the crew after we have raided this fat merchant ship. Unfortunately, I will also have to let in our allies on the *Swantje*, and they will want a share in it."

"You wouldn't have to tell them why we want to sail to the West Sea. You could suggest that there is more and bigger prey. I think it wouldn't be advisable to tell everyone the exact reason, including your own crew."

"Spoken like a real pirate! You have left the honesty and gullibility of a child behind. Well, that's not necessarily the best, but certainly not the worst. Especially not in our business."

Nikolas had forgotten the reason he had come to the cabin and was instead eager to study the charts. He fetched his own maps and spent the rest of the day comparing the charts with his own records and, with Ben's consent, supplementing and correcting them. After scouring all the charts that were already on the table, he took some other parchments from the wall shelves and found that many of them showed seas and coasts that he had never seen before and did not know where they were.

A whole series of other documents were bound diaries of sea travellers, most ending with the ship getting into a storm or running onto a reef. The hours flew by, and he had not even looked through a third of the charts and records when Ben ordered him out for the first night watch. Nikolas could hardly break away from this treasure trove, but he did not dare to oppose his captain.

During his guard shift, he pondered the wealth of knowledge Ben had accumulated in his cabin. It seemed that never before had anyone made a map containing all the information about the West and the Baltic Seas. Moreover, all the charts had regions on the open sea that were shunned, probably because no one dared to attempt routes without a view of the coast. But with a directional compass and a method to measure their speed, one should also be able to orientate oneself on the open sea. And maybe, yes, maybe there was a country somewhere that no one yet knew about.

# 11

## Fight and Defeat

With sunrise, activity arose on deck. It promised to be a clear and hot summer day again, and they could see the allied *Swantje* at their agreed position. The *Gundelinde* was ready to strike, and now it was time to wait for the merchant ship. The wind was favourable and would drive them directly towards their target, the sails were ready to be lowered, and the men checked their weapons once more.

Nikolas had finished scrubbing the deck when Henning saw a red flag rising on the mast of the *Swantje*. At his call, Ben gave the order to set sail. Everything went smoothly. The sail rushed into position and billowed in the wind. They quickly picked up speed, and when they got out of the bay and into the open sea, the *Swantje* had already forced the merchant ship to change course. It was a holk of about twenty-four steps in length, with three masts, but its size made the ship cumbersome, and so the two smaller and more nimble cogs soon caught up with the holk.

The *Gundelinde* was coming alongside when arrows suddenly rained down on them. The arrows slid over the planks or got stuck trembling in the wood. Fortunately, no one was seriously injured. Only Klaas dragged himself behind the mast, pulling one leg behind. There, he slid to the ground and pulled out the arrow stuck in his thigh with a pain-distorted face. He tied his leg above the wound with his belt.

The others had just taken cover when a second shower descended on them. At that moment, Jan came to deck to see what the unfamiliar noises were, and an arrow hit him in the shoulder. He stared, aghast, at the piece of wood that was now protruding from his body before his eyes turned inwards and he fell down the stairs.

A terrible battle cry from the other side of the holk told them that the *Swantje* had now reached the merchant ship and was getting ready to board. Without waiting for an order from Ben, they all jumped out of their hideouts and joined the hollering. No new arrows came over, for already some men of the *Swantje* had swung on board the merchant ship and raged amongst the sailors with their falchions. Other looters from the *Swantje* and the men of the *Gundelinde* climbed the holk to engage in the fight. Only Nikolas stood with a dagger in his hand in the middle of their deck and could not believe what was happening before his eyes.

Until now, they were able to conquer all their quarry without much force and had renounced raw atrocities, but so far, none of their victims had defended themselves much. Moreover, they had always been in the majority and had found poorly or unarmed crews. But this time, they were far inferior, and ever more men armed to the teeth seemed to be pouring out of the belly of the merchant ship and onto the deck. They defended their ship and their cargo with as much stubbornness as the pirates showed in their attempt to board and plunder the ship. Their only advantage was that they attacked their opponents from two sides.

Nikolas saw Pitt fighting two men at the same time with a falchion in each hand. Just as they were threatening to break his defence, Klaas emerged out of nowhere, repelling a blow with an outstretched sabre that would otherwise have slashed Pitt from top to bottom.

On the afterdeck, Derek took a fencing position in front of another man, and their duel was almost well mannered.

Ben bravely battled with a man who was fighting with a sabre and an axe, but he, too, had already received a blow or two, as his shirt was blood-soaked.

Henning knocked off a man he had pierced with his blade and immediately turned to the next.

Jens and Niels both attacked one man together and stabbed him in cold blood with his back against the mast.

But the men of the *Swantje* were even crueller. They did not wait until their opponents could fight and defend themselves, but instead slayed them from behind so that they did not even see their misfortune coming.

Nikolas was still standing in horror when a man swung on a rope over to their ship. The man directly approached him and was about to grab him when Nikolas evaded the hand and ran away as fast as his legs would move in his fright. He heard the man behind him laughing all the way. Nikolas crashed against the closed door of the captain's cabin and turned around with his dagger stretched out.

"You're not really a pirate. Stands there trembling with his back to the wall and can't go anywhere. When we have finished you, we will sink your ship with man and mouse." The man grinned and tapped the dagger in Nikolas's shaking hands with his own blade. Then he raised his sword for a last blow, and Nikolas closed his eyes in anticipation of the agony of death that the blade would inflict on him. But instead, he heard a thump, and when he opened his eyes, Hein had jumped from the afterdeck and pulled the man around by his raised arm.

"Who attacks a defenceless child?" Hein growled as he punched the stunned assailant in the head, who staggered backwards and fell straight into the dagger, which Nikolas was still holding outstretched in front of him. The man's weight was on him as he sidestepped, leaving the attacker to fall to the ground. The last crooked expression on the face of the man froze, and he laboriously pulled himself up the stairs to the afterdeck. Then he turned to Nikolas, who still stood like a statue but with a pounding heart and wide eyes. The man took a step towards him and opened his mouth, but instead of words, blood poured out. The dagger was still stuck in his back as he turned around and dragged himself to the railing. It seemed as if he was trying to retreat to his ship, but then the strength left him, and he plunged headlong into the sea.

*I killed a man.* The thought repeated in Nikolas's head in an endless loop, and it was only when the call for fallback sounded across the sea that he detached his view from where the man had disappeared.

The men of the *Swantje* and the *Gundelinde* fought their way back and fled to their own ships. Derek had shouldered Henning and struggled to get over the gap between the railings, while Ben was still fighting with the man with the axe. A final bloodcurdling scream rang out across the deck as the axe hit Ben's hand and got stuck in the railing. While his opponent was struggling and pulling to free the axe, Ben rammed his knife into his side and he sank, badly wounded, to the ground, but Ben's fingers were already severed.

Blood poured out of Ben's finger stumps as he swung himself with the last of his strength onto the deck of the *Gundelinde* and remained where he had landed. White as a sheet, he stared at his hand as if stunned. Klaas rushed to him with a cloth and a strap and staunched the blood supply on Ben's upper arm, then pressed the cloth onto the wound. Ben let everything happen to him without any reaction.

Hein had steered the ship out to the open sea, where the *Swantje* had already sailed away. The merchant ship did not follow them, as they were probably busy nursing their own wounded.

"Someone has to look after Jan," Klaas shouted to the others, who also took care of their own injuries.

Nikolas, who was the only one unharmed, rushed off and stumbled down the steps belowdecks. In the sudden darkness, he didn't see where he was going and fell over Jan, who was lying at the foot of the stairs. On hands and knees, he fumbled on the ground until his eyes got used to the twilight, and he saw Jan lying motionless but still breathing. The arrow in his shoulder had broken off during the fall and pierced his back. Nikolas shook Jan carefully and called his name, but the man didn't come to it. Eventually, he picked up a bucket and splashed cold water in his face. Just as Jan opened his eyes, Klaas limped down the stairs.

"He's already awake again, can't be that bad, then." Klaas picked up Jan and leaned him against the stairs.

Nikolas fetched a candle and illuminated the injured shoulder. Jan had lost a lot of blood, judging by the puddle on the ground, and when Klaas pulled out the arrow through the back, the puncture began to bleed again. Klaas ripped Jan's shirt off his body, pushed it against the wound from the front and back, and finally wrapped a long cloth several times around his shoulder and chest.

"It'll be alright, my boy. Soon, you can boast about your first battle wound. You don't have to say that you just laid around during the actual fight," Klaas said cheerfully. Jan returned a dull but grateful smile. "Come on, little one, we have to put him somewhere where no one else can fall over him," Klaas said to Nikolas, and as he turned away from Jan, Nikolas could see how worried Klaas really was.

Back on deck, Klaas took Nikolas aside. "He lost a lot of blood because the wound wasn't immediately tied off. He must not lose any more, it already looks bad enough. Check the bandage regularly and make sure that the cloths are always firmly pressed on the wound so that the bleeding stops."

Nikolas nodded and saw Klaas tighten the belt around his own thigh as he limped off.

Ben was still sitting on the stairs to the afterdeck with a pale face, pressing the already blood-soaked rag against his left hand. He explained, strangely smiling, that in this profession, one had to expect such injuries, and that this was what made a real pirate.

In front of the forecastle, Derek knelt next to Henning. Nikolas went to help them, but then he saw Derek stroking two fingers over the eyelids of the man in front of him and closing his eyes. Nikolas knew that no help was needed here anymore.

He sat down on the railing and buried his face in his arms. The face of his attacker appeared in his mind and stared at him with his crazed eyes, and every time he opened his mouth, a swell of blood gushed out. Nikolas could not bear these images and climbed into the crow's nest, which Henning would no longer claim to himself, and stared across the wide sea. He tried not to close his eyes, not even blink, until his eyes burned and his gaze was blurred by tears.

As the sun went down, they had put miles between themselves and the scene of the fight. The *Swantje* anchored beside them, and now the two ships lay quietly and almost peacefully side by side.

They had shortened the sails and gathered around Henning, who was lying on a plank. On board the *Swantje*, the crew had also come together around their fallen comrades. Ben sounded the ship's bell, and the bell from the *Swantje* joined in. When Ben rang it the second time, they let the dead man slide from the plank into the water, and Henning sank into the dark and unfathomable depths of the sea. On the *Swantje*, they beat the bell four more times, and with each ring, they handed one of their dead comrades over to the sea. It was a lacklustre but functional procedure, nothing like the committal of old Christian.

Nikolas pondered how many men were lying on the bottom of the sea, and images of pale-green corpses rising from the depths haunted him as Ben ordered them to sail towards the coast.

The next day, the *Swantje* separated from them, and the *Gundelinde* called at a small port in the east. The inhabitants of the village rushed to their landing as if no ship had visited this port since time immemorial. The pirates pretended to be traders who had been attacked and were welcomed in the friendliest way.

Jan hovered a few days between life and death, but after another week, he was able to spoon a clear soup by himself. Ben's fingers had been severed to the second joint, and the flesh around the stumps had become inflamed and began to rot.

Fever and chills plagued him when they lifted him one morning from his bedside and placed him in front of the large fireplace of the empty inn where they had found shelter. Klaas stoked the fire and put an iron rod in the embers. Pitt forced a mug of clear liquor into Ben and then held him down with Hein.

"You might better go outside," Klaas said with a glance at Nikolas, but he shook his head. Klaas was probably right, but Nikolas wanted to see with his own eyes what his father's stories had always left out.

Klaas put a saw to Ben's wrist, and once he had started to cut off the hand, not even the patient's screams stopped him from finishing the procedure quickly and precisely. The black-tinted hand fell to the ground, and Ben briefly lost consciousness until Klaas cauterized the wound with the glowing iron rod, which immediately brought Ben back to his senses and almost made him jump out of the chair.

The sight of the rotten hand on the ground made Nikolas's stomach churn, but it was the smell of the burnt flesh that made him stumble, choking, into the open.

After the amputation, Ben fared better again, and soon he boasted that a missing hand suited him well as a pirate captain.

They stayed in the small village for a total of one month. Nikolas often roamed the area or played with the other children on the street, as he had not done since his father's death.

The village was surrounded by extensive forests with pines, spruces, birches, and aspens. Often, Nikolas came across clearings, which were overgrown by marshy meadows and forced him to make larger detours. He observed eagles circling above him looking for prey, and on one occasion, he even saw a lynx crouching on a rock and watching him with yellow eyes. He had never seen a lynx before, but he instinctively knew that this animal was dangerous, and slowly re-treated without taking his eyes off the big cat.

In the mornings, shortly after sunrise, a dense fog always hung between the trees, which only dissipated when the warming rays of the sun made their way in. In the evenings, when he was lying in his bed, he could hear eerie howls from afar, and sometimes he wished to be in his hammock on the *Gundelinde*, where none of these creatures that the forest housed could surprise him in his sleep.

Over time, he understood one or two words of the local language and learned that they had landed in an area ruled by the German Order, and that they, in fact, had not seen a ship for years. The people made everything they needed to live themselves, and as they had so often before, additional workers were appreciated to help build houses and barns, or simply offer a pleasant distraction in this seclusion.

When they finally got back on board on a September morning, they took with them, besides good timber, some small barrels of the strong liquor, which seemed to be excel-lent for cleaning wounds. Jan was still paler than usual and a little weak, but his wound had healed without complications. Nevertheless, he confided to Nikolas that he still felt a stab-bing in the shoulder when he moved his arm, and that should never change again. Ben's wounds had also healed, and he had been sewn a stuffed pigskin glove, which he now wore over the fleshy arm stump.

# 12

## Finnish Steam Bath

$\mathcal{D}$espite the heavy defeat against the holk, everyone was eager to bring up a new ship. Ben gave the order to sail back to the West Sea, but Derek openly opposed him, even though he was again outnumbered without Henning. But to Ben's and Nikolas's surprise, Klaas and Pitt also sided with the critical voices. As winter approached, they did not want to make an unnecessary trip and would try their luck in these waters and then find a cosy place where they could spend the cold season.

Ben followed his crew's wishes, and thus the opportunity to sail back to the West Sea and search Helgoland for Störtebeker's treasure was again postponed for the time being.

They sailed farther north, and the days quickly became shorter. Nikolas still often dreamed of staring eyes and blood-spluttering mouths and secretly vowed never to kill a human being again. It had been so easy and quick to take the man's life, and if he had not done so, he would probably be at the bottom of the sea now. And yet Nikolas wished it would be as easy to give him back his life.

He took over the position in the crow's nest. In the last few weeks, he had grown so much that even the then too big clothes from Anna were now a few inches too short on his arms and legs and the wind blew mercilessly into his sleeves when he sat freezing in the lookout.

They encountered two small merchant ships heading south, whose flags showed a blue cross on a white background, which they plundered without much trouble.

In his little spare time, Nikolas busied himself with the maps in Ben's cabin and found that this northern part of the Baltic Sea was mostly inaccurately recorded, but he was pretty sure that they were now in the Gulf of Finland.

One night, the weather turned and those who had slept were torn from their dreams. The wind whipped hail into their faces and pushed the ship into a strong heeling even without a hoisted sail. Hein had to put all his strength into steering the ship head-on into the wind, providing the least-contact surface. The storm lasted all night, and when it finally subsided in the morning, it continued to rain without interruption.

They hadn't been dry for five days when, after more than a hundred miles, they found a sheltered bay with a small fishing village, where they set their ship on a small beach.

They had landed in Finland, which had been under the rule of Queen Margaret I of Denmark since the founding of the Kalmar Union. Despite his little knowledge of Danish, which he had acquired in his first winter, Nikolas managed to quickly organize accommodation and food for them in return for labour. After so many defeats and only small successes, they needed this little bit of luck. Despite the disputes between the Kalmar Union and the Grand Duchy of Moscow over areas in this region, the small village flourished, not least because of the nearby commercial centre Ulvila, located on the river Kokemäenjoki.

The men of the *Gundelinde* were already thinking about how they could make great booty here next spring, but for now, they were happy to have found shelter from the icy winter weather.

It snowed for almost two weeks, and during that time, they barely took a step outside the door, at most to relieve themselves. Since one could hardly see through the dense curtain of snowflakes, they never went to the intended latrine, which resulted in them often stepping into the yellow and brown residues of their predecessor.

But one morning, Nikolas opened the door and a bright-blue sky arched over him. He had never seen such a sight. Snow mountains piled up, gleaming on both sides of the log cabin, and the landlord Martti Holkeri, with the help of Klaas and Pitt, was already digging lanes into the white walls.

He was fastening his fur-lined jacket when Nikolas was hit by a cold snowball right in the face. Jan stood on top of a snowdrift and grinned down to him, but as he took a step, the edge of the hill gave way and Jan toppled with the snow onto the cleared path.

"Hey, you dimwits, do you think we're doing this for fun? Get a move on and help us. And clear up that path again!" shouted Pitt, whose dripping red nose protruded from under a thick fur hat.

They grabbed two shovels but couldn't help themselves putting a handful of snow down Pitt's collar as they passed by, and he responded by pushing them left and right into the snow. Shortly afterwards, Ben stepped out of the door, and as he slammed it shut behind him, an avalanche broke free from the roof and slid onto his head.

"That's also a way to build a snowman." Jan laughed, and the other men joined in as they saw Ben coated in white and apparently stuck to his knees.

They had gotten sweaty shovelling snow and cooled down quickly after the work was done, which resulted in severe cold. But the Finns knew a tried-and-tested remedy against the illness and indicated to them to come along.

They wandered one after the other on a narrow path into the forest. The forest was strangely quiet under its snow cover, and Nikolas discovered here and there fine traces of small animals such as mice and hares. A large area of churned snow mixed with soil, however, also indicated the presence of larger animals, such as wild boars, that had been foraging for food there at night.

As the forest thinned, Nikolas saw an icy, glittering lake between the trees. On the shore stood wooden huts, and men ran busily between them back and forth. The huts were covered with thick grass sods currently piled high with snow. Stone stoves were embedded in the walls of the huts and were fired from the outside. More men stood on the frozen lake and punched holes into the ice with iron-clad and sharpened poles.

Then, everything seemed to be ready, but what happened next surprised them all. One after the other, the Finns began to undress, and one by one, they entered the huts. Two men, whom Nikolas knew as Paavo and Esko, told them to take off their clothes as well.

"They're bonkers, those Finns. I don't take my clothes off in this cold," Pitt whispered.

They looked at each other uncertainly, but when they noticed that even Hein was already standing naked next to them, they followed his example.

"But I won't let anyone touch me, and if someone tries something in this cubbyhole, he'll have to be spoon-fed for the rest of his life," Pitt muttered as he dropped his pants.

The hut had a small front room, where they were instructed to wash themselves. It was much warmer here than outside, but the water in the buckets was still cool and small pieces of ice swam on its surface.

Even in the twilight, Nikolas could see all the fresh and faded scars on the bodies of his comrades, and he wondered if they would have had as many if they hadn't become pirates. Maybe in a few years he, too, would be littered with scars...or maybe even dead.

When they were all washed, they were allowed into the main room, and a warm haze struck them. The Finns sat on a kind of staircase with wide steps. On one wall, the back of the oven protruded into the room and an enormous amount of heat emanated from it. Nikolas preferred to sit as far away from the furnace wall as possible. When everyone was finally in the chamber, one of the men drew water from a bucket with a wooden trowel and poured it onto the oven stones. In no time, the whole room filled with vapour.

The Finns leaned back, sighed, relaxed, and let the warmth act on their bodies or whipped their backs with birch branches, which Pitt commented on with an incredulous headshake. Nikolas found it strange to breathe air so warm and enriched with moisture. The heat penetrated every fibre of his body, soothing his muscles and calming his nerves. After the steam had dissipated, another infusion was made, and Nikolas did not know whether he was sweating so much or if it was the water vapour that settled on his skin.

Shortly thereafter, Pitt stumbled with a red face from the highest level to the door. With him, a large amount of the fog also left the hut, and a third infusion was necessary. Finally, the Finns rose with satisfied smiles, and the men of the *Gundelinde* followed, relieved.

Outside, the cool winter air surrounded them and tickled their spirits. The Finns laughed and jumped through the snow to the shore of the lake. Some kicked in the frozen-over ice holes and hopped into the water. The water reached up to their stomachs, and with loud hollering and jeering, they quickly dived a few times and then let the next one have his turn. Nikolas watched the spectacle from a safe distance as Pitt gave him a push from behind.

"Hop on, little one, that's the best about this whole affair," he said and grinned widely.

Nikolas went to the lake and after a short hesitation jumped boldly into one of the ice holes. He thought his heart would stop and break into thousands of ice shards. Everything in and around his body pulled together so much that it hurt. This was how the Danish soldiers must have felt during the Battle of Stockholm when they fell victim to Master Hugo's cunning and drowned in the icy Baltic Sea.

Snorting and beating the air around him, Nikolas reappeared and crawled stiffly to firm land. Dripping wet and trembling, he staggered back to the hut, where he was given a towel. Luckily, his belongings hung near the hot oven. When he finally laced up the warm fur jacket, he had stopped shaking, and a pleasant warmth spread inside him. Wrapped up like this, he watched Hein and Ben, who rose out of the icy water with pointed screams and then ran over the snow with shrunken manhood to their bundles of clothes. It was surprising to Nikolas that sweating in the sauna and the subsequent extreme cooling in the icy lake promoted their health, as one seemed to be more of a sign and the other a reason to get sick. For the Finns, the sauna session was a weekly ritual, and every year on the birth of Christ, a day-long sauna visit was carried out to celebrate the day.

In mid-March, they began repairing their ship and replenishing their supplies. Again, they removed most of the barnacles and algae from the hull, but this time, they had suitable tools at their disposal. The smooth hull would reduce water resistance and thus increase their speed in an attack.

When they set sail, they first headed a little farther north to reach the mouth of the Kokemäenjoki, where they wanted to find their next target. Before long they had found the river, and a fully loaded merchant ship came their way. But now that they were alone again, they did not dare to strike such great targets and they let it pass in peace. They scouted the coast and discovered a protected spot behind one of the many smaller islands, where they could not be seen from the river but were able to emerge quickly and take advantage of the surprise moment.

They waited a few days and let two more cogs pass with wistful glances until they spotted a merchant ship that suited them. It sailed under the Swedish flag and had considerable draught, which slowed it down. They waited until the trader sailed past the other side of their island and then launched a fast attack. The anchor was hauled up, the sail set, and they shot around the island so that the merchant ship had to go hard starboard so as not to ram them. It almost came to a standstill, and it was only a matter of minutes before they were on board the trader and kept the crew at bay by force of arms. They seized a load of tanned skins and fur, along with a few chests of ore intended for further processing in Stockholm, and a box of clothing.

The merchant had just gotten away, considerably relieved but with their skins still intact, when a smaller and faster ship caught up with them. They didn't even know what was happening to them when they were forced to fight on their own ship. Fifteen gargantuan men attacked them, and to their surprise, Paavo and Esko were amongst them. Although they still had their weapons at hand, they had to give themselves up quickly and finally watched, with their hands and feet tied up, as their cargo, including their own supplies, were carried off board.

Two men collected all their weapons and threw them overboard.

"*Se olla me,*" said the largest of the men. "*Toimia tai se tulla jokiskin saada huono.*"

"What does he want?" asked Ben.

"He said we should bugger off, next time we won't get away so lightly," Nikolas translated.

"This son of a bitch, I will smash him to bits should he step into my sight again. He could at least have expressed himself in an understandable language," Pitt cursed, trying hard to get rid of his restraints. Exhausted, he gave up, as the more he writhed and tore, the more the knots tightened.

They lay on deck for more than an hour until Derek finally managed to cut through the ropes with a small knife that had been tied to his arm, hidden.

The bandits had long since disappeared, and the men of the *Gundelinde*, despite Pitt's swearing of revenge, rushed to leave these waters. Luckily, the robbers had not searched for other treasures, and so the personal belongings and their shares in coins from their previous loot had been preserved. The box containing the garments had also been left behind.

Since Paavo and Esko were involved in the raid, the crew decided not to sail back to the small village again but to leave the Gulf of Bothnia without further supplies on board and to find the passage to the Baltic Sea in the south. Without weapons, they did not dare to carry out any further raids. Luckily, the sea here in the north was rich with perch and zanders, but without lard and onions, Jan had no choice but to serve dry fish seasoned with the salt of the sea.

As they were soon sick and tired of these meals, and the loss of their weapons forced them to act, they decided to go to Stockholm. They left several small fishing villages behind until Ben finally gave the order to take course on an estuary.

"Niels, up to the lookout, Nikolas, sound for any shallows, and helmsman, course on these archipelagos, there is the river which will lead us to Stockholm."

The river was a crossing of countless coastal islands, and they had to change direction several times when the passage between two islands was too narrow or the depth of the water only a few fathoms.

It took a few days before they saw the city with its huge fortifications. Apparently, the inhabitants were already accustomed to being attacked, and had therefore begun to protect themselves as much as possible.

# 13

## Well Dressed

They anchored on the riverbank, where there were already several other ships, which no longer had cargo and wanted to avoid the expensive mooring fees in the port. They spent the first evening inconspicuously obtaining information about the city.

As in other cities, the gates were closed at sunset, and no one came in or out unseen during the hours of the night. Moreover, Stockholm itself lay on an island and could only be entered via bridges from the south or north. On the bridges stood massive defensive towers and heavily armed guards who also controlled everything and everyone that came into the city or was to be brought out again. That way, the city on the river was able to monitor who could get further into the country and to Lake Malar, which was the inland trading centre of Sweden. It seemed almost impossible to steal weapons or anything else here without raising some eyebrows or worse.

The next morning, they set out to inspect the city itself. Only Jan and Hein stayed on the ship. The remaining men reached the north gate after an hour of walking and were permitted entry when they declared that they were merchants in transit who wanted to rest a little in the city.

On the main street, they had no other choice but to follow the jammed stream of people into the centre of the city and to the market. There, they split up and agreed to meet again on the ship in the afternoon. Nikolas wandered alone through some streets and soon arrived at the southern gate. He made slow progress, as many people thronged into the city so early in the morning to sell their goods. In front of him, a pregnant woman pushed her way through the crowd followed by her husband leading a donkey with huge bundles on his back. It took the guards a long time to examine the bundles, but finally they let the couple through.

Outside the city, Nikolas overtook the pair with the donkey by sidestepping onto the field next to him. He walked for a while until he reached a fork in the road and the crowd of marketers diminished. He turned to the left and inspected the city from the outside. The wall surrounding it was seamless and the same height everywhere, with no obvious way to overcome it easily.

He made his way through a thicket to get closer to the city wall and then sat on a stone on the edge of the field contemplating their slim options of stealing anything. Voices behind him pulled him out of his thoughts. A man whispered in a foreign language and a woman's voice answered. The bushes behind Nikolas rustled, and the donkey's head appeared, looking at him briefly and then continuing to eat the young grass from the roadside. Behind the donkey, he recognized the man and his pregnant wife. The woman made a contorted manoeuvre and then grabbed under her raised skirt. Nikolas wondered in amazement if she was giving birth when she suddenly pulled out a bundle of fabric between her legs. The man took it from her and stowed it in his backpack. Then he approached the thicket where Nikolas was hidden and fetched their donkey. The branches of the bush swung back, and the couple disappeared again from Nikolas's view.

Apparently the two had managed to smuggle something out of the city. On his way back, Nikolas observed that plenty of men on the streets also had bulging stomachs. Maybe they could steal a few weapons that way.

The others arrived on the ship shortly after him. Niels and Jens had spied on a blacksmith's shop, where a whole bunch of knives, daggers, and swords were waiting for their delivery, but they, too, had noticed the controls at the city gates. Nikolas told them about the pair of smugglers, and Ben was at once enthusiastic about the plan, but Nikolas also convincingly explained the risks of this undertaking.

"We should at least make sure that we go into the city with big bellies, in case we are recognized when we leave," Nikolas explained. "Klaas, Pitt, and Ben are probably the most credible."

"What's that s'pposed to mean? Are you sayin' I'm fat?" Pitt protested.

"Not yet," Nikolas countered.

"Hold your tongue, little one."

"And if something goes wrong, only the best fighter in the world can find his way out." That argument pleased Pitt.

They searched the ship for things that they could push under the shirts of the three chosen ones to model credible beer bellies. But the only thing they had were their own coats, which barely formed a dented little paunch, which would draw even more attention to the otherwise stocky and well-trained men.

"The clothes box," Nikolas remembered.

The box was quickly brought on deck, and Klaas pulled out several simple linen dresses with blouses, aprons, and capes. When he held up one of the dresses, everyone on deck seemed to come to the same conclusion.

"You said the couple acted as if the woman was pregnant?" asked Klaas. "You and Jan would make two pretty chickens."

"What, but, no, you can't ask for that," stammered Jan.

"With your three bellies, we can smuggle out more weapons, maybe even a bag of flour," Nikolas said, also trying to distract from the idea.

"It's better to have two safe bellies than three asses on the scaffold," Ben said. "The guards will be less touchy about frisking a man than a pregnant woman."

"We'll paint your lips and pad your blouse real nice. You could become the next May queens. I can already imagine it." Pitt smirked, and everyone joined in with his laughter.

Nikolas couldn't come up with a better reason to change the plan. So, in the middle of the night, he and Jan stood on deck dressed in two grey work dresses for maids, including capes and aprons, which were a little too short for them but made the two youngest crew members look deceptively like real milkmaids.

At dawn, they set off. Jan had neatly shaved his upper lip, and Nikolas also enjoyed shortening for the first time the sparse hair that had been sprouting on his chin. Klaas and Pitt accompanied them as their husbands and did not miss the opportunity to pinch their bottoms. The others followed in small groups in front and behind, and only Hein had remained on board alone.

They entered the city without any problems, and, in fact, the guards showed no interest at all in the two alleged women. Nevertheless, Nikolas was nervous, his heart was racing, and he was unusually hot for such a mild spring day. He and

Jan followed Niels and Ben discreetly through the crowd, while the other two followed Jens and Derek. It was agreed that Ben and Derek would eventually start a diversion to lure the blacksmith and any assistants away and lead them around town for as long as possible until they could find the opportunity to disappear into the crowd. Jens and Niels were then to enter the smithy and wrap the weapons in two rags so that they could be pushed under the dresses.

Jan and Pitt were already waiting at one corner of the alley when Nikolas and Klaas arrived at the other end. Ben and Derek knocked on the door with the sign of the blacksmith, and when he opened, they persuaded him to come with them to inspect their goods, which were supposedly too heavy to bring along. The blacksmith took his assistant with him, and they walked along the alley to the main road. When they bent around the corner, Jens and Niels emerged from a niche in the row of houses and walked to the forge. They knocked briefly, and when no one answered, they picked the lock and opened the door. It seemed to take an eternity, but finally they came out with two well-laced bundles, closed the door, and walked away in different directions. The bundles disappeared under the dresses of Nikolas and Jan, and another cloth was pushed in to form their bellies into well-rounded shapes.

As they set out, the blades of the stolen weapons pushed against Nikolas's legs, and he plucked on his dress to keep everything hidden. If he had been walking unhindered in the morning, he was now waddling along the streets like a heavily pregnant woman. It took them twice as long to get back, and when they arrived at the ship, the others were already waiting for them.

"Well, finally! We should set sail right away. The alarm has already been raised, and it won't be long before they turn every stone upside down to find the stolen weapons," Ben said.

They had already prepared for departure, and while Nikolas disposed of his unfamiliar clothes and their loot belowdecks, he heard the anchor hitting the outer wall of the ship.

They reached the open sea untroubled, and with their new shiny weapons, they felt a bit more invincible again. They sailed farther south, and a few days later, their weapons came in handy when they ponied a trader who had loaded metal dishes and bags full of grain. So, in addition to fish, they also got to eat porridge again, but even that didn't keep them happy for long.

After sailing along the coast for two weeks, the route was finally changed.

"We're heading for Visby," Ben proclaimed on a rainy morning, and excitement spread amongst them. "I hope that we can sell our cargo there to the highest bidder and also hire some fearless pirates to be able to hunt for bigger fish again."

Yes, Visby seemed very suited for this. The capital of Gotland had once been the refuge of the Victual Brethren, from where they held dominion over the Baltic Sea for several years. And although the German Order had expelled them from the city, and the port was now again a prestigious trading centre of the Hanseatic League, there were still many men who earned their keep in illegal manners and found shelter behind the high walls and towers.

But before they reached this fabled pirate stronghold, they had to progress for a few more days in continuous drizzle and unsettled seas.

On the fifth day, they finally saw the rainy coast of Gotland appear dark in the distance. A few hours later, they were able to identify dense forests and the first church towers and knew that they would be able to dry their clothes on a warm fire in the evening.

This time, they headed directly to the port and moored their ship at the quay. Ben paid for the berth, which also covered the guard, and so they all set out to look for a night's lodging.

The rain and nightfall had swept the city empty. Magnificent merchant and townhouses lined the main street and were testimony to the prosperity of this commercial centre. They passed the cathedral church and turned from the forecourt to the right into an alley where all the inhabitants of Visby seemed to have gathered. Balconies and overhanging roof ledges protruded far across the alley, stopping the rain, and transforming it almost into a long corridor between the houses.

"Welcome to Parsley Alley, handsome. Come with me and I'll give you everything you ever dreamed off," a courtesan purred into Klaas's ear as she stroked over her low neckline with her fingertips.

"It's a tempting offer and I might come back to it when we have done our business and I can provide the compensation you're sure to demand. Or am I wrong?" said Klaas.

"Not wrong, that's why you should move on for today. But if you have successfully completed your business, ask for Regina Caritatis and I'm sure we'll come to an agreement." The courtesan shook her fire-red hair before returning to her friends at the roadside. The women giggled as they walked on. One of them blew a kiss to Nikolas, which aroused him so much that he desperately tried to think of the swampy bilge on the ship, where the rats multiplied, to distract himself from the embarrassment of his tightening trousers.

The next tavern was bursting with chanting sailors emptying one jug after another, and they ordered a round for themselves whilst Ben began to look for potential traders. He spoke for a long time with the landlord, who pointed to some of the men around the bar, and Ben thanked him. While a young lad brought them their beer, Ben was busy talking to those men. And when they were served their second round, Ben joined them happily.

"Just agreed on a fair price for the grain, and I'm sure I'll find a buyer for the dishes as well," he said, downing his tankard in one big gulp to keep up with them.

Nikolas's tongue became heavy and his eyes glassy from the drinks. The noises around him blurred when an argument broke out in one corner. Punters who had previously played cards together faced each other, and two men clashed violently.

"Cheater!"

"What are you calling me?"

"I say that you are a wretched fraud and a bad one at that!"

"Give me my money back."

"Pah, dream on."

"I'll beat it out of you, then."

The man took aim and thrust his shoulder into the ribs of the other. That one was thrown back by the force of the impact, but he stayed on his feet and started a counterattack.

"Bar fight!" someone shouted, and the whole room transformed into a battlefield. Fists flew and chairs and tables were smashed. The whores cleared out, and the landlord stood resigned behind his counter trying to bring his goods to safety. Jugs flew through the air, and since most were of burnt clay, they shattered when they hit walls, floors, or heads. The men of the *Gundelinde* were also in the midst of the brawl and beat anyone who got in their way. Even Nikolas wrestled with a grown man who was even drunker than him, so they were equal opponents.

When Nikolas awoke in a corner of the tavern the next morning, some boys were about to clear the smashed furniture aside and a few maids swept the shards together. Ben talked to the landlord again.

"Have you already sold your load of dishes?" the landlord asked.

"Well, there are several people who all want to have a share, and I think I'll get rid of them in the next few hours," Ben replied. "You would have been better off if all your pitchers had been made of metal." He watched a girl who was dropping a whole pile of broken cups into a bucket.

"If I take the whole load, then you have what you want in one deal and don't have to spend your time negotiating," the landlord suggested.

"I want a quarter of a guilder for every item you take, food for our next trip, and free beer during our stay here."

"Five shillings for every item, and free beer. You'll have to pay for the food."

"Fifteen shillings per item."

"Seven shillings."

"Ten shillings, and beer and accommodation for me and my men as long as we are here." The landlord mulled things over. "And we're going to pay for our food," Ben assured him.

"Agreed," said the landlord, and the deal was sealed with a handshake.

They stayed only a few days, but they lived well. The beer flowed like water, and so they ate less than the landlord had hoped, but what was done was done.

The last evening, they spent aboard their ship. The food and fresh barrels of thin beer had been loaded, and five broad-shouldered men had joined their crew.

# 14

## Helgoland

The rain had given way to bright sunshine, which now burned mercilessly down on them. They sailed with a light breeze farther along Sweden's coast, and Nikolas went after his usual work. But the mood and tone on board had changed since Visby. With the new crew members, the conversations on the ship had become rougher and arguments broke out easily. Jens and Niels had made friends with the new arrivals, and Klaas and Pitt also seemed to get along with them reasonably well. Derek was rarely seen in their company, but they all seemed to respect him and did not even try to provoke him. Jan, in particular, suffered from their jokes and pranks, and Hein became even more uncommunicative than usual. They badgered Nikolas because of his breaking voice, but he didn't rise to their jokes, so they soon lost interest and left him alone. A new custom that quickly started was to play dice for their belongings or to test their courage with perverted games.

"Well, you scaredy-cat, let's see how long you last," Olof said to Jan.

Thorbjörn and Ingvar grabbed him and fixed Jan's hand on a barrel.

"Let go of me! I'm not doing this," Jan yelped.

"Oh, come on, don't be like that. If you stay calm, nothing will happen to you."

"Exactly, don't be a dog in a manger and treat us to some fun," Gustav and Birger bawled.

Olof played with his knife and rammed it without warning between Jan's thumb and index fingers. "Stretch your fingers away from each other, or they'll be gone soon."

He began stabbing with the tip of the knife between Jan's spread fingers, first slowly and then faster and faster. The others stood around them jeering while Thorbjörn and Ingvar were still holding Jan down. The blood drained from Jan's face, and with a determined jerk, he pushed the two off. Unfortunately for him, his attempt to escape resulted in exactly what Jan was trying to avoid, and Olof's knife pierced his hand and nailed him to the barrel.

"Are you crazy to move?" Olof exclaimed angrily, pulling his knife out of Jan's hand. "That's on you, you scaredy-cat."

At least Jan did not faint this time but collected his thoughts enough to quickly press a handkerchief firmly on the wound.

Nikolas and Klaas found Jan crying in a dark corner belowdecks.

"Let me see," Klaas said, and as he took off the bandage, blood ran over his hand. "Well, no bone got hit, but he's an idiot, nonetheless. Little one, get a bottle of the devil's stuff from last year, I've hidden two more flasks in my chest."

Nikolas went to Klaas's seafarer chest and opened it. Under a shirt and a fur vest, he found the bottles and a stack of neatly folded cloths.

"This stuff is incredibly good for cleaning wounds, but you shouldn't drink it, it burns your intestines and probably makes you blind," Klaas said, pouring a little over Jan's hand.

Jan briefly groaned when the home-distilled spirit wetted the open wound and washed the blood away. Then Klaas dressed Jan's hand anew and pulled the bandage so tightly that the fingers were squeezed together.

"Why do they do this?" Jan asked in a choked voice. "I don't want to be part of it anymore."

"All cowards. Next time, punch them up the bracket and they'll leave you in peace." Jan looked at Klaas, only more disgruntled. "Or stay close to me and I'll gladly do it for you."

This proved to be a good advice for the first few days, but Olof and the others would have left Jan alone anyway, as somehow, they seemed to have a bad conscience and continued their games amongst themselves.

Their looting rides also became frighteningly brutal with the new arrivals. In their first attack since Visby, just three people survived seriously injured, and only because Ben stepped in, stopping his men from brutally slaughtering innocent people.

"When I say you should keep them at bay, that doesn't mean you should kill them all," Ben screamed, red blotches spreading on his cheeks.

"They are easier to keep at bay when they're dead."

"Yes, and it's more fun that way," Birger and Olof sneered.

"If you call this fun, I suggest you murder each other and don't go after people who have surrendered already. And besides, I'm still the captain, and what I say is being done!" Ben said with a bright-red head.

"A captain can also be demoted," Olof said challengingly. "We're not bound by laws and rank; majority is what counts."

A deadly silence hovered in the air as Ben and Olof eyed each other.

"Get the cargo over and take the wounded, we will bring them ashore. I'll say it one last time: under my command, you are not murdering for fun." Ben said these last words so masterfully and with so much determination that no one thought to contradict him.

Everyone went to work in silence. Klaas cared for the injured as best he could until they dropped them off in the nearest fishing village.

Their next raids were mostly without deaths, but with many injured amongst the attacked. Although Ben still did not agree with this brutality, he could not help noticing that they were very successful and could even bring up larger ships and seize more valuable goods. After a good three years during which they had lived more badly than right and had made more profit in the winter as temporary workers than the rest of the year on the high seas, they led the pirate life that they had set out to live. But it was only Ben and Nikolas who gave some of their booty to the poor.

For the next few years, they sailed between Reval and Königsberg and repeatedly headed for Visby, where the trade in stolen goods flourished. Although he never had anything left for it, Ben's experience as a trader paid off and he was able to quickly convert goods they didn't need into cash. In Visby, the team changed often, but the hard core of the comrades remained true to the *Gundelinde*.

A few times, they passed the small village where they had amputated Ben's hand, but they didn't dock there again, as they knew that they wouldn't be able to convert any of their loot into profits. In Riga, Ben had a prosthesis made, which let him variably to attach a hook, a knife, or a fork to his arm stump. He wore the hook most often, as it allowed him to better find a holding when the sea was rough.

Unfortunately, their successful raids in the Baltic Sea also resulted in the larger merchant ships being equipped with more mercenaries and archers. Thus, the men of the *Gundelinde* experienced more and more resistance and were often pushed back hard and fast.

Five years after they had left Hamburg, Ben was finally able to enforce sailing to the West Sea again. Here, too, they achieved some success, and because of the less guarded merchant ships, they went into the winter break with some prosperity for the first time. They spent the cold months in Jutland and could not wait to build on their success in the spring.

Nikolas had hidden his share of the loot under a loose board beneath his seafarer chest. Without having to make a living, he had enough time this winter to think about the compass and the Jacob's staff. If he would be able to reliably measure their speed, he could use the compass to determine their position on a map even on the open sea. To do this, he would simply have to draw a straight line from its starting position in the direction of travel with a length according to their speed. In the event of a change of course on the open sea, the end of the first line would serve as a coupling point for a second line leading in the new direction. But first, he needed an accurate chart, and so he did everything he could to complete his own documents.

Now that they were back in the West Sea, they had to consider the tides. It suited Nikolas that he was tasked with sounding the depth of the water most of the time. He watched, intrigued, as large parts of the sea fell dry at low tide and the dangerous sandbanks, gutters, and basins became visible. He estimated the tidal range, which indicated the difference in height of the water level between low and high tide, to be about one step. One had to know the area well to find the entrances to the rivers, and reliable pilots, as Hein had been once, were of great value.

They raided a few smaller merchant vessels, but the loot was so meagre that it was not worth heading for a port. Instead, Ben ordered they head to Helgoland to carry out repairs on the ship. But Nikolas suspected that Ben had another ulterior motive, and he saw his hunch confirmed when Ben called for him and disclosed his plan.

"You can imagine why I chose Helgoland. I can feel it in my fingers, albeit only in my right, that we are close. You remember old Christian's words? What do you think?" asked Ben.

Nikolas was surprised that he was asked for his opinion but had made a discovery that he had wanted to share with Ben for a while now.

"Here, I got that from the bottom of the sea in the lead arming." Nikolas reached into his pocket and pulled out a handful of fine white sand riddled with pointed shells, like needles.

Ben could barely hold on to himself. "Ha, I knew it, fine and white, shells and needles, surrounded by water."

They put the ship on land in a small bay, which lay between towering red-and-white-coloured sandstone cliffs, and the next morning, the repair work began.

"Derek, I will explore the island with a small squad and see if there is anything to take. You're going to monitor the work here in the meantime," Ben ordered after breakfast, and he seemed unaware of Derek's suspicious look. But the second helmsman agreed, and so Ben set off with Nikolas, Klaas, Pitt, and Hein.

The stony path led them steeply uphill. Here and there, stubborn lichens pressed against the rocks, and tufts of salt marsh plants grew stubbornly in cracks and crevices. They reached the plateau and saw from the nearly 250-foot-high cliffs far over the sea to the mainland. You could have watched every ship approaching the island for miles, and they saw that this was indeed an ideal base for raids.

A few small huts stood in a sheltered hollow, but as they approached, everything was lying still and abandoned. They entered the first house and determined that no one had lived here for years. The clay crumbled from the walls, and here and there stones had already fallen out. The few pieces of furniture were covered with dust and salt, and through the dilapidated roof, the sun sent shy rays into the gloom. They turned to the next house, but as they were about to enter, an old man hobbled around the corner and pointed an armed crossbow at them with trembling hands.

"Stop, or I shoot," the man shouted.

Klaas let go of the doorknob and raised his hands as a sign that they were coming in peace. "Listen, old man, you'd better lower the weapon before you hurt yourself."

But the old man did not seem to want to be persuaded. "One step closer and I pull the trigger," he threatened as Pitt approached him.

"You don't think we're scared of you," Pitt said.

"Maybe not, but if not of me, then maybe of him." The old man whistled sharply through his missing teeth, and a huge black dog appeared out of nowhere, snarling at them.

"Good grief," Pitt gibbered and stumbled backwards. "Call back the mutt, we won't do you any harm," he lamented as he hid behind Hein.

"Now you're not so brave, eh? You better behave, otherwise Anvil here will make minced meat out of ya," the old man jeered.

But then Hein stepped forward and built himself up in front of the dog, who growled at him wildly.

"Anvil, sit!" thundered Hein, and to everyone's surprise, the dog pulled his tail between his legs and sat on the ground in front of Hein with expectant eyes.

The old man gasped for air. "So, you betray me now too? Well, then, come on in."

They looked at each other and then followed him to his hut.

"I don't have anything I could offer ya, and I wouldn't do it anyways. So, say what ya want from me, and then get off my island," he grumbled as they crowded into the small room.

"Are you living here alone?" asked Ben.

"Me and my twelve mateys, as ya can see." The old man mockingly waved his arms about.

"What happened to the others? There must have been more people here once."

"They ran off when the Victual Brethren landed here. Only me and Anvil appreciate the quietness of our island... And what do ya want here?"

"Klaus Störtebeker is said to have been here several times?"

"It's rude to answer a question with a question."

"It's just as rude to let your monster of a dog loose on guests," Pitt interrupted, still looking frightened at Anvil. But the dog had lain down on the floor next to Hein and seemed relaxed, listening to the conversation.

"Yes, I saw this Klaus Störtebeker when he arrived here with his men to rest from their raids. Back then, there was still life on the island. Countless men like ya have since been here looking for the treasures. But no one has found anything."

"It seems our intentions are easy to predict. You don't happen to know where to find these treasures?" asked Ben, smiling kindly.

"That's new. Nobody ever dared to ask about it outright." Expectantly, everyone stared at the old man as he continued. "I've seen treasures you'd just dream of, but since Störtebeker's execution, I haven't seen anything sparkly here anymore...only the sea. They probably brought the treasures somewhere else."

"Again, somewhere else? I'm tired of chasing a treasure that's always somewhere else," Klaas burst out.

For the rest of the day, they roamed the island, climbed rocks and glide down into caves, but nowhere did they find any sign of a hidden treasure. The ground was of hard stone almost everywhere, unsuitable for digging holes and burying something. They did not even find another message that the treasure had been indeed moved, and so they returned bitterly disappointed to their ship at sunset.

The next morning, everyone mucked in to repair the ship, and after a few days, they set sail again. Ben, who still hadn't given up hope of finding the treasure, or at least a hint, gave the order to sail around the island one more time.

Nikolas explored the depths around Helgoland, and when they arrived again in front of the small bay, he had noticed that the island was surrounded by reddish sand with many different mussels. Only in front of this small bay was this white sand with the pointy shells. It had already darkened, and they were getting ready to head for the open sea when Nikolas sounded one last time and examined the lead arming.

He found, as expected, the white sand and the needle shells, but on top of it was a tarnished ring with a large, encased ruby. Nikolas held it in his hands in amazement and watched as the gemstone sparkled blood red in the light of the stars. Someone must have been very careless to drop something so precious into the sea, and what a coincidence that the lead had landed exactly on the ring.

Nikolas put the ring in his pocket and climbed into the lookout, where he polished it with his sleeve, unobserved by the others. In the moonshine, he could see an inscription inside the golden hoop: *amicus dei et hostis omnes orbis.*

God's friend and the world's fiend.

# 15

## Mutiny

In the following days, Nikolas tried time and again to tell Ben about the discovery of the ring, but Ben was so shaken that Helgoland had also turned out to be a dead end to his treasure hunt that he avoided speaking to anyone.

He couldn't trust the others either. Hein was visibly fed up chasing treasures; with Jan, he was afraid that the wrong ears would eventually hear the secret; and Klaas and Pitt were never alone as they were busy with the most absurd games and tussles that culminated when Gustav and Birger caught a few rats.

Instead of breaking their necks and throwing the rats overboard, as would normally happen, they locked them in an empty box. And now began the spectacle that Nikolas thought was the most incredible and disgusting thing he had ever witnessed.

"Hey, Olof, I bet I'll bump this rat off faster than you," Birger challenged him.

"What's the catch?" asked Olof.

"No catch, but, of course, it shouldn't be too easy, where else would be the fun?" Birger held a squeaking rat by the tail up in the air.

"Well, I'll beat you one way or the other, even if you tie my arms behind my back."

"You guessed half the game. Whoever kills the rat first with his bare teeth wins."

Ingvar and Thorbjörn, who had sat on the railing, approached to watch this spectacle. Birger pushed the large bucket, which Nikolas used whenever he scrubbed the deck, with one foot into the middle of the deck and put the rat in it before covering it with his coat.

Olof grinned confidently, knelt next to the bucket, and lifted the coat slowly. The rat blinked at him with its black button eyes. Like a seagull that descended into the sea to catch fish, Olof plunged headlong into the bucket and tried to crush the rat. But the animal had jumped out of the bucket at lightning speed, and Olof slammed his forehead against the bottom of the bucket.

Another rat was taken out of the box, and now it was Birger's turn. Birger proceeded more cautiously and managed to grab the rat with his teeth by its tail. Then he hurled it through the air and thundered it against the edge of the bucket to break its neck. But the rat started a counterattack. Birger howled as the rodent bit his right cheek and hung from his face like an ulcer. Against the rules, he ripped the rat off his face with his hands and, like a wild animal, dug his teeth in its neck until it died twitching.

Loud jeers rose when Birger spit out the dead rat and took a big gulp from his tankard. The more beer and wine flowed, the more rats died that night.

The next morning, they sailed north again despite the all-night bender.

"Ship in si—" Birger, sitting in the lookout, broke off his call and held his head. Not only did his skull buzz, but the others winced as if Birger had thrown stones at their heads.

Only slowly did everyone rise from their twilight state and look over to the small merchant ship, which sailed in the same direction as them.

"What are you waiting for? Normally, you can't be stopped when it comes to slaughter!" Ben seemed to want to replace his disappointment from Helgoland with new enthusiasm. "When they're on our level, set the sail into the wind and go alongside." The crew only hesitantly moved. "That's a command," Ben exclaimed angrily.

"What are we supposed to do with such a small ship? Conquering rotten fish again?" asked Derek, to a murmur of approval.

"Such small traders may also have loaded valuable goods."

"Or not. I say we have a strong crew and can afford to attack large merchant ships that promise a guaranteed loot." The calls of support for Derek grew louder. "If I were the captain, I would spare us the time and not chase every little fish. For too long, we have listened to a prissy man chasing treasures that do not exist. It's time for a new captain to give you all that you deserve." Now there was a strong roar of support on board.

"If we pursue such a strategy, the Hanseatic League will rise again and send a whole host of warships after us," Ben argued. "We can only allow ourselves to attack a large merchant ship from time to time. Or do you want to end at the gallows?"

"We should vote!" Olof interrupted loudly. "Captain is who holds the majority. This is what it was and always will be."

Unfortunately, Ben had lost his majority as he took more and more men on board in Visby. The crew voted and Derek was appointed as the new captain.

From then on, there was a different tune in the air. Derek knew how to avoid quarrels amongst the men, but he made those who voted against him feel that they no longer enjoyed the goodwill of the captain. They had to take on the night watch more often and were assigned to the lowest tasks, such as scrubbing the deck and draining the bilge room, while the others were almost bored.

Soon after, they spotted a ship with a strong draught and larger than the *Gundelinde*. Derek gave the order for pursuit, and as they were lighter and more agile, they quickly closed the gap. But that warned the trader, and when they caught up with him, his crew was ready to fight. They were greeted with a hail of arrows, but they took the opportunity when the archers redrew their bows and stormed the merchant ship. The carnage began. After the archers were crushed, the last men swung over to throw themselves into the bloody battle. To Nikolas's dismay, a bunch of innocent sailors soon piled up, slaughtered like cattle. The cargo, bales of Flemish cloth, barrels full of beer and sacks of grain, were distributed amongst both ships so that they could hold about the same speed. They manned the two-masted holk named the *Cecilia van de Hoornse Hop* and sailed on with two ships.

The beer barrels were tapped that very evening to celebrate their success under their new captain, and everyone got an extra portion of cured pork.

The next morning, they touched at the coast, and Derek set out to sell their loot off the books at the next market town. But he proved to be far more inept than Ben, who had been relieved of all duties. The amount of money they distributed that evening was only half of what Ben would have eked out for the goods.

Their next raids were as bloodthirsty as they were successful, but displeasure spread over the small proceeds. So, four weeks after the mutiny, Ben was reinstated in the pirate community once again to sell the loot, and from then on, they were unstoppable. They did not even try to take prisoners, as they had only had trouble with them.

Instead, Derek hired ten more deckhands and sailed with two fully manned ships under his command. Captured ships were sold as well as their cargo. Derek took over the two-master and brought Ben on board to keep an eye on him. Olof was in command of the *Gundelinde*. Although Olof spread fear and terror amongst those who did not execute his orders quickly enough, he rarely gave orders, so life on the *Gundelinde*, except in combat, was quite contemplative.

Since Olof also had no sense for the devices in Ben's cabin, he allowed Nikolas to take the compass and the Jacob's staff. Nikolas spent his sparse free time using his maps to determine their position, but without knowing their exact speed, he often miscalculated their actual location by several miles, even with short distances.

He also found that when the swell was stronger, the compass needle repeatedly touched the bottom of its case and could no longer freely align. He thought about how to prevent this and made dozens of sketches to develop a suspension for the needle, which not only allowed it to align horizontally to the north, but also vertically to compensate for the movements of the ship. He had the idea to hang the compass rose into a ring, which, in turn, was mounted movably in another ring so that the needle always remained horizontally in one plane, even at sea.

Another problem occurred when he placed the compass on a barrel. The compass needle was distracted by the metal hoops of the barrel. In contrast, wood did not seem to influence the needle at all, but even flexible wood such as hazelnut or yew, as was used in bow making, wouldn't make a perfect ring. He pondered for a long time but found no solution for how to construct the suspension.

One evening, when they were anchored and enjoyed their beer, Nikolas sat on deck again, lost in thought. The first barrel was empty, and since it was already old and almost unusable, they threw it overboard. Nikolas was looking at the barrel, which was now bobbing on the water next to their ship, when he had an idea. It had nothing to do with the compass, but he now knew how to measure their speed.

If the ship was moving, it would be driven by the wind, but the barrel would more or less maintain its position, as it would hardly be affected by the wind because of its smaller surface area. If he could now measure the distance between the barrel and the ship that was covered within a certain time, he could calculate their speed. Using the compass, he could determine their direction, then enter their path on a chart and thus determine their position.

Excitedly, he jumped up and searched belowdecks for old wooden parts.

"Have you gone completely bonkers? Stands there and throws wood into the water!" cried Jens.

The others looked at him and then over to Nikolas, who ran along the railing throwing pieces of wood into the water all around the ship. He didn't even notice the others watching, and it wasn't until a strong hand on his shoulder arrested him that he turned around.

"Stop that, or you can jump in right after, fishing it all out again! Do you understand?" Olof growled.

"It's just waste wood."

"I don't care. If I don't give the order to throw even a wood chip overboard, you won't chuck whole pieces into the sea. Understood?"

Nikolas was about to make a nasty remark about Olof's often nonsensical orders, but since he was finished with his preparations anyway, he refrained from starting an argument. He wanted to watch the pieces of wood and see if they drifted off or not. They all stayed where they were, and even the next morning, they had moved only little away from the ship.

When they set out again, Nikolas had no opportunity to verify his assumption. They attacked a ship that did not greet them with arrows, but whose crew was skilled in close combat, so that they also suffered some losses.

Ben lost his right eye when a sword hit him along his face, and for the first time, Nikolas also suffered a severe wound to his stomach. As Ben had predicted, the merchants were apparently warned by the increased disappearance of ships. They had prepared themselves and now took paid mercenaries on board as they had eventually done in the Baltic Sea. Nevertheless, the men of the two pirate ships managed to loot the merchant vessel, but the celebration in the evening was subdued.

Klaas had his hands full to take care of the wounded on both ships. Nikolas lay sickly in his hammock after Klaas patched his side with the sewing equipment they otherwise used for the sails. Ben's eye wound surprisingly bled little, but Klaas had to remove the eyeball completely and fill the eye socket with a clean cloth before putting on a head bandage.

The next raids were also much less favourable than at the beginning, and to top it all off, the weather also changed.

The *Gundelinde* tried to keep as much distance as possible from the two-master so the two ships did not accidentally ram each other. Despite the raging storm around them, Nikolas heard screams. He blinked through the rain whipping him in the face, and the foremast of the two-master broke in the middle as the ship was caught by a huge wave. But Nikolas had no time to worry about the crew on the other ship, as he himself fought against mountains of waves that repeatedly flooded the deck, and as a precaution, he had tied himself to the mast with a rope. He often hung like a dog on a leash when the water ripped him off his legs, and he slipped on the deck.

He was getting up again when a body fell from the rigging into the water.

"Man overboard," a shout rang out over the deck.

Nikolas clung to the railing and saw Niels, who got lifted up by a wave.

"Help me, help me!" cried Niels in despair, but as he sank back down between two waves, his voice faded away.

"Help him, he can't swim!" shouted Jens, and it was the first time Nikolas saw him so desperate and worried about his brother.

"A rope, quickly!" Olof barked at the crowd standing around. They fetched a rope, but Niels had disappeared without a trace.

"Where is he?" screamed Jens, his voice toppling over. His gaze was so contorted near insanity that no one dared to venture near him, but when he attempted to jump after his brother, they grabbed him and dragged him away from the railing.

"Stay here, or do you want to throw yourself into disaster?" Olof told him.

"But he's my little brother!" Jens tried to free himself with all his strength.

"You can't help him anymore. He's gone."

As the waves smoothed out and they were able to exchange messages with the *Cecilia*, they learned that there had also been losses on the two-master. Two men had been slain by the falling mast and were delivered to their watery grave the following evening.

# 16

## Back in Hamburg

$\mathcal{D}$erek ordered to sail back to Helgoland to make the ships fully seaworthy again after the murderous storm. They would not be bothered there, and the location of the island was convenient to set off for booty quests. Nikolas again sounded the depth of the sea and studied the sand on the seabed as they approached the island: first red sand from the sandstone rocks, then fine white sand in the bay, where they anchored again.

But this time, Nikolas was not allowed to go ashore. Hoping that the ring had not just landed on the bottom of the sea by chance, he took the heaviest lead they had on board and let it slide into the water at short intervals around the *Gundelinde*. Near the cliffs and on their backboard side, he found only reddish sand in the lead arming, but as he made his way around the railing, the red sand was more and more interspersed with fine white grains until it transitioned completely to the expected fine white sand with pointed shells on their starboard side.

He let his gaze wander along the cliffs. At the northern tip of Helgoland, he could see in the distance the surf gate that the waves had eaten into the soft rocks over time. The rock cliffs around the small bay also looked as if they were giving in to the gnawing of the water. This explained why he found red sand around the island. The white sand was most likely being washed up with the tide from further out and deposited here due to the shape of the bay.

Since he had found the ring in fine white sand, as described by the inscription in the cave on Rügen, he stayed on the starboard side. He pondered where he would hide a treasure himself. No one would look underwater, but then he wouldn't get to the treasure either. So, it was better on land. Buried near a marker like a large tree or boulder that only he knew, somewhere where he would be undisturbed and unobserved. But it would be noticeable if he disappeared for a long time; after all, he had to dig up the treasure first and then make it disappear again in the earth. If he could reach the hiding place from the ship, he would only have to wait until everyone was asleep. There was still a risk of being discovered, but it was the most workable solution that came to his mind.

While he was lost in thought, he had worked his way up to the bow, and he was not even aware at first that he was peeling a gold coin out of the lead arming. He stared at the shiny coin in his hand. Then he looked around cautiously, but no one was watching him. He quickly put the coin in his pocket and lowered the lead back into the water. He had to renew the lead arming two more times until he retrieved another coin. Subsequently, he saw only imprints of coins that had probably fallen off again, but then he managed to pull up a small, dainty silver bracelet from the depths. After that, he found nothing more.

He looked around again, but still no one took notice of him. Could this be the treasure of Störtebeker? Did the notorious pirate hide his treasure underwater? Of one thing

Nikolas was sure: there were more coins and trinkets down there. But with the lead, it would take months to lift everything. If only he could swim. The water here was only a few fathoms deep, and with a little practice, he would be able to dive down to the bottom.

He would have liked to talk to the old man up there on the rocks again, but when the first squad of men came back, Nikolas learned that they had only found the rabid dog sitting next to a decomposing corpse, and when he attacked them, they had killed the animal.

Nikolas took note of their next raids in passing, and it was only when the rumour spread that they would go to Hamburg the next day to sell their loot that he woke up from his musing.

Hamburg. He had been a boy of thirteen years when he turned his back to the city on a foggy night, and he had never thought of returning to the place of his childhood. Outwardly, he was calm and collected, but on the inside, he was both troubled and curious. At night, he dreamed that he would walk along the Alster with his father laughing by his side, but then his father was dragged into the river as if by an invisible hand. Nikolas desperately tried to grab him, but he could not reach. The Alster had turned into a stormy sea, and he saw his father vanish between the waves. He jumped into the water and swam toward his father.

"You can't swim," his father shouted before he could reach him, and Nikolas was suddenly no longer carried by the water but pulled into the depths without being able to do anything about it. The pressure on his body increased the deeper he sank, and his heart seemed to stop when he hit the ground.

Nikolas woke up and lay in his hammock with his eyes open. He stared at the ceiling, through which he could hear subdued steps on deck. He still felt the pressure on his body that pushed him down, and he remained motionless until the images passed and he was able to get up.

Muted, he climbed on deck. The sun was just coming up, and he had seen the same view of the coast on another morning five years ago, travelling in the other direction at that time.

Before they reached the estuary of the Elbe, they loaded their goods from the *Gundelinde* to the *Cecilia*, as the cog would be recognized too easily in her former port of registry. Then they left the *Gundelinde* near Cuxhaven behind, only minimally manned. The men greeted each other happily as their small original crew was reunited.

"Well, little one, now we're going back home. Do you know what you'll do first?" asked Pitt.

"No idea. I will stay away from the St. Nikolai School, though, otherwise the master will send me to the cathedral school of Cologne after all."

"Oh pish, I think he's hardly going to recognize the lanky pale boy of yesteryears, even if you'd laugh right in his face," Klaas said.

"And what are you going to do?" asked Nikolas.

"Oh, the usual. First put all our savings in the collection box of the next church and then make a comprehensive confession about our misdeeds."

"I think you mean to say that you're going to carry your money to the next brothel," Nikolas scoffed.

"I haven't even thought about that. Maybe the lovely Irma will hear my confession."

"She's probably going to do that for a few extra pennies, but she won't be able to provide for your soul," Klaas said.

"I'm not sure whether a priest could do that either, considering your load of sins." Nikolas laughed.

"True words, but Irma can give me at least relief for my earthly suffering, and she's proven that many times before. What about you, Ben? Will you support Derek?"

"I will keep myself under cover. If someone recognizes me, I can probably expect the worst punishment of all of us. And not only the well-known prostitutes, but also some of Hamburg's most respectable and influential citizens might recognize me and would like to betray me for a small reward."

"You haven't looked in a mirror for a long time, have you? Hardly anyone will dare to look at you."

"Thanks very much. Do I really look that bad?"

Ben's face was covered with a shaggy beard that did not quite cover the weather-tanned cheeks, and behind the eye patch that he was now wearing, and the long scar protruding up and down from underneath it, no one would suspect the rosy-cheeked son of Mister Bartholomew.

"Don't worry, true beauty comes from within anyway, and we've long known how much loveliness is in you." Nikolas grinned, and even Jan, who had stayed in the background, laughed aloud for the first time in a long time.

Yes, they had all changed a lot since the day they had first met, and even a bath couldn't have altered their appearance that much.

Nikolas was glad to have his friends around him and looked forward to his return home. Hein stood at the helm and steered them confidently along the coast. Here, he was again in familiar waters.

Hamburg had changed just like them and prospered in the last five years, and Nikolas could not remember ever having seen so many people on the streets.

Ben, despite his altered appearance, had pulled his hood far into his face as they walked between the workers at the port to the city.

"So, then, let's dive into the shamblin' and swayin' life of this city," Pitt exclaimed joyfully, rubbing his hands together.

They walked along the Dike Street, and Nikolas viewed the houses that still looked exactly as he remembered.

"Mister Hinricus Hoyeri lived here with his wife at the time. They had a son I used to play with while my father cleaned the Nikolai canal behind the house."

"Well, maybe they have a daughter you can play with now." Klaas punched him in the shoulder.

Nikolas got hot ears. He had never spent a night with a woman, at least not in the sense that Klaas and Pitt always suggested. A few years ago, he would have admitted this without hesitation, but now he was too embarrassed, as he himself often bragged about his adventures in the back rooms of respective quarters.

"This was the house of a trader who only let my father in when his personal dock had been affected, and I always had to wait here on the street. And that there..." Nikolas pointed to a once magnificent warehouse.

"That was my father's house," Ben concluded.

"He always gave me small sugar biscuits." Nikolas and Ben looked at the old house.

Ben swallowed hard, and they all looked up and down the now dishevelled facade. Apparently, no one had taken on the old trading house after Ben had disappeared.

"Come on. Only ghosts are dwelling here now, there is no food for the living." Klaas wrapped his arms around Ben and Nikolas and guided them along the road.

They arrived at the hop market, and the memories swirled in Nikolas's head so that he barely noticed his friends heading for a tavern.

"We should treat ourselves to a stuffed pork snout and a decent measure of beer before we turn to other things," Pitt said, opening the door of the brewery.

As much as Nikolas was lured by a warm meal, he had something else on his mind that he wanted to see to first, and so he said goodbye to his friends for now.

He had refined the design of his compass suspension and wanted to commission his construction with a craftsman.

"What nonsense are you talking about? Don't you have anything more important to do than deal with such malarkey? I have, for sure. Do you see all these barrels? The staves must be bent by the end of the week." The hooper, with whom Nikolas spoke first, was about to grab him by the collar and throw him out on the street.

"But, good man, I am going to pay you appropriately if you can help me. And it will hardly cost you much to at least listen to my idea. A man like you will surely find an excellent solution to my problem in no time." Nikolas jangled his purse. The man's eyes grew big like children's eyes seeing a sugar plum, but there was also the greed of old age in them.

"What did you say you wanted to build? A compass?"

"No, I already have the compass. I just want to hang it differently so that it can move in all directions and level the swaying of a ship."

"Hanging it, you say? Like from a rope?"

Nikolas realized that the man could not follow his verbal explanations. He rolled out his sketches and hoped that the hooper would now understand what he was talking about. But after the craftsman asked again fifteen minutes later how he would imagine this compass thing to be able to spin in all directions, Nikolas gave up.

"Well, I see that you can't help me. Thank you, nonetheless, for your time." Nikolas wanted to leave the workshop.

"And what about my pay?"

"Payment on delivery. But maybe you can give me a piece of your fittings."

"I have sacrificed my time here and abandoned my work because you offered me money."

"But only for a fair trade. What about the iron, or what do you use?"

"That's the best iron you can find, and for that, you'd have to pay out two shillings."

"I don't need much. I am happy to give you two pennies and you give me what you can spare for it."

"Pah, for two pennies, you get this little piece from me. I'm not a fool." The hooper took a finger-size rusty cut of iron from a metal pile. "But first, I want to see the money. I don't trust you; I'll tell you that much."

"There, then, we have something in common," Nikolas said, fishing two pennies from his leather purse.

He went to two more forges, but they could not help him either. Nonetheless, he bought pieces of the metals they used for nails, horseshoes, and weapons.

Then he walked along the Burstah to the Mill Bridge and marvelled at the colourful facades that hard-working craftsmen had renewed on behalf of wealthy citizens. At the Hahntrapp, he bought half a fried chicken before he went to the Alster Lake, where he sat down in the shade of a tree and ate while looking over the water surface glittering in the evening sun. The wind carried the biting stench from the tanners across, the smell of his childhood.

When he had finished eating, he walked in the cooler evening air along the dam at the water mills and past St. John on his way to the St. Nikolai School, his curiosity having dispelled his reservations about the place. He stood across the street looking at the ivy-covered stone wall that surrounded the school's courtyard as the small back gate opened. A bent old man came out, briefly glanced at him, and then scurried away along the street. Nikolas stepped back into the shadow of the house and his heart beat high in his throat. He had just seen Master Deubel. The master had become even more haggard and his hair almost white, but this stubbornly disparaging look left Nikolas in no doubt. After this uncomfortable encounter, he quickly rushed through the small streets back to the harbour.

Back on the *Cecilia*, Nikolas found that all the metals he had purchased distracted the compass needle and were therefore unsuitable to build the suspension. He decided to go to a carpenter the next day and try his luck there.

"So, you need two rings that are hung into each other on axes," the slender man said, looking at Nikolas with bright eyes.

"Exactly," he replied, surprised. "Do you think you could build something that is stable enough to use on a ship even in harsh weather conditions?"

"I think I could. How big is this suspension supposed to be?"

"About one and a half feet in each direction. I will bring you the compass as soon as possible. How long will it take you?"

Nikolas was excited and quickly waved aside any caution when the carpenter told him that it wasn't going to be cheap. The man estimated half a week, and after putting down a small deposit, Nikolas went back to the harbour.

Unloading the *Cecilia* the next day had never been easier for Nikolas. With Ben's help, Derek had been able to negotiate a good price for all the grain, wax, cloth, and spices, and now they were about to load everything under the watchful eyes of the buyers or their assistants into barges, which would then take the goods to the warehouses along the canals in the city. It took the whole day, and the *Cecilia* rose from the water as she lightened.

As things got quieter at the harbour in the evening, they assembled belowdecks at the wooden table where Derek had already divided the coins into several stacks. Those who had suffered serious injuries during their battles received correspondingly more, and Derek had also awarded himself some additional coins as captain. As ruthless as they were in attacks, as fair they were amongst themselves, they all went to the city that evening in high spirits and with bulging purses to pursue their pleasures. Only Jan had not appeared on board to collect his share.

In the city, they bought something to eat and then got wasted in a drinking hole while playing dice. They caroused all night, and Nikolas slept half the day after.

# 17

## Mathi

$\mathcal{N}$ikolas tolerated their night-long binges better than Klaas and Pitt, and while the two were still holding their buzzing skulls, Nikolas went to the carpenter to deliver the compass.

He then met the others in the bathhouse, where they washed away the dirt of the last few months, got shaved and their matted hair cut short. Their old, tattered clothes were left behind, and instead they put on their last pair of clean trousers and shirts. In the next few days, they would have enough time to buy new robes before continuing with their chosen profession.

For lunch, they went to the Pork Market at the Dam Gate, and then they took a few pints along the way to the Hop Market, as Pitt claimed that the best remedy for a hangover was simply to keep drinking. After they had knocked back a few litres of beer, high spirits overcame them. They crossed the Consolation Bridge into the direction of the bailiff's quarter and entered the Eimbeck House.

It was a risk, as the Eimbeck House was a popular society venue for the upper citizens of Hamburg and accommodated, besides a drinking room, also the meeting chambers for the city council. The three friends had fun sitting between all these respected lords who, if they had known who they were, would have brought them straight to the gallows. But since they looked so well-groomed after their visit to the bath-house, they didn't stand out in the least. And as at this late hour even the finer gentlemen had already enjoyed plenty of wine, they were not exactly in inappropriate company either.

"I thought the moneybags had better manners," Pitt muttered as a fat man with a bright-red face and a feisty grin pinched the landlord's wife, who had brought him another jug of heavy red wine, in the backside.

"What can I bring you?" asked a sublime-looking servant, who wore his nose a little too high for Nikolas's taste.

"*Amici mei et ego prehendemus tres urnae de vestrum vino optimo,*" Nikolas said with a firm voice, but he could not suppress the laughter for long, as the man stared at him so incomprehensibly that his suspicions were confirmed.

"Pardon?" the man asked, blushing.

"I thought this was a house of the upper society and you would speak Latin. Excuse my mistake, I didn't mean to embarrass you," replied Nikolas, still supressing an outright smirk.

"We take three jugs of your best wine," Klaas said.

"Certainly," said the servant and bustled off.

"I thought you couldn't speak Latin," Nikolas said, grinning.

"I can't, but when it comes to drinking, I understand that in every language."

They amused themselves for a long time watching the smug lords, who behaved amongst the likes of them like animals, when they otherwise always pretended to be so dignified. Apparently, they thought it unthinkable that a few outlaws had mingled in their circle, and they gave themselves up to ridicule.

The wine paralyzed Nikolas's muscles and a pleasant warmth spread in his neck. Everything seemed possible to-night, and so they moved on in the balmy summer evening in search of another inn.

In a small lane, they stumbled, more by chance than planned, into a cosy tavern, which was almost bursting out of all seams, and yet there was a more respectable atmosphere here than in the Eimbeck House.

"Three beers for me and my friends," Pitt shouted to the innkeeper.

"Where are the women? A different activity would be nice," Nikolas asked cockily.

"You won't get it up anyways," Klaas teased him.

"I always can!" boasted Nikolas.

They sat down at the only free table in the centre of the tavern and a lad about Nikolas's age brought them their drinks. It wasn't long before three other men joined them and challenged them to a card game. They agreed with a handshake, but the alcohol was already affecting Nikolas's attention, and he made some stupid mistakes and lost the first few rounds.

He tried to pull himself together and concentrated on his cards when someone swiped against his back. Annoyed about this distraction, he turned and wanted to give the trouble-maker a telling-off when he saw a brown braid dangling in front of him. As if his hand had its own will, he groped vigor-ously at the shapely bottom, which formed under a simple linen dress.

The girl stopped in her tracks without turning around.

"Hey, my lovely, sit down with me. There's still room here on my lap." Nikolas pulled on the braid like on a rope for a tower bell and grinned at his friends.

"That's enough. May I?" The girl placed six empty jugs on the neighbouring table and turned around to smile sweetly at him.

"Well, here's a loose girl and the prettiest I've seen in Hamburg so far."

Klaas and Pitt hooted, but the other men at their table fell quiet.

"What did you just say?" the girl asked, still smiling.

"I said, I've been waiting for something like you to roll around with in bed."

Nikolas didn't know what had happened to him when he found himself on the ground. He stared at a wooden beam on the ceiling, and slowly a throbbing pain spread in his jaw, exactly where the girl's fist had clocked him.

"Mathi! Not again. You're scaring away the guests," shouted the innkeeper from behind the bar.

"He asked to roll around," the girl replied.

Nikolas raised his head, dazed. A large, broad-shouldered man pushed his way through to him, picked up his chair that had also toppled over, and reached out his hand. "I'm sorry, my friend, but she can be quite hands-on when she doesn't like something."

Nikolas held his chin and sat down again. Somehow, the situation seemed familiar to him.

"May I bring you another beer, it's on the house." The innkeeper smiled kindly.

Nikolas nodded absentmindedly and stared at the girl, who still glowered at him. She picked up her beer jugs and was pushed along by the landlord, who whispered tensely in her ear on their way to the bar.

"That was a sight I won't forget for my entire life. Nikolas, our great fighter, is knocked down by a little girl," Klaas teased.

"But you have to admit it wasn't a bad hook to the chin." Pitt slapped his friend on the back. "You'll have to endure a lot if you want to win her over. And it seems you're not the right person for the task."

"Stuff it, she just surprised me," Nikolas grumbled, but he knew it wasn't true. This girl with the boy's name could deal a damn good blow.

"Don't worry about it. She's already knocked down many of us." One of the other gamblers smiled.

"Do tell," said Nikolas.

"She is the daughter of the innkeeper."

"So what?"

"Well, he is Eberhart 'The Boar' Buring. Twenty years ago, he was a well-known prizefighter and taught his daughter how to fistfight. So, there is no shame in being sent tumbling to the ground by her."

"But she's a girl," Nikolas muttered.

The other looked at him with a shrug. "Of course, each of us would rather roll on the floor with her doing other things. But if she doesn't knock you out, the old man certainly will."

They continued to play for some time and allowed themselves another round of beer, but Nikolas was no longer in it and continued to lose game after game. His only luck was that, thanks to his inattentiveness, he did not put in excessively high stakes. Instead, he watched stealthily as Mathi served other guests.

She didn't immediately draw the eye, but once you noticed her, one wondered why this pretty girl with the hazelbrown eyes; the small round nose, which had been broken but professionally set again; and the well-rounded curves had not already attracted more attention. Nikolas hoped she would come past their table again, but she didn't even look in his direction. Instead, she and the tables around them were served by the lanky lad.

"I demand revenge. Shall we meet again here tomorrow night?" asked Pitt, who had lost a lot of money.

The men agreed with delight.

"What do you say?" Pitt nudged Nikolas on the shoulder.

"What?"

"Tomorrow, back here? Then we'll get our money back."

"Definitely. Here. Good idea. And tomorrow, we will drink less, and then we won't be knocked off our feet so quickly."

"You mean they won't turn our pockets inside out?"

"That as well."

For Klaas and Pitt, it was obvious that their young friend would not only return to this tavern to win back any lost stakes.

Nikolas slept restlessly. He dreamed of flying apples that laughed at him and awoke just as an apple hit him on the head.

He got up early and disappeared into the city alone. After wandering aimlessly around for a while, he finally discovered the little lane where the Wild Boar lay. He didn't find it right away, as he was too drunk last night, but eventually, he saw the weathered wooden sign with the image of the wild boar on a green background. Determined, he walked along the narrow lane and then just as determinedly past the door to the Wild Boar.

He stood for a while lost in thought at the other end of the lane, and an increasing stream of people pushed past him. Suddenly, a figure in a linen dress and blue apron broke out of the crowd and veered into the very lane where Nikolas leaned against the corner. She carried a large wicker basket with her shopping stowed under a cloth. As the lane was so narrow that she couldn't just walk past him, she approached and at the same moment recognized him. "What do you want? Haven't you had enough?"

Nikolas's heart was pleased by this unexpected sight, but she had hardly finished speaking when injured pride also knocked on his chest.

"I haven't. You caught me in bad shape yesterday."

She had walked on and answered him over her shoulder. "They all say that."

Nikolas followed her to the door. She turned around and looked him directly in the eye, leaving him stunned. "And what now? Do you want to beat me up?"

"No, I'm not hitting a woman," he said.

"They all say that too, and behind closed doors, they beat their wives black and blue."

She opened the door and walked in, not bothered about him following her inside. They crossed the bar and entered the small kitchen behind the counter, where she placed her basket on a wooden table.

"I don't have a wife, but I wouldn't beat her."

"How do you know if you don't have one?"

Mathi put butter and milk in a compartment under the small window which faced the backyard. Then she put a small bag of flour on a shelf and filled a bowl with fruit and vegetables.

"I suppose you've only dealt with whores so far. With women who are so kind and willing to give themselves to you for a few pennies that one might think they are angels on earth. But do you really think that even one of them would be so affable if she did not receive the corresponding payment?"

Nikolas didn't know what to say, he had never thought about why a woman might sell her body like that.

Mathi walked through another door and Nikolas trotted grimly after. She passed across the yard to a well that was shared between the residents of the adjacent houses. A few chickens scratched in the dirt, on the back wall of the tavern was a small wooden shed from which animals bleated, and on a crossbeam hung a large sack with some sand piling up underneath it.

"Every woman can have her own opinion and expect the respect she deserves. But instead, the so fine and better gentlemen treat them like their property and let their fists speak for even the slightest misconduct. As if they don't have a mouth to express their worries in a reasonable manner." Mathi had drawn two buckets of water and carried them over to the wooden shed.

Nikolas wanted to help her, but she scowled, reminding him of the naughty brat he had in front of him.

"You don't seem to be a friend of many words either." She put the buckets down and opened the shed. "And you seem to be one of those men who think they can do what they want with a woman."

"That's not true," Nikolas protested, but she ignored him.

179

Mathi entered the stable and poured the water into a trough. Inside stood four sheep that had been shaved for the second time this year a few weeks ago and, as usual after such a procedure, looked skinny and disproportioned. Then she poured a handful of oats in front of each and tied them to a beam. She fetched a stool from the yard and began milking the first sheep. Nikolas watched her for a while. An apology was on the tip of his tongue, but he didn't bring it over his lips. Instead, he took the water bucket and began milking the second sheep. Although they hadn't carried goats on board for years, he hadn't forgotten how to milk. They didn't say a word, but he noticed Mathi watching him from the corner of his eye.

She thanked him after they were done, and Nikolas noticed the hint of a smile.

"Where did you learn to milk?"

"As a shipboy, I had to take care of the goats on board."

"Are you still a shipboy?" There it was again, that little smile.

"Something like that. But we don't have goats anymore."

Mathi opened a hatch that led under the tavern into a vault and descended with the buckets. Nikolas stood a little lost in the yard when she shouted to him from the darkness, "Do you want to help me or not?"

Surprised, he walked down the steps. Mathi had lit a torch that was stuck in a wall bracket and waited for him with a candle in her hand. The room was so low that they had to duck their heads. Planks crisscrossed the ground as large puddles spread everywhere. The groundwater in Hamburg was too high to be able to build deep cellars, and water penetrated even this shallow vault during high tide. On the walls stood several beer barrels and just as many wine casks placed on planks above the water level.

A small door led to another room. When he entered with Mathi, Nikolas was struck by an icy breath and a shiver ran down his back. In the glow of the candle, he saw that Mathi's fine hair on her forearms had straightened up. Shelves were distributed in the second vault, so many that the room resembled a small labyrinth. On narrow boards lay countless small and larger cheeses in different colours, from milky white to strong yellow. Round wooden frames were stacked in a rack. Mathi filled the milk in a clean bucket, added some whey, and covered everything with a cloth.

"Who makes all the cheese?" asked Nikolas.

"Me, obviously. And I sell them on the market too." She went out into the first room again. "We need two barrels of beer and a barrel of wine." She placed two planks over the stairs, forming a ramp.

They rolled the barrels together into the yard and through the kitchen behind the counter. Then she lit a fire in the kitchen oven. She got up again, her nose blackened, when Eberhart "The Boar" Buring stepped in. He eyed them.

"What's going on here?"

"Don't worry. I can handle this one on my own," she replied, then walked into the taproom.

The first guests arrived for an early lunch, and the lanky lad who had served them yesterday showed up for work. His name was Frank, and he took care of the roast they wanted to serve to the guests.

Mathi had a lot to do now and kept disappearing into the kitchen to come back loaded with the orders. She skilfully balanced several plates in one hand and three jugs of beer in the other. The innkeeper stood behind the counter and handed out more drinks.

Nikolas had sat down in a corner and ordered something from the roast and a thin beer, as he wanted to keep a clear head. The guests came and went, but to his disappointment, there were always so many other people in the tavern that Mathi hardly noticed him. He sat there all day and only went out to relieve himself. Mathi talked to the innkeeper every now and then, and they looked at him for a while, but none of them came over to talk.

As it darkened outside, Klaas and Pitt joined him, and shortly afterwards, the rest of their gambling round turned up so that they could start their revenge. Unfortunately, they were only served by the lad again, while Mathi took over all the other tables.

"Well, have you been around here all day?" Klaas murmured.

Nikolas nodded, morose.

"The way you look, you haven't gotten any satisfaction in that respect?"

Nikolas shook his head.

"Well, maybe that's a good thing. If she had beaten you again, we would have to take the girl on board and leave you here," Pitt quipped.

"I'm not beating a woman. I have a mouth to express my feelings. And women also have the right to their own opinion," Nikolas hissed back.

"So, you chatted her to the ground all day, or what? The girl seems to have turned your head quite well, if you ask me."

"She only dislocated my neck."

Nikolas was now concentrating on the game, which paid off as he won one round after the other. After he had recovered his and Pitt's losses from the night before and a little bit beyond that, his opponents capitulated, but instead of instigating a brawl, they remained cheerful and accepted their loss as fair game, especially as Nikolas paid for the next round of beer. So, they continued to sit together and let the evening go on in a wet and jolly manner.

Nikolas took every opportunity to look out for Mathi. She stood behind the counter and watched the guests to see that everyone was served and happy. At some point, their eyes met, and for the first time, she smiled openly at him. Nikolas smiled back as his heart performed a dance of joy. But it was a brief moment, as at a table behind a pillar, a guest asked for service. Mathi walked over and Nikolas's gaze followed her. He looked at her slender figure from head to toe. Her bosom was perfect. It was a reasonable size, but not too big. Her belly was flat, and her bottom arched under her dress. A few strands of hair had separated from her braid and framed her face. She had just picked up the order and turned around when a hand came out behind the pillar and held her around her waist.

Nikolas jumped up so suddenly that his chair struck the man behind him. Klaas and Pitt cast a warning glance at the neighbour so that he stayed calm and turned back to his beer. Mathi had detached herself from the stranger's grip and said something to him, sweetly smiling, while Nikolas struggled to get through to her between occupied chairs and tables. But before he could come to the rescue, the man fell to the ground, laid flat by Mathi's potent punch.

"Ha, did you see that? He fell over like a house of cards!" Nikolas laughed, looking back at his friends.

"Like you yesterday. Are you satisfied now that it's not just you?" Pitt grinned.

"She's just got an incredible right-hander, that's all."

# 18

## Unknown Waters

The next day, Nikolas went back early to the Wild Boar and found Mathi with the sheep.

"Where did you learn to punch like that?" he asked when they finished milking.

"Eberhart, the landlord, taught me."

"You call him Eberhart?"

"What else should I call him?"

"I don't know. Father or something."

"He's not my father. My mother used to work for him, as I do today. And when she had me, she left me with him, and ran off. I don't know who my father is. Eberhart is certainly not." She said it so indifferently that her story hit him even more.

He had never known his own mother either, yet he missed her and would have liked to know her. Maybe the difference was that his mother had no other choice when death came for her, whilst Mathi had been abandoned deliberately.

"What about your parents?" she asked.

"Both dead... Why did they call you Mathi? That's not a name for a girl." Nikolas had no desire to talk about himself. He wanted to know more about her.

She smiled as if she knew what he was up to.

"My name's Mathilda. But the other street boys didn't want to play with me that way."

Nikolas raised his eyebrows in amusement. "I guess you made them understand with a few right-handers."

She laughed.

The morning passed far too quickly. He ate lunch and stayed in the tavern again for the rest of the day, but this time, he sat down at another table, hoping to finally be served by Mathi, but again only this lad Frank saw after him. Nikolas changed the table twice more, but it didn't help. At least he was pleased to notice that she looked at him from time to time.

"I thought we'd find you here." Klaas patted him on the shoulder, and he and Pitt joined him at his table.

That evening, someone again assaulted Mathi, but tonight, Nikolas stayed seated and was looking forward to her teaching this daredevil some manners. But nothing happened. Mathi kept her distance to the man and looked at him, disgusted. He spoke to her until the landlord appeared and placed his arm protectively around her. Nikolas stretched his neck to see who the man was she hadn't knocked down, even though he was harassing her. He saw an old man with hollow cheeks who wore his blond hair combed backwards. As a young man, he probably hadn't looked bad, but now the first wrinkles emphasized his arrogant lines, reminding Nikolas strangely of his new captain. Despite his slender figure, a belly arched under his jerkin, which was ornately decorated, and the shirt underneath also had fine lace on the sleeve hems, which only rich officials and merchants could afford.

Eventually, the man sat down at a table and ordered wine. While he was drinking, he followed Mathi around the room with his eyes, but when his jug was empty, he left the tavern without further ado.

The next days, Klaas and Pitt had guard duty and so Nikolas sat alone in the Wild Boar in the evenings. When the tavern began to empty the next night, Mathi sat down with two full jugs of beer.

"How are you?" she asked him.

"Good, and you?"

She stared into the foam of her beer before answering him. "Why do men think that if they want a woman, they can just take her?"

Nikolas looked at her, indecisive.

"I mean, I've already made it abundantly clear to that sleazebag that he should put his money and his name somewhere else. Of course, I didn't say it like that; after all, he is the reeve of Ritzebüttel, but he could still finally stop chasing after me."

"You mean the man from yesterday?"

"The pig made up his mind to make me his mistress. Apparently, he tried the same with my mother."

"Maybe words are not enough here, and you should show him his place with your beating arguments."

She snorted contemptuously. "I did that before I knew who he was, and that was a mistake."

"Why?"

"That's what excites some men. It awakens their hunting instinct. You are like that."

"I can go now." Nikolas got up demonstratively.

"Stay," she asked him, quietly adding: "Tell me about the sea."

And so, he sat down again and collected his thoughts, as this was not a light question. "The sea is the most beautiful and the most terrible I have ever seen. When the sun goes down, it shimmers mysteriously, and when you look into its depths to discover the secrets, you'll find that it only allows you to look at the surface, not as deep as your ship's hull. One day it is gentle and carries you away, and the next it tries to devour you, and if it doesn't succeed, it will show you its grim face until you long for firm land. And yet every sailor is drawn out again until he finds his damp grave in the abyss of the sea."

She looked at him, mesmerised. "I've never been to the sea. Sometimes I go swimming in the Alster and float in the water imagining that I am in a large ocean."

"You can swim?"

"Of course, you can't?"

"No. Hardly any of the sailors on our ship can do that."

"What? I would have thought that if you went to sea, it would be something like a prerequisite to be allowed on board."

"A good sailor will never be in a situation where he has to swim."

"I don't believe that. If the sea is as cruel as you say, then anyone, good or not, can fall into the water."

"But even if you could swim, it wouldn't help you in a gale. I always tie myself to the mast when it storms."

"And what if you can't do it in time or the rope splits?"

"Then you are at the mercy of the sea."

They spoke for a long time until the last guest had left and Eberhart put the chairs on the tables and asked Mathi to sweep the floor.

Nikolas thought about her words when he went back to the ship. The message they had found in the cave at Cape Arkona, carved in stone, came to his mind. Being able to swim might not be helpful when you fell into the water during a storm, but it was all the more useful to lift a treasure that was underwater.

He found Mathi at the market the next day, where she sold her cheese at a small stand. It was difficult to have a longer conversation with her, as customers were constantly asking for something.

"Can't you calculate? A loaf costs seven pennies, so half a loaf costs three and a half," he bawled at an elderly woman who had asked again about the price. Insulted, she left Mathi's stall.

"You're scaring my customers away. She probably really couldn't count," Mathi said indignantly.

"Can you teach me how to swim?" he interrupted.

She thought for a moment, wrinkling her nose. "On one condition. Apparently, you can calculate very well and probably also read and write, otherwise you would have been really presumptuous to snap at the poor woman like that. I'll teach you to swim if you teach me to read and write."

Nikolas looked at her in surprise but remembered that he had often wrongly assumed being able to read and write was more common.

"When do we start?"

"I won't have time today, as my cheeses need to be turned. How about tomorrow?"

"Deal."

"Good, meet me tomorrow morning at the Dam Gate."

When he arrived the next morning, she was already waiting for him. She was wearing a light cape that kept her warm in the cool morning hours and had pulled the hood over her head so that she would not be easily recognized, as it was not fashionable for a young woman to meet a man alone. Underneath, she carried a small bundle across her shoulder.

They left the city through the Spital Gate and walked for a while on the road towards Papenhude. On the way, Mathi tried to show him different swimming movements, which made him laugh. Outraged, she looked at him and said he would see who was laughing once they were in the water.

After a short mile, she left the road, and he followed her across a meadow that would be used for haymaking later this autumn. But for now, the grass was still high and morning dew wetted their legs. Eventually, they reached some trees, between which dense blackberry bushes grew, but Mathi knew where they could get through unscathed. Their path led them slightly downhill, and when they stepped out of the shadow of the trees, Nikolas saw that they were standing on an embankment. A sheltered sandy bay opened in front of them, which was only visible from their position.

"That's my favourite spot," Mathi proclaimed, hopping down the small slope.

The sun had risen higher and began to warm them. Nevertheless, they waited another hour until the early-autumn sun had unfolded its full strength. Nikolas drew the alphabet with a stick in the sand to pass the time, and she tried to imitate him.

"You have already made a good start in fulfilling our agreement. Now it's my turn, otherwise it will be too late." She got up and laced open her dress over her chest.

Nikolas stared at her.

"Oh please, don't think I'm going to undress in front of you," she said, laughing as she noticed his look. "You should also take off your clothes, or do you want to go into the water in full garb? It's going to be pretty hard to swim when the fabric is soaked," she continued as he kept looking at her in amazement.

Nikolas hadn't even considered this, and when she stepped out of her linen dress, he, too, finally took off his jerkin and shirt. She was already wading into the water when he removed his shoes and pants. He still couldn't take his eyes off her, as she only had her undergarment on, the sleeves of which he had already seen peeking out around her wrists.

The water reached to her navel and the tips of her hair touched the surface when he, dressed only in his braies, also walked into the stream. The water had a pleasant temperature. Without waiting for him, Mathi plunged headfirst into the river, leaving foam behind where she had stood. Nikolas waded deeper into the stream and felt his feet submerge in the wet sand. Mathi reappeared in the middle of the river and laughed at him, and with a few quick strokes, she swam back.

"You've got to get a tad farther in," she cried when she had ground under her feet again.

He continued to approach her, slightly discomforted as the water reached up to his chest.

"Well, as long as you can't swim, you stay where you can still touch the ground. The first thing you must learn is to let yourself be carried by the water."

She lay down on her back. Her hair floated around her head like algae, and her thin undergarment drifted ghostly to the surface.

"Now it's your turn," she said.

She positioned herself behind him and reached under his arms. "Come on, put your legs up."

Nikolas did as he was told. She held him as if he had no weight, and he felt her warm body against his back. A tingling sensation spread farther down his body.

"And now try to lie down, relax."

He stretched his body out. Mathi got down on her knees behind him, and his legs drifted to the surface.

"When you breathe in, you become lighter, and when you breathe out, you go under. Can you feel that?"

He tried it and experienced how the air in his lungs made him more buoyant. He was so concentrated on his breathing that he barely noticed that Mathi was just holding his head. But when she let him go, he slumped a little deeper into the water, and flailed with his arms in terror. Mathi grabbed him tightly by the arms.

"Get on your feet! Knee deep in the water and half drowning. The water carries you, you sheep. Try it again."

He tried and Mathi held him up again. When she finally let him go, he held his breath and forced himself to stay calm. Carefully, he let a little air escape from his mouth until he finally was breathing shallowly. Then he noticed Mathi drifting beside him. They looked into the sky for a while, saw white veils of clouds sweeping over them, and Nikolas relaxed more and more into the weightlessness.

"You learn quickly," she praised him. "Now try to move your arms like rudders in the water and swim with your legs like a frog."

She showed him what she meant, and he followed her example. Unbelievably light, he slid through the water until his bottom touched the ground on the shore.

"And now the whole thing on your front." Mathi showed him again what to do, and he watched her clothes and long hair wafting around her body again.

This time, he allowed himself an indulgent look, but she was soon too far away for him to see more. He imitated her movements, but where she elegantly glided through the water like a nix, he looked more like a young dog who had involuntarily fallen in. At least he didn't go under. He tried it again and again, and slowly he got a sense of how he had to coordinate his arms and legs.

The sun indicated noon, and they were still in the water. Nikolas's hands were wrinkled, and his stomach growled as Mathi swam towards him. The last half hour they had practiced diving, and Nikolas was fascinated by the peaceful silence that this underwater world offered.

"I think that's enough for today. I shouldn't stay away for too long." Mathi waded to the shore and half turned around. "Are you coming?"

Nikolas had stopped and his eyes clung to her bottom like the wet fabric of her undergarment. Her bosom was barely hidden either. His loins tingled and he quickly dived back into the water.

"I'll stay in a little longer," he said, and as she walked up the embankment, he took a few deep breaths and whispered incantations to rein himself in again.

Mathi had taken her bundle and had disappeared between the trees to put on her dry undergarments.

When he was sure that she couldn't see him anymore, Nikolas rose from the river but was unsure as he hadn't taken dry clothes with him. So he took off his wet braies to slip into his trousers without them, but as he stood naked on the shore, he saw Mathi smiling from the top of the slope.

He jumped to his pants and struggled to pull them over his wet legs. When he finally laced them up, he looked to Mathi, who was still watching him unashamedly.

"What? Have you never seen a naked man?"

"Never one who was so embarrassed by his own man-hood, you sheep," she said and laughed.

As he finished dressing, Mathi sat on her coat and pulled a piece of bread, some cheese, and a bottle of beer from her bundle. They sat silently next to each other and gobbled their provisions while the sun above them already sank lower. The wind was rustling in the trees and a few seagulls were scream-ing in the distance.

On the way back, they spoke little, and it was almost a re-lief when Nikolas saw a familiar face coming around a cor-ner.

"Hey, where were you? You didn't pick up your share," he told Jan, who looked at him, terrified. "What happened?"

Jan eyed Mathi and pulled Nikolas aside. "I got a new job in Lübeck."

"On a ship?"

"No. As a cook for a merchant. He'll be back next week and then I'll go with him."

"So, you won't come back with us?"

Jan shook his head. "Please don't tell on me. I'm worried they might kill me as a traitor."

"Don't worry. I'll miss you." They hugged to say goodbye and Jan hurried on. "Good luck," Nikolas shouted after him.

Nikolas accompanied Mathi to the Wild Boar, and they arranged to meet up again the next day so that he could con-tinue to teach her to read and write. He surprised himself when he put his hands on her hips, and even more so when she did not deny him. She looked him in the eye, smiled as if he had poured out his heart in love, but then she shook her head. He understood, and so he gave her only a fleeting kiss on the forehead.

Lost in thought, he walked down the alley and didn't notice that she was looking after him.

After Mathi returned from Sunday Mass, they sat down at a table in the empty taproom of the Wild Boar. A thunderstorm was raging outside, and everything that was not nailed down in the streets was washed away. The canal watchers would have their hands full as soon as the rain subsided.

Mathi wrote everyday words like *tree, market,* or *house* on a slate, which Nikolas dictated to her. She had learned the alphabet quickly, but now the challenge was to put the letters together into one word. He wouldn't have thought it was so difficult to teach someone to read and write, but he had the patience and Mathi the will, and so they progressed well.

He enjoyed being close to her and assumed that she, too, liked his company. And if he could have spent more time with her, he might have stayed forever. But his shipmates could not afford to stay in Hamburg for the winter, and so the final farewell came far too quickly. They politely shook hands and wished each other luck. It was unlikely that they would see each other again.

# 19

## Victory

The next morning, Nikolas finally picked up his compass, which had been ready for days, and brought it to the *Cecilia*.

"What is that supposed to be? A carousel for fleas? Are you hoping to get rid of your vermin?" asked Gustav.

"If any of you even has the slightest the idea of touching this flea carousel, you'll have a surprise coming." Nikolas was in a miserable mood, although the suspension of the compass worked smoothly.

The sky was overcast as they sailed downstream, and Nikolas sat in the lookout with an equally cloudy mood, looking wearily at the landscape. In Cuxhaven, they stocked up on provisions and a little later they rejoined with the *Gundelinde*.

This time, Nikolas stayed with Klaas and Pitt on the *Cecilia*. Unfortunately, he had not managed to retrieve his treasure under the loose plank on the *Gundelinde*, as someone untrustworthy was always near him belowdecks. To top it all off, he quickly discovered that the moist sea air had expanded the fine wooden mechanics of his compass suspension, which completely disabled the mechanism.

Twice as many masts, sails, and ropes on the two-master also meant twice as much repair work, which left him no time to think about navigation problems. The smaller *Gundelinde* was faster and more nimble, and manoeuvres could be carried out quickly. Here, on the *Cecilia*, everything had to be done in a more coordinated way. Otherwise, except for the size and an about fifty times larger load capacity, the holk was built in the same way as their old cog.

At least their raids went without major injuries, which, of course, only counted for their own men. They sold or exchanged their loot with merchants, farmers, or even smugglers on deserted beaches, and when winter came, Derek gave the order to return to Helgoland.

Nikolas was excited, as he hoped to learn more about the treasure and find an opportunity to lift it. But when they reached the small bay and prepared the huts on the rocks for winter, it was too cold for Nikolas to try out his newfound swimming skills.

The mood deteriorated rapidly. The winter quarters that Derek had chosen for them were not at all to their taste. They had enough food and alcohol in stock, but they sat grumpily in the dilapidated huts day in and day out and got bored. They missed the sizzling atmosphere of the sailor's pubs and without question the whores who would have normally warmed them on those cold days.

They lasted until February, and when the snowfall stopped and the sun shone again from the pale and frosty sky, Derek announced that they would leave this cursed island. Not a day too soon, as there had been plans to escape, which included letting Derek freeze to death on this island.

They put all their belongings back on the ships, and this time, they kept west, past the East Frisian Islands as far as

Amsterdam. Amsterdam, with its canals, reminded Nikolas of Hamburg, and although the city was one of the most beautiful ones he had ever seen, he was glad to leave it again, as, he thought, it was not worth staying in a city without a tavern like the Wild Boar.

But life didn't get any better on board either. They had hired nearly a dozen more men for both ships, and it was getting cramped. On the *Gundelinde*, they even had to share the hammocks in alternating shifts.

The summer began to blister, and the crews were irritated and sluggish. The merchant ships that ran on the Dutch coast were all fully loaded, but therefore also well-guarded. After a few costly defeats, they stuck with raiding coastal villages, which also meant that they could no longer land in these areas and were confined again on board.

However, these raids had one advantage. Nikolas had been able to extend his nautical charts by the Dutch coast before they sailed across the Strait of Dover to England and back north. Already from the distance, could Nikolas see the huge white chalk rocks and, at night, the beacons of two towers. Around Dover, they had been able to bring up a few ships, making rich booty, and now they were looking for cosy winter quarter.

Almost everywhere they went ashore, monasteries and churches rose grey and venerable from the green hills of the rainy country. Nikolas felt miserably small and insignificant in the face of these imperturbable buildings, and yet, whenever possible, he was drawn to the uncomfortable wooden benches that reminded him so much of the St. Nikolai School and the church service. If he hadn't run away then, he might now be a scholasticus at a cathedral school or even on his way to being a doctor and would now teach the scholares sub jugo reading and writing, as he had taught Mathi. And when he contemplated sailing across the seas as a pirate for the rest of his life, he felt empty and useless. How many poor and sick had he helped so far?

High in the north, in Bishop's Lynn, Nikolas lit a candle at the St. Margaret Church for his mother. Except for her name, he couldn't remember anything about her. But he found peace and confidence in the thought that there was more to life than chasing adventures.

In the end, they decided to spend the winter in Bishop's Lynn. It was not quite to their liking, as the inhabitants were all ultra-Catholic, and a strict curfew was kept in the only tavern. But it had been the same everywhere they had landed on the island, and the chance of finding a more amusing lair seemed slim. So, they paid the port fee and prepared for an unspectacular winter. But after only a few days, they gathered that there was a small place only a little walk farther away, where a landlord flouted the rules and stayed open until well into the night.

Even this small ray of light in the rainy solitude was, however, soon undone. Apparently, this happened every few months, as it did not go unnoticed, of course, where the sailors retreated to every evening, and regular checks were carried out.

On such an evening, Nikolas had already gotten so drunk that he followed a pretty girl with a long brown braid out the door without much thought. The girl, who had introduced herself as Libby, wandered on an invisible path through the fog to a barn, and he trotted willingly behind.

She placed the little lantern she had carried on a box and held out her hand. Nikolas clawed three coins out of his leather bag, which disappeared between the folds of her dress. Then, she lay down on a pile of straw and bared her snow-white legs. He stared at her hands, which slowly stroked along her thighs until they paused just before her pubic area.

"You've never been with a woman, have you?" Libby asked suddenly.

"Why would you say that?" asked Nikolas.

"You look so uncertain."

Nikolas was indeed uncertain, and if she had not seen through him, he probably would have backtracked. It wasn't that he didn't want to, quite the opposite. But this was a matter he could not learn from books or figure out through trial and error. It took two to do it, and he had always been reluctant to do anything he hadn't had time to practice. And he hadn't been able to get any practice as, even before Mathi told him so, he always had a hunch that his potential playmates would not volunteer to participate in his exercises.

But this girl with the brown braid, who was about his age and had spoken kindly to him about everyday things, let his inhibitions drop, and so he untied his pants before he could talk himself out of it.

He lay down on her, and she led him with one hand until he entered her. He was surprised when she continued to give him instructions, but this also alleviated his worries, as he knew if and how he was doing it right.

"Slow down."

"Does it hurt you?"

"No." She giggled. "I just want to have some fun, too, before you're done."

Nikolas tried to control his movements, and she guided him by letting her hips circulate rhythmically. She didn't stop him when he got more intense, so they slid through the straw with each push and piled it into a heap.

Faint voices sounded from outside, and torches wandered through the fog as if carried by invisible hands, but Nikolas was too occupied to notice until, as he reared up in a final ecstasy, someone knocked on the locked door.

Frightened, they separated. Nikolas rolled on his back to close his pants, and then walked toward the door. He was only a few steps away when a foot crashed through the boards. Surprised, he backed away and stumbled against a box, toppling the lit lantern. The spilled oil drew a burning trail that quickly captured the straw. If Nikolas had been able to gather his thoughts, he would have nipped the fire in the bud. But he stood frozen and completely thoughtless, staring at the lapping flames.

Libby grabbed him by the arm and dragged him to a ladder leading to the hayloft. Dust swirled as they ran to the hatch in the gable. The heat in the small barn became unbearable, and thick smoke rose where the flames hit damp straw.

They could barely see the ground outside, so they hesitated to leap into the unknown. But when they heard men downstairs entering the barn and breathlessly starting to extinguish the fire, she took him by the hand and jumped.

They ran in a wide arc around the rapidly forming crowd. Now that they no longer had a lantern, and with the glow of the burning hut at their backs and the fog in front of them, Nikolas saw little and sprained his ankle when he stepped into a rabbit hole. Libby did not wait for him, so he stood alone in the darkness with a sore foot, while far behind him, the fire spread to the whole barn. He did not know where he was, and so he had no choice but to limp back towards the fire.

He trembled from exhaustion as he reached the barn and was stopped by guards, who took him to a group of men who were already guarded by mercenaries.

Eventually, after a few miles of painful walking, they were locked up in a musty dungeon cell, where Nikolas was greeted by Klaas and Pitt.

"We thought you had escaped; after all, you got away with this hussy in time," Klaas whispered.

"What's going on?" asked Nikolas.

"The church detains people here every few months to show that it is doing something about neglect and fornication," Klaas said.

"And what happens to us now?"

"We'll probably be kept here for a few days and then let go again. But they want to be paid for the forgiveness of our sins rather well."

"I'm just wondering what half-wit set this hut on fire," Pitt said.

"How much would a confession cost me?" Nikolas grinned.

"You? Did your mother never tell you not to tumble around too hot?" Pitt looked at him with big eyes.

Klaas was right, and after a few days, they were all released. For the rest of the winter, though, Nikolas returned to their ship after curfew instead of visiting secret drinking holes.

So high in the north, spring came late, and when they finally departed, the wind was steadily blowing from the southeast, leaving them with no choice but to sail farther north. They raided a few smaller traders who had loaded dried cod, which offered them sufficient provisions for the coming weeks. But it was frustrating to be at the mercy of the wind and to have little chance of crossing in front of it or even sailing in the opposite direction with their square sail.

When the wind finally turned, they sailed east, where they hit the Norwegian coast. Since spring had come late and the following winter had arrived quickly, this season was short and they caught little prey, which they had difficulties selling in Bergen.

As soon as the weather allowed it the next spring, they sailed south again and crossed back to the English coast. The farther they came, the larger the merchant ships became and the more valuable their goods. But these ships were again better guarded, and often they had to deal with strong resistance.

After every successful loot, there was a big celebration in the evening, either on a beach in a sheltered bay or on board at sea. They had managed to raid a medium-size merchant ship with valuable ores on board, promising a good profit, which warranted another celebration with high spirits and a lot of wine.

Small shreds of clouds moved across the deep-black sky, where the stars twinkled on their course. Nikolas lay on the afterdeck numbed by alcohol and counted shooting stars. The haloed moon dipped everything in its silvery cool light.

Many of the men had not even made it to their sleeping quarters, so they lay crisscross on deck, leaning against boxes or stretched out on the stairs. Even the night guards had gotten overwhelmed by sleep. The last chip of pinewood burned down on deck, and Nikolas's eyes were overcome with sleep. He heard the waves gently beating against the bow, the wind rustling in the sails, and thought that they had better shorten them so that the anchor chain wouldn't break.

But he couldn't move, and he didn't want to. His arms and legs lay heavy on the planks, themselves like an anchor.

From afar, he heard whispering voices carried over by the wind. The fluttering of the sails increased, and he rolled to the side to look astern through the posts of the railing. He watched a ship which was shortening its sails at some distance in quiet activity. The ship approached them straight on, and suddenly Nikolas was wide awake. That was not possible. Had the anchor of the *Gundelinde* loosened? And then it hit him like a blow. This was not the *Gundelinde* but a fully manned three-master.

As if the alcohol had completely evaporated from his body, he jumped up. He stared across the water and could see the golden letters at the bow of the ship in the bright moonlight: 'Victory'.

"Oh shite," Nikolas cursed as he turned around and saw two more ships heckle them from the other sides. His heart raced as he ran to the small bell on the afterdeck.

"We are under attack! Up! We are under attack!" screamed Nikolas as he swung the bell's clapper back and forth, out of his mind, until it tore off. But that didn't stop him, and he continued beating the metal from the outside with the clapper until a hand silenced the bell.

"Stop the row and get your weapons." Hein took the clapper out of his hands.

Nikolas stumbled belowdecks and found his holster with the falchion. His long knife was still in the sheath on his belt, and a smaller knife was hidden in his boot. It was too late for an escape, and so they had to face the fight. The men on the holk and on the *Gundelinde* had gone into combat position and awaited the attackers with drawn blades.

Nikolas tightened his belt when he heard the opening battle screams. First, they were met by a flock of arrows, and Nikolas took cover behind the mast. Twice more, arrows sliced through the air until the attackers were close enough to embark.

Hordes of soldiers flying the English flag raced on board. Enter hooks and planks connected the ships, and more soldiers flooded over. Nikolas had climbed into the ropes and intercepted one or the other rope swinger already in his flight. Eventually, he jumped on a bridge plank and stood in the way of the advancing soldiers. He pushed the first three attackers into the water, but then he had to face off. It was a struggle he had never experienced before, a matter of life or death, as the soldiers had not come to steal their cargo but their very breath.

Nikolas fought with a tall man on the swinging plank. He leaped over the attacker's blade, setting the board into vibration and making his opponent lose his balance for a moment. He quickly stomped on the board again so that the soldier flailed helplessly with his arms and gave up his cover. Instead of stabbing him, though, Nikolas kicked him in the legs, and the soldier also ended up in the dark sea.

Then Nikolas stormed onto the enemy ship, where two more soldiers grimly received him. The first dead people were already lying on the decks of both ships as they began their battle.

His arm became heavy, and his opponents pushed him backwards when he stumbled across a dead soldier. He was looking in the blank eyes when a blade punctured his hip, and he repelled the next blow aimed at his heart, seized the fallen soldier's sword with his left hand, and plunged it deep into the stomach of his surprised assailant. He rolled to the side before the fatally wounded man tipped over. For the second time in his life, he had killed a man, but he had no time to think about it, as the next attacker was already rushing at him, seeking revenge for his comrade. However, it was precisely this revenge that blinded him with anger, and it did not take long for the third man to receive death from Nikolas's hand. Unnamed horror spread in him, and without thinking further, he now slaughtered everyone that stood in his way. No man could stop him, and the wounds that were inflicted upon him didn't bother him, he didn't even feel them. It was only when no one in his proximity was alive anymore that the pressure in his head dissipated and he could think straight again. He looked around. The English three-master had now also sent its men into the fight, and in the turmoil, one could hardly put one foot in front of the other.

Nikolas was looking at the *Gundelinde* with a warship docked starboard when the sail of their old cog fell and fluttered in the wind. The two ships moved forward side by side and faster and faster—like a gliding pair dance on the deep-black sea in the glittering moonlight, accompanied by terrifying battle music.

Desperate shouting behind him made Nikolas look up. Pitt hung from the mast with a rope around his neck and kicked for his life. Above him, two soldiers had settled in the rigging and tried to capture the pirates like cattle and hang them on the spot. Nikolas jumped towards a battle-axe that was stuck in a timber beam, but he slipped in a pool of blood. He picked himself up and jerked the axe out of the wood. Pitt's strength left him, and with protruding eyes, he pleaded silently. Nikolas took aim. The axe slipped from his hands, but it hit its target nonetheless and got stuck in the mast. While still in flight, it had cut the rope from which Pitt hung, and the pirate then fell to the ground.

Nikolas swung himself into the rigging and landed like a fly in a spider's web next to the two soldiers, but who the spider was had yet to be determined. Again, the element of surprise was on his side, and he quickly shook the first of the two soldiers out of the ropes. The second retreated upwards and struck back down with his short sword until he reached the lookout. Here, he had the more favourable fighting position, but Nikolas did not give up. Bit by bit, he worked his way up until he was level with the enemy. Each held on to the flagless top with one hand and tried to stab the other around the mast. The blows went back and forth, but eventually, Nikolas had enough. In a conniving act, he struck the soldier's holding hand and cut off his thumb. The soldier fell into the depths with a piercing scream.

Far below, the falling man hit someone whose one hand was a pointed hook and who was struck down, unmoving. Nikolas descended the rigging fast like the wind and pulled the soldier, whom he had just pushed to his doom, to the side. Ben lay unconscious, but his chest lifted and lowered. His right leg had become entangled in a broken plank, and the weight of the falling man had dislocated his lower leg at his knee, and bone fragments spiked through his blood-soaked trousers.

Nikolas ripped a tie from the dead soldier's uniform and strapped it around Ben's thigh, but before he could finish treating his old captain, a blow hit him on the back of the head and he slumped forward.

When he came to, he was leaning against the board wall, his hands bound behind his back. Next to him lay Ben, still unconscious. The last surviving pirates were being gathered and tied together like livestock.

Eventually, the English admiral came on deck, miraculously unharmed, his feather hat sitting precisely on his head, and walked along the chain of prisoners.

"Who is the captain of your damned crew?" he asked in a loud voice. When no one answered, he asked again, "Your captain?"

Nikolas could hardly believe his ears when Derek, who had fear and cowardice written all over his face, spoke up.

"He's our captain!"

The Englishman turned to Derek: "Who is your captain?"

"He." With a nod of the head, Derek pointed to Ben.

Nikolas was gobsmacked.

Two soldiers lifted Ben up by his arms and dragged him to the captain's cabin. The remaining prisoners were locked in cells belowdecks on the English three-master.

# 20

## London

Nikolas was woken up by a clanging noise with a hammering headache. He opened his eyes and found himself in a cell under the deck of a moored ship that was pulling and tugging at the anchor chain without making headway. The clanging sound came from a soldier who swiped along the metal bars with a key chain to let them know that they were going to be picked up soon.

Their ties had been replaced by iron shackles on their hands and feet to prevent them from cutting the ropes with a hidden knife.

Nikolas's body felt smashed, and he would have liked to fall back into a numbing sleep, in the hopes to later wake up from a nightmare.

Instead, he sat in a puddle of seawater and piss, in musty air that almost took his breath away, under the deck of an English warship, and he could imagine what would happen to him and his surviving comrades. Hanging from the neck was the most common punishment for piracy. On the coasts, the bodies of the dead sea bandits were often left dangling as a deterrent to other buccaneers, where they gradually dried up and were cured by the salty sea air, if not torn apart and eaten by seagulls and other birds of prey.

Or they were beheaded, as had happened with Störtebeker. Then their heads would be spit on pikes as a reminder for everyone. The rest of their bodies would get buried somewhere outside the city, where wild animals would unearth them and take them to their burrows to feed their young.

But at the moment, Nikolas found this hardly frightening, if only this cursed scumbag with his keys would finally shut up. He tried to sit more comfortably, but a pain shot through him as if a burning blade had penetrated his body. The wound on his side must have gotten inflamed, and his hip felt hot and swollen all the way down to the thigh. In the twilight, he saw a dozen bruises and many more cuts on his arms alone. Blood had trickled over his skin and marked it with dark and dried streaks.

Four other soldiers came belowdecks. Finally, the rattling on the bars stopped and the cell door was opened. As the prisoners rose one by one, Nikolas's eyes fell, to his delight, on Pitt, who also looked rather battered. He had a dark-red bruise around his neck but was alive and nodding with a pain-stricken face. Not far away, Klaas, the left half of his face covered in blood, was tied to Birger. Derek was also amongst them, and at seeing him, cold anger overcame Nikolas. At least, he thought, he sits in this hole just like we do and hasn't received a reward for his betrayal. He couldn't find Ben anywhere, nor Hein, Olof, or Jens.

The men stood up, pulled back and forth between the men in front and behind. Astonished, Nikolas discovered that the ship had two decks. The first prisoners had already climbed to the upper deck, while the rest of them scurried behind, still in the dark, accompanied by the clattering of their ankle shackles.

When he finally emerged from belowdecks, Nikolas blinked into an overcast day. The sun, diffused by a layer of clouds, shone over a thousand-feet-wide river, which moved in its bed quickly and relentlessly to the sea. A massive bridge rose to the west, casting its shadow over the waves. It must have been truly a master who cast a bridge over such a wide river and build its stone foundations into the floods. But Nikolas had no time to admire the architecture of the bridge. The line of prisoners disembarked over a connecting plank, which bent worryingly under the weight of so many men. If only one of them stumbled, they would all fall into the grey-green river and drown miserably.

Nikolas was the last to set foot on firm ground. The city was huge. From the ship, he had seen roofs two miles away and estimated that this city had to be about twice the size of Hamburg. But now, on ground level, he could only see the harbour and the adjacent houses, and that was no different than in his hometown. The buildings were mostly made of wood, a few with stone plinths, and covered with straw.

They were herded eastwards like cattle to the slaughter-house. The track was led by two soldiers in blue skirts, one of whom carried a flag. Behind them walked two more soldiers with haltered swords, ready to use them at any time. They had been received by just as many watchmen on land, who were guarding the row of prisoners on both sides.

The ground was softened by heavy rain, and their steps made squelching noises that rhythmically interspersed with the clatter of their irons. Streamlets of rubbish and faeces swam towards the river, mixing their vile stench with the sultry air. Breathing not only became difficult but required some conviction to continue.

A few guttersnipes had joined the posse and shouted insults at them. Some reenacted scenes of an execution and pretended to be hanged. Shortly before the city gate on the riverbank, they began throwing hands full of mud. As Nikolas walked at the end of the line, he could see most of the actions of these little devils without becoming their victim. A few lads crowded together, and one of them picked up a brown lump that had very much the shape of a heap of shit. Then he took a step forward and threw. The ammunition splattered on a blond head a few men in front of Nikolas.

"Beat it, you little twats," Derek shouted.

Nikolas's disgust for the brazen thrower turned into fierce admiration when he saw who the recipient was.

The busy stream of people faded once they were outside the city walls; in fact, there were no other people on this street, and when Nikolas looked ahead, he guessed why. In front of them stood an enormous fortress. Behind a moat rose an outer wall, after which extended another wall with four towers. In the middle of the fortress was a mighty white tower with small turrets and fluttering flags at the corners which stretched even higher.

They were brought to the fortress via a drawbridge. A troop of blue-uniformed officers exercised inside the fortress wall, following the barking orders of an officer. Courtyards with residential and commercial buildings nestled against the outer wall, and the even blows of a hammer on metal echoed from the fortifications. In one corner, several magnificent black horses were groomed, and the scent of a fat roast wafted to them from a building with a smoking chimney.

Nikolas hoped that they would soon get at least a corner of hard bread when he discovered the execution block, and his hunger was suddenly only a trivial earthly feeling that meant nothing in the face of death.

They were taken to an underground dungeon. Below the low ceiling were two narrow and barred windows through which the noise of the nearby river penetrated. The floor was covered with straw, which was surprisingly dry.

There were three more cells in this dungeon, where countless men were already awaiting their fate. Some looked like evil chaps who could probably commit any atrocity, but were Nikolas and his comrades any different? Nikolas discovered Hein, Olof, and Jens in one of the other cells, but Ben remained missing.

Exhausted, they sat down in the straw and tried to find some relief for their aching limbs. Nikolas opened his shirt and gently detached it from his weeping wounds. He was relieved to find that the injuries looked worse than they were. Then, he carefully pushed down his trousers at the hip to take a closer look at the stab wound.

"See to it that this stays clean." Klaas had scuffled over and settled next to him with a groan. His face was still blood encrusted, and his left eye swollen shut. Soon after, Pitt joined them.

"Thank you," Pitt croaked, rubbing his neck, which Nikolas had saved at the last minute.

"Deferred is not deterred," Nikolas said resignedly, tying his shirt back up.

"There is nothing worse than a young pessimist. Not everything is lost yet."

"But we're high up shit's creek." All hope had faded, and if he had to die anyway, Nikolas would prefer to fall asleep now and never wake up again.

"So what? There's still land on both sides," Klaas said, his words almost unintelligible. Apparently, he had lost a few teeth too, judging by the whistling that accompanied his every word.

"I can already see the lovely brown mountains of turd."

"Stop making me laugh, I think I broke a few ribs," Pitt said as he pressed a hand to one side.

"I'm just glad that they don't give this traitor any special treatment," Nikolas scoffed with a look at Derek, who was trying to wipe the excrement from his hair with a bundle of straw. "Caught together, hung together."

After a few hours, they were finally brought the hard bread crusts and a few jugs of very thin beer that Nikolas had longed for. They were also given two buckets of water and a few old rags to wash their wounds so as not to attract rats with the smell of their blood.

Most of them didn't look as battered anymore, and their spirits lifted after they had cleaned themselves up. But some were so poorly that they wouldn't make it long without medical help.

They talked in low voices, but each conversation always amounted to their execution. They were all the more astonished when, in the evening, a few soldiers visited them, accompanied by a wound doctor and two helpers. The doctor examined them briefly, gave instructions to his helpers, and then had the seriously injured taken away. Their wounds were cleaned again and professionally dressed. Afterwards, they were even stripped of their shackles so that they could move around freely.

Nikolas regained some hope. It made no sense to take care of their physical well-being if they were to be beheaded soon. But even in conversations with the other inmates, he could not find out what was going to happen with them. An old, toothless man named John, who had been arrested for breaking the peace, could at least tell him that they were in the Tower of London. When King Henry IV was in the city, he lived in the white tower, and even the crown jewels were guarded here after they were once stolen from Westminster Abbey. John assumed that he would be banished from the city and the neighbouring lands, which, for an old man like him, was synonymous with death, and so he rejoiced at every day he remained in the tower. Nikolas liked to talk to him and improved his knowledge of the English language.

Dozens of French prisoners sat in the other cells; they were picked up in groups at irregular intervals and never returned. Nevertheless, their number seemed to remain the same, as prisoners arrived all the time, be it that they had just been arrested or were relocated from other dungeons of the extensive fortress. Nikolas would have liked to talk to them and learn their language as well, but none of the French even considered exchanging a word with a non-countryman, whether English or not.

Gradually, the seriously injured returned from the nearby St. Catherine's Hospital, but they did not bring any news. Some had lost limbs, others showed, not without pride, foot-long scars, which had been tacked together with coarse stitches. Others never returned.

Finally, Ben was brought back to them, which no one had dared to hope for anymore. He was supported by two men, as they had taken off his right leg above the knee. The trouser leg was knotted under the stump, as was the left sleeve, where they had removed the prosthesis with the hook. Otherwise, he looked well fed and freshly washed, which one couldn't say about the rest of them.

They were given food twice a day, sometimes even a warm soup in the evening, and bones once a week with some meat still on them. But the cleanliness decreased every day, so the dirt in their facial hair, mixed with leftover food, now formed rigid shapes. This, of course, attracted the rats, and one night, Pitt woke up screaming when a fat rat squatted on his chest and gnawed at his beard. Even the guards rushed in with a torch to find out the reason for the tumult, but when the flickering candlelight illuminated the scene, it was cause for general hilarity.

"It tried to eat me," Pitt vowed, to counter the mockery.

"Yes, of course, and tomorrow it'll bring her family, and then they will celebrate Christmas with you as a roast." Klaas laughed loud as he patted his friend on the back.

"Maybe you can negotiate with them, and they'll dig us a tunnel if you let them nibble at your cheesy feet," Nikolas said, ridiculing poor Pitt, who was still shaken by the encounter.

The weeks turned into months and no news arrived regarding their fate. Never in his life had Nikolas been so bored that he almost wished for an execution order to arrive. Maybe they were part of a cruel experiment to see how long a person could survive without freedom and stimulation? To distract himself, Pitt began carving small figures from the bones of their barren meat meals. He used sharp-edged stones that had broken out of the wall. At first, his figures looked disproportionate and sometimes he accidentally broke off limbs, but he got better with every item. He named a horse that he had otherwise done quite well, but lacked the right hind leg, Ben.

Time dragged on, and nothing offered variety in their days, so Nikolas and a few others also started carving little shapes, but none of them showed as much perseverance and skill as Pitt. After a few weeks, he had a small farm, with horses, dogs, cats, cattle, and even a rooster, complete with comb and feathers.

"Why don't you create something useful for once?" said Klaas one day as Pitt devoted himself again to carving another horse.

"What would you like?" he asked, blowing a few chips from the newly worked area.

"Maybe a game of draughts or dominoes, something to distract myself."

"You could play with these figures. See?" Pitt took a cow, marched it over the straw and mooed along. Then he took a dog and chased the cow with snarling noises.

"My highly developed mind longs for something more challenging." Klaas grinned at his friend's childish behaviour.

"Why don't you make a domino game yourself? Your mind might just be bright enough to deal with something so simple."

"My delicate hands are not made for such rough work." Klaas lifted his chunky and coarse hands, looked at his fingers with pride, only to scratch out some dirt from under his nails.

Klaas and Pitt continued to squabble for the rest of the day, each praising their own virtues. But the next day, Pitt carved small rectangles, pressed dots into a flat side, and rubbed a little clay from the ground into the dents to make them more visible. He was about to give the third domino the basic shape when Klaas looked over his shoulder.

"Well, have you bowed to my superior mind?" he exclaimed enthusiastically, taking one of the stones in his hand to inspect it. "I'm proud of you. You're going to make it to something under my leadership."

These two were like two peas in a pod, and Nikolas could not imagine what one would do without the other. After three days, Pitt had finished all the dominoes and they played their first match.

But Pitt didn't stop carving. He built a small box for the stones, which he composed of many different parts connected with small wooden pegs, and flowers made of snow-white bone were inserted into the brown wood on all sides. It was a masterpiece with a movable lid.

His art did not go unnoticed, and one day, the guards collected all the figures and the domino game, including the box. But the setback didn't last long, as the guards came back the next day, followed by a lieutenant who wanted to talk to Pitt. Nikolas translated as best as he could.

"He says that he has seen your work and that he likes it very much," Nikolas said.

"Tell him I really liked it too," Pitt murmured.

"He offers you a deal. For each figure, you get an extra portion of meat."

Pitt's attention was piqued. "I want a jug of beer with every meal, and I need better tools," Pitt negotiated.

The beer was approved, but not the tools, as they could also serve as a weapon.

To general surprise, the officer made this offer to all prisoners, which started a veritable carving frenzy amongst the starving convicts, and over their evening meal, the first fisticuffs broke out about the best pieces of bone. Eventually, they were brought the bone waste from the entire tower and smaller wood scraps from which they made brooches or fine inlays for jewellery boxes.

They didn't know what their work was worth outside on the open market, but they all assumed that the officers were making a good profit.

The improved food not only bettered their spirits, but slowly their emaciated faces became fuller again, and that was a lifesaver as they quickly approached winter.

In the cold mornings, the steam rose from their warm bodies, and fog moved along in dense swathes outside their windows. The basement dungeon was even wetter than before, and their clothes were constantly damp. Soon, many of them suffered from debilitating cold and frostbite on their fingers, feet, and ears, which made most activities impossible. At least the stench of faeces and unwashed bodies decreased, and the spread of fleas was stopped by the freezing temperatures.

The cold grip of winter eventually claimed its first fatalities. Derek woke up one morning and frightened everyone as he crawled through the straw to get away from his cell neighbour. That one had already coughed his lungs out for days and was now staring with glassy eyes into a void, a clear, smelly liquid trickling out of his nose and mouth. But that was just the beginning. In the weeks and months that followed, until the first warm rays of the sun encouraged the birds to their spring song, several men had to be pulled dead from the cells.

With the songs of the birds, the soldiers came back. They collected Ben and several other men, including Nikolas, as representatives for their crew, and chained and handcuffed them. Ben got two crutches so he could keep himself upright, and they were herded across the city once again. The ground was still frozen, and the pigs and chickens in the streets had to rely on enough waste being thrown out for them. This time, no alley boys ran after them but instead turned away in fear and disgust, as the prisoners looked petrifying after months of neglect in a dirty cellar.

They passed a large cathedral, the largest Nikolas had ever seen, with a length of seven hundred feet and a quadruple tower that rose six hundred feet into the light-blue sky. To the west of the cathedral stood a stone house with a huge chimney. The sign above the front door identified it as 'Saint Paul's Bakehouse.' A seductive scent of warm bread passed through the cold air, but they were pushed into the next alley at the edge of the Corn Market. Countless traders were pushing forward to the markets in the city and parted as best as they could for the stinking and disease-riddled parade. Shortly before the Newgate, they were taken to a large building, whose windows were reinforced with grates and doors were clad in iron.

"Take a ride to Tyburn, eh?" asked the guard, who had stepped out of his niche in the gate to look at the new arrivals.

"Going to see how they're dancing the Tyburn jig tomorrow." The soldier who led their train laughed.

John had told Nikolas about Tyburn. There stood the gallows, where the common criminals were hanged for the amusement of the people, those who were too unimportant to blunt the executioner's hatchet.

Compared to Tyburn, the basement dungeons in the tower had been cosy. Here, the scum of England awaited their punishment, and when the door was closed behind the pirates, they were shrouded in complete darkness at first. Slowly, they got used to the sparse light coming in through small shooting ranges, and they saw frightening grimaces appearing all around them.

A man with cut-off ears stood in their way. He rose to his full size, which might once have been frightening, but the long time that he had spent in this place had taken away all the horror. So, Nikolas only compassionately raised his bound hands and patted the man's cheek. The man was so astounded by this reaction to his appearance that he simply hid in the darkness again.

That horrible night, someone next to Nikolas emptied his intestines and countless others pissed into the middle of the room. Everywhere there was constant rumbling, accompanied by distressing whining and moaning.

They were glad that they were picked up the next day and did not have to endure any more time in this hellhole.

After a short walk, they turned into Basinghall Street, where they again stepped through a gate, but this time, there were no bars but bullion glass in the windows. The building had three floors of stone and every few steps, torches lit up the long corridors. They were taken to a long and high room with wooden benches on the side. In the middle was a large oak table with a stack of parchments bearing the royal seal. Soldiers and two admirals had lined up in front of the windows. Behind the table sat a man, wrapped in a heavy red cape, and next to him stood a monk in a black cowl overseeing the procedures.

"Are you Benedikt Bartholomew, the captain of the ships named *Gundelinde* and *Cecilia van de Hoornse Hop*?" the caped man asked Ben.

Ben had not understood anything except for his name and looked uncertainly into the round.

"May I?" Nikolas asked cautiously.

Since they were given the opportunity to audition, he wanted to make the most of this opportunity, perhaps even avert the gallows. But before he could explain their case, he was cut off with an impatient hand wave. The official pointed to a sealed scroll and explained long and wide their options.

In short words, Nikolas translated to the others that they were offered a caper letter to disrupt French trade and shipping. They would be given the necessary ships, crew, and food, and they would be allowed to keep a tenth of their loot. Of course, they would also take on all the dangers and risks that came with the job of privateering. If they did not accept this generous offer, they would be brought to the gallows the next morning.

The offer was far from being as generous as they were led to believe, but the prospect of escaping death for at least a little while longer enthused them all. They signed on behalf of their crew, and Ben was noted down as captain once more.

They would not be sent off alone but sail under the sovereignty of English officers, who would also ensure that they did not defect and break their contract.

# 21

# Punishments

They had been brought back to the tower, where they told their comrades everything that had happened at Basinghall Street, and unbridled cheering erupted.

A week later, they were brought aboard their ships. Amazingly, it was the *Gundelinde* and the *Cecilia* that awaited them. Another ship already known to them lay on the quayside and was clear to leave. It was the three-master that had overwhelmed them three-quarters of a year ago but would now sail with them as their strong ally. The *Victory.*

In addition, a cog like the *Gundelinde* had been converted into a warship under the English flag. At her bow gleamed the name 'Seizor'.

They were not the only men to board. Any space that was not needed for food was occupied by ordinary seaman. Apparently, many other prisoners had received and accepted the same offer.

Nikolas guessed that about thirty-five men would sail on the *Gundelinde,* and on the *Cecilia,* fifty. In addition, there were about fifty soldiers who would serve on the *Victory* and the *Seizor.* Seeing the troops and armament they would now fight alongside made Nikolas anxious. He had already come to question their pirate life and hated violent raids, and he could not reconcile his dislike with the new scale of violence that they were tasked with, regardless of their official letter of marque. The only peace he found was the thought that they had escaped death and their future had still to reveal itself.

Most of the equipment had already been loaded, and only a few lonely bags of crushed oats and barrels of apples were left on land. The physical work felt good, but every fibre of his muscles told the story of how long he had been squatting idle in the dungeons of the white tower.

Ben stood with two officers on the deck of the *Cecilia* and oversaw the work. From time to time, he tried to communicate by hand with the Englishmen, which didn't work out well, and Nikolas decided to teach Ben a few words at the next opportunity.

Ben had a wooden leg now, which he could tie to his stump with a leather attachment so that he could walk without the hindering crutches. He had also been given his hook for his left hand, and once again, Nikolas thought of all the pirate captains from his father's stories when he looked at him. If he had seen Ben today for the first time, he would have been frightened, but he also remembered the rosy-cheeked trader he once was.

Derek was about to shoulder a bag of grain and bring it on board. He had been the only one to complain about their contract with the English. It did not suit him being patronized, which, of course, did not prevent him from taking full advantage of the offer.

Nikolas had told him in front of the assembled crew that he should finally keep his mouth shut, and if all this was against his wishes, then someone would surely fulfil his desire and cut off his head at dawn. Derek had looked aghast and snapped for air, but no more words of discontent came across his lips. Nevertheless, he had been whispering with Olof ever since, and Nikolas only hoped that the arrogance of these two would not bring them all to ruin.

The first night, they remained at the harbour. The captain's cabin had been taken by a handful of English soldiers to ensure law and order on the ship, so Ben slept with his crew belowdecks.

To Nikolas dismay, the converted compass and the nautical charts had been taken away; however, he was relieved when he was able to open his secret hiding place under the loose plank on the *Gundelinde* and find the coins and trinkets from Störtebeker's treasure. He put them in his small leather bag, which he carried day and night on a strap under his shirt.

It was still dark when the four ships cleared the anchors and set out to do their bit on the French coast. The *Victory* sailed first, then the *Cecilia*, the *Gundelinde*, and finally the *Seizor*. They began their journey with the ebb, so they were swiftly dragged to the sea. The Thames became ever wider and snaked through the land before Nikolas finally saw the vastness of the open sea again.

It was delightful to let the fresh salty sea breeze blow around his nose again. He had often wondered how people preferred to live in a crowded city, especially in the summer, when thick swarms of flies flew through the alleys like small black clouds, lured by all the rubbish.

He decided that he would never move back to a city, and he was just as sure that he did not want to sail the seas as a pirate forever. But he hadn't learned a profession. He had run away from school and thrown the chances to learn at the Cathedral School in Cologne into the wind; instead, he had moved out looking for the adventures from his romantic childhood dreams and initially believed that he had found them. But now his dreams had become reality, and all romance had been lost in the struggle of real life.

Perhaps, if they were ever released from this contract, he could sign on to a merchant ship or buy a small fishing boat. But until then, he would continue to spend his time and risk his life as a robber of the seas under the dictates of the English crown.

He did the former by drawing a nautical chart depicting France's Atlantic coast and had ample time to do so as they were to sail along the entire West Coast. Unfortunately, there was also more than enough opportunity for the latter.

First, they transferred to Calais, which had been under English rule for several decades. From here, the four vessels of the privateers sailed along the coast of France and looted ships and coastal villages.

They attacked the village of Dieppe at dawn, which had also once been under English control but had been recaptured by the French. It was the best time of day for such surprise attacks, as after a quiet night, the attention of the guards had declined, and the sleeping city dwellers were still relaxed. Some guards had sought a sheltered corner at dawn to take a catnap, believing that nothing would happen now. Nikolas found these raids abhorrent, as everyone was harmed, whether poor or rich, man or woman.

They reached the port with the first light on the horizon, and as usual, it was only the men of the *Gundelinde* and the *Cecilia* who went ashore, while the precious soldiers of the royal fleet stayed in the background and spared themselves.

The pirates positioned themselves in small groups along the main roads before kicking in doors, throwing burning torches through windows, and devastating the whole village from all sides in one all-encompassing swoop. Many of them murdered the inhabitants, whether of high standing or simple workers. Women were raped and parents slaughtered in front of their children.

This behaviour was unbearable for Nikolas, and in desperation, he beat down one of their own men, who had rammed a knife into a small child in sheer bloodlust. It was a blond boy of maybe six years, and the intestines were bulging out of the gaping abdominal wound. Shocked, Nikolas took the boy's head into his lap and gently stroked his hair from his forehead. There was nothing else he could do, and he just sat there.

"Everything will be good," he said, reassuring the boy, who reminded him so much of himself. The boy's blue eyes flickered restlessly and looked around, tormented and frightened, without any recognition. Then his breath became shallower, and after one last jerky gasp, the child's head slumped to the side and the eyes stared dead into the void.

Hot tears ran over Nikolas's cheeks. It was as if part of him died with the child, a part that had been preserved from his own childhood.

It took him a while to get up. He closed the boy's eyes and gently picked up the lifeless body, not wanting to leave him in the street. The innocent child's blood clung to his hands and wet his shirt as he carried him to a nearby hut. With his foot, he opened the door hanging only half in its hinges. Inside, he spotted a woman in a corner, who fearfully grabbed two other blond children and pulled them deeper into the shadows. Nikolas put the boy on the straw bed.

"I'm sorry," he said.

He was already outside when he heard the lamentation of the mother, who had been hit to the core and was crying for her son. He accelerated his steps to get away from this place as quickly as possible.

Many such cruel experiences already haunted him during the nights, and this was another that would plague him until the end of his life.

Somewhere a woman screamed in panic, and when Nikolas looked around, he spotted a young girl with long brown hair lying in the middle of the street. A broad-shouldered man was pinning her to the ground with all his weight, almost squeezing all the air out of her, so that her cries for help fell silent. She continued to resist when the man tried to push up her blue apron and coarse linen dress. Eventually, she managed to bite her rapist in the face. The man screamed and brutally punched the poor girl in the face, leaving her dazed and bleeding under him with no strength to fight back.

Nikolas pulled the man to his feet. He was a giant, but that was just right for Nikolas, and he lashed out with all his irrepressible hatred, his counterpart withstanding his blows formidably. The giant reciprocated with full force, so that Nikolas also received potent hits. They pounded each other through the street and may have forgotten to retreat had Klaas and Pitt not pulled them along to their ships.

As quickly as the men broke into the towns and villages, they disappeared again, leaving behind chaos and devastation.

Whenever they attacked merchant ships, they took prisoners, and when they reached the Channel Islands, they delivered the prisoners at St. Peter Port on Guernsey. In Jersey, they replenished their supplies and took a few new men on board to replace the dead.

They circumnavigated the Brittany peninsula as far as the Bay of Biscay and continued their terror campaign without much difficulty. At the mouth of the Loire, they turned back, as they had already used up half of their food supplies, but they would need less on the way back, as the number of men had decreased.

Derek had hardly made an appearance during all this time and had received and executed all the orders of the English without even a sign of disagreement. But Nikolas had watched Derek rally around him a handful of shifty men, who, in turn, secretly exchanged messages with others.

In the middle of the night, the mutiny finally broke out. Nikolas, like most others, was overpowered in his sleep and tied up. But it didn't all go as smoothly as Derek had imagined. The soldiers on the *Cecilia* and the *Gundelinde* sent signals with beacons to the *Victory* and the *Seizor*, which reacted at once.

Trapped belowdecks, Nikolas heard the fight raging above him. It was strange to sit almost safely and uninvolved in the dark, yet so close, knowing that the men above were knocking each other's heads off. Feet scraped and bodies rumbled on top of the deck. From a distance, the clattering of swords rang out, accompanied only by screams and commands. Then, it was all over.

The men who were detained in the belly of the ship were quickly found and freed, and when Nikolas came to deck, he saw the insurgents disarmed in a corner. In another corner, the dead were piled up.

The mutineers, who had fought back to the end, were brought aboard the *Victory* and locked up in the cells belowdecks. Amongst the half dozen were Derek and Olof. Those who surrendered immediately were allowed to stay on board and were not further punished. But the men found guilty were to be sentenced the next morning.

Hardly anyone ate their sparse breakfast, and when the convicts were brought to deck, there was a depressing silence, interrupted only by the rattle of the chains that tied the mutineers together.

All crew members had to appear on the deck of their ships, and the captains had been brought aboard the *Victory* to witness the punishment up close. The smaller cogs anchored so close to the *Victory* that everything could be seen from there as well.

Then the first sergeant ordered the punishment to begin. Derek was the first to be punished, as he had been branded as the leader by his comrades. Unrest spread and a lust for sensation gripped the spectators. Nikolas had climbed into the rigging of the *Gundelinde* and followed the events over on the three-master. Derek was led to the afterdeck with his hands tied behind his back. The admiral nodded his head, and Derek was led to a plank that protruded over the railing, which had been specifically attached for this penalty.

A scramble for the best places erupted on deck, and bets were made on how long the convicts would survive.

Suddenly, the murmur and the rumbling died down. Derek climbed onto the plank, panic was written all over his face. A rope was noosed around his legs as he looked desperately into the crowd, but no one dared to look the poor devil openly in the eyes. Hesitantly, he approached the end of the plank and the end of his life. A moment later, Derek disappeared. It happened so quickly, as if he had dissolved into thin air, but the splashing of a body revealed that he had fallen into the water.

The other end of the rope around Derek's legs had been thrown over the railing and led under the ship to the front deck, where it was attached to the capstan. Four men turned the drum on its levers, pulling the rope back in. Since they had not waited for Derek to jump into the water by his own will, he had unexpectedly and suddenly been yanked into the depths by the rope. The windlass turned slower and slower until they pulled a limp body on deck at the other end of the ship.

They turned Derek with a foot on his back, and the wound doctor, who had remained in the background, stepped forward. He looked down, disgusted at the damaged body.

"Few drown when keelhauled. The shells on the hull cut them open and that leads to their demise," explained Klaas, who had also climbed up the rigging.

Nikolas recalled how he had his hands slit to the blood on barnacles and sharp-shelled duck mussels at the time and could well imagine what happened to a man who was dragged underwater along the hull without being able to protect himself. A shiver ran down his spine, and he wished Derek a quick and painless death if he had to die.

The doctor knelt and checked the pulse on the delinquent's neck. In those few seconds, the tension was almost palpable. But then he barely shook his head, and a murmur went through the crowd.

Two soldiers grabbed the dead man by his arms and legs and dragged him down to the main deck. Those who stood in front turned away, terrified, and those who stood in the back stretched their necks to see better. The clothes hung in shreds around Derek's body and gave a clear view of what had once been a human being. The sharp shells of the mussels had stripped back the skin in large pieces. Flesh, veins, and bones had been laid bare and were equally shredded and mutilated. From the left ear to the cheekbone, skin and tissue were peeled off, and the exposed skull bone shimmered wet and cold in the sunlight. Teeth were visible through deep cuts in the cheeks, and intestines pressed through open wounds in the abdomen. Insights that were otherwise reserved only for knowledge-hungry doctors who made their way to unknown deathbeds at night.

The crowd around the grisly remains split, and the admiral appeared in their midst. Even though he spoke English and hardly anyone understood his words, everyone knew what he was saying. An example had been made and had its expected effect. There was none amongst them who would ever think of a mutiny again.

Next, Olof was brought forward from the group of convicts. It was shocking to see this rough, strong man, whom Nikolas had gotten to know as an unpredictable pirate, collapsed and sobbing like a small child.

"Have pity. Do all of us need to be punished? I swear on all that is sacred to me that I will never desire more than I am entitled to," he implored the soldiers, who had a hard time dragging him, as his own legs no longer carried his weight.

When they dropped him off to sling the rope around his legs, life returned to him.

"Help me, please, they want to kill me. They will kill us all. Listen! If you do nothing now, you will all die! What cowardly dogs you are!" He screamed and kicked so violently that two more soldiers had to hold him down.

Olof had made only few friends, and they were either already dead or standing bound behind him in anticipation of their own fate. And so, he faced only pitiless faces, who turned away, disgusted, when he looked at them whimpering and whining.

Derek, as the leader of the rebels, had been dragged alongside the keel. The remaining five convicts, and Olof, were to be keelhauled a shorter distance, from one nock of the main yard to the other.

Since they had tied Olof so that he could no longer move and walk the plank by himself, they had to hoist him over the railing.

"You sons of bitches, you devilish butchers, in hell you shall fry, you rag pack," Olof's voice sounded up from the floods, for the rope still had to be led over the nock before four strong men pulled it in. With a final curse and a quiet glug, Olof was dragged into the depths and silence ensued again.

Eventually, they pulled him back aboard. No sound was heard from him when his body hit the planks. He, too, had countless wounds that reached deep into the flesh, but when the doctor bent over him to feel the pulse, Olof's eyelids fluttered, and a nod from the doctor confirmed that the unfortunate man was still alive. The wounded was brought belowdecks and looked after, for even if the keelhauling was a harsh punishment and usually resulted in death, it was not meant to be an execution.

The remaining mutineers were also keelhauled. Four of them survived, albeit seriously injured, and were suspended for an indefinite period.

The dead were weighed down with stones from the bilge and thrown into the sea, where they were to await in disgrace the day of the Last Judgment.

# 22

## The Rats Leave the Ship

*A*fter the gruesome punishment of the mutineers, the work on the four ships was carried out with quiet diligence, and although the distribution of alcohol had not been banned, in the following days, there were no cheerful jokes with music and games. They continued their journey back in grim peace, but now they passed the towns and villages they had already destroyed, and attacks on land were rare. The few raids they carried out were all the more cruel, as the men released their swelling frustration about being penned up on a crammed ship.

Nikolas could no longer bear the bloody carnage, and so it was he who roused the guards of the town of Quimper out of their sleep by sneezing thunderously, and thus giving them time to sound the alarm.

It was also he who ran from the protective fringe of a small grove across the open field to the city wall of Brest and warned the inhabitants in time of the impending privateer invasion.

Once in battle, he ran away screaming from men he would have normally knocked down with one punch. And when he faced a fight, it often happened that he hit his own mates in the turmoil, which, of course, did not happen by chance.

After sabotaging five of their raids, he was transferred to galley service. In doing so, he had squandered every chance of going ashore, but he accepted it gladly, as it meant that he would not be part of spreading more senseless grief and destruction. He also found time again to think about navigation without sea marks and to complete his nautical charts.

But this personal peace did not last long. Nikolas was one of five men who was emptying the bilge from the permeating water when a warning call rang out from the *Victory*.

The bucket with the rotten water poured over Nikolas as the next man failed to catch it. The other men in the line had already rushed to deck to see what was going on when Nikolas jumped out of the darkness and into the dazzling morning sun. And indeed, there were warships under the French flag coming from a nearby estuary. The first ship was already in battle with the *Seizor*, and more and more French ships were approaching. The caravels were all as big as the *Victory* and manned with rested soldiers who would give their lives to destroy this English pirate plague.

Orders echoed across the innocently glittering water. A French sailing ship approached the *Gundelinde* and got into combat position.

Soldiers wearing red shirts with a coat of arms over light armour entered the small cog and challenged the pirates to fight. If they had sat together in a merry round, Nikolas's opponent would surely have been the target of taunts, as his waistband under the open helmet was embroidered with colourful flowers, which testified to the prosperity of the Lord, but made a ludicrous impression on a battlefield. But this image did not last long when Nikolas quickly found himself pushed back by perfected blows. Luckily, the fighting was so rampant that the Frenchman could no longer perform his sophisticated fighting technique. Years of life and fighting in a confined space of a ship gave Nikolas an advantage, and so he swiftly pushed his shorter falchion between the ribs below his opponent's raised arm. The soldier staggered backwards, fatally wounded, and soon he was one of many trampled under the boots of the fiercely fighting.

Nikolas no longer counted how many lives he had taken; he was only concerned with saving his own. Just as his arm became heavy, the French withdrew. With the courage of the desperate, the privateers pushed after the French, and it was only when the caravel were out of reach that an incredulous howl of victory spread.

The caravels moved farther and farther away and were no longer reachable for bows or crossbows when they formed a semicircle around the pirate ships. A cool breeze arose, and a cloud obscured the sun. Nikolas shivered. The men had been cheering when they fell silent. Everyone stood by the railing and observed the strange arrangement of the French fleet. Nikolas noticed a lot of activity on the ships, but he couldn't find rhyme nor reason for it.

Then, iron pipes on wheels were pushed to the railing of two large caravels until they protruded over the sides of the ships. And suddenly, a bloodcurdling thunder sounded over the sea. Nikolas climbed up in the rigging to get a better view of what was happening. While his feet were still looking for a safe hold, it boomed again, and this time, he saw what was happening. Large stone projectiles hurled out of the guns and fell into the water around their ships. No sooner had he recognized the danger when a cannonball hit the ship wall of the *Gundelinde* and smashed the planks. Pirates and Englishmen scrambled to get themselves to safety, but there was no escape. They were trapped on their own ships and could only wait for the sea to take them down.

After the next thunder, the mast splintered, crashed down, and buried two men on the afterdeck. Nikolas was thrown down with the rigging and hit the planks hard.

"That's the devil's work," someone next to Nikolas muttered. He looked up and saw Hein crouching there with his hands folded and his eyes closed. His lips moved in silent prayer, and it seemed unreal to Nikolas that this bearish man was now kneeling so broken and despaired beside him. But everything around him seemed unreal. The stern of the ship had begun to sink, and water was already coming out of the door of the captain's cabin.

With aching limbs, Nikolas crawled out from under the tangle of ropes that trapped him like a fish in a net. His face burned where it had hit the deck, and he tasted blood. With his tongue, he felt a tooth hanging from the root and jerked it out with his left hand, as he could barely move his right arm due to a heavily bruised shoulder.

The ship sank faster and faster, and Nikolas's trousers were already soaked. On deck, no one was alive except him and Hein, but desperate cries for help came from the sea.

"We have to get off the ship," Nikolas called, but Hein did not respond.

His lips were still moving mutely, and his eyes looked in rigid horror at the rising water filled with floating dead bodies.

"Come on, we have to leave." Nikolas shook Hein's shoulders firmly. A chorus of squeaks made him look up. Rats crawled and jumped out of crevices and cracks and ran to the edge of the ship, which was only a few feet above the surface now.

"So that's what it takes for you to voluntarily bugger off," Nikolas muttered. "If the rats leave the ship, then it is high time for us."

He hoisted Hein to his feet, but a severe wound on the helmsman's thigh caused him to collapse again, and only with Nikolas's help could he hold himself upright. Hein followed him to the edge like a lamb to the slaughterhouse.

Everywhere, Nikolas saw broken planks, a few barrels, rope, and tarp swimming in the sea. In between, some mates were scrambling for air, but most had already lost their last fight and their bodies were bobbing lifelessly between the wreckage. The *Victory* was missing her topmast and hung to the portside incapable of manoeuvre, but not sinking any further. A French caravel headed towards her, presumably to capture any survivors. The *Cecilia* was no longer recognizable as a ship, and most of the parts in the water had to have come from her. From the *Seizor*, only the tip of the topmast with a flag rose out of the water.

Nikolas tried to remember the weightless feeling, the lightness, and the trust that the water could carry him, just as Mathi had shown him. Then he took a deep breath and smiled cheerfully at Hein.

"Trust me," he said, and without thinking about it, he grabbed the bewildered Hein and took a last step into the depths of the sea. *Trust me,* he heard Mathis's voice as the water closed over his head. A moment later, he emerged again, holding Hein by the arm.

The sinking ship displaced the water around it, and a strong suction pulled them down. Horror spread in him, and additionally, Hein, who previously was apathetic, was now thrashing around and clinging to everything he could grab. Desperate, Nikolas tried to calm him, but every time he opened his mouth, he swallowed seawater. Over and over again, Hein pulled him under and Nikolas ran out of air. With a strong swim stroke, he dived away from the clawing hands. Seconds after he surfaced again, Nikolas saw his friend spluttering and gurgling before going under for good. Full of fear and with pricks of conscience, he dived behind. Blindly groping around him, he searched underwater for his mate's body. But he didn't find him. Once again, he took a deep breath and found an arm. He grabbed and pulled the limp body to the surface.

Hein had fainted, but he was breathing. Struggling, Nikolas managed to get a few feet between them and the ship when something hit his head. It was one of the barrels that had been stored on deck. He looped a rope that was tied to the barrel around one arm while holding the unconscious Hein with his injured arm. But then Hein opened his eyes and started screaming and writhing again, making it almost impossible for Nikolas to hold on to him.

"Calm down, calm! I can't hold you if you fidget like that," Nikolas scolded the big man. "Here's a barrel, listen to me! A barrel to hold on to. You won't go under."

With his last strength, he managed to turn the panicked Hein so that he saw the barrel and got him to hold on to the rope.

Heaving and frightened to death, Hein looked at him. "I can't swim."

"Do you know how the frog moves its legs? That's what you need to do. We are now two frogs in the water. Frogs can swim well. Do you hear?"

Hein nodded. He started to pull his legs to his stomach and stretch them again, like a frog, and finally they slowly moved from the spot.

Nikolas had his eyes firmly on the coast and tried to hold on to the hope that there was a beach there, not just rugged cliffs. He didn't realize they were leaving a red line behind them. Hein's wound was deep and had not stopped bleeding.

"What's up, are you out of puff?" Nikolas turned around when he found it harder to make headway.

Hein hung limply on the rope that cut into his arm, for his hand no longer held it.

"No, Hein, no! Come on, don't let me down now." Nikolas swam back to his friend, but his head had fallen backwards and was rocked by the waves like a toy. Had Nikolas not been so exhausted, he would have cried, but the droplets on his face were just the salty sea.

Completely shattered, a final large wave washed Nikolas onto a rocky beach. He turned on his back and looked into the grey sky. Eventually, he closed his eyes. He felt nothing more, he didn't want to feel anything anymore. Not the waves that bathed his legs, not the wind that stroked his face, not the cold that crept into his limbs, not the sorrows that tightened his heart.

He didn't know how long he had been lying there, but the sun wasn't setting yet when he heard voices and crunching steps.

"There he lies and kips."

"I could think of a better place to sleep."

"His standards have dropped considerably over the last few weeks."

"Hey, wake up, milord."

Nikolas was roughly shaken. The pain in his shoulder re-turned and he noticed stones pressing into his back. When he finally opened his eyes, he looked into the worried face of Klaas.

"Well, this must be a featherbed, judging by your deep sleep."

"There's still room here, just lie down with me," Nikolas said throatily.

"Ha, and we were worried," Pitt's voice sounded from the other side.

"I was hoping you'd bugger off again and leave me one or two more hours of peace."

"If it's so homey for you here, then we can come back lat-er." With that, Pitt and Klaas looked at each other and turned to go as if they had made a joint decision.

"Well, I won't be able to fall asleep again anyway." Strug-gling, Nikolas leaned on his healthy arm and tried to stand up. "I'm afraid I need some help here."

His legs did not want to carry him, so Klaas and Pitt grabbed him under the arms, and together they stumbled towards the cliff that surrounded the small beach. A gorge divided the cliff and allowed for a steep and daring ascent to a grassy plateau.

It had started to darken when they finally reached a set-tlement, but they could not dare to enter the place. On the one hand, they had no money, and, on the other hand, they would attract attention, since none of them were able to speak the French language. Tired and drained, they leaned against a large boulder and watched as more and more warm, flickering lights winked from the windows as night fell.

"I could fall asleep on the spot, but I'm afraid that my hunger will insidiously murder me in my sleep," Pitt said.

"I'm afraid I'd succumb under such an attack too," Nikolas replied, and an unmistakable growl from Klaas's stomach made any further agreement superfluous.

Klaas and Pitt set out to find something edible, and Nikolas collected wood for a fire. This turned out to be the more difficult task, as neither tree nor shrub grew within fifty steps. Instead, other oversized stones stood on the plane, almost like statues, and in the last of the twilight, Nikolas recognized that they had not been arranged arbitrarily but to form a circle.

When Klaas and Pitt returned, Nikolas had lit a small fire in the shelter of one of the boulders.

"But that won't last all night," Pitt remarked when he saw the small supply of twigs and dry grass that Nikolas had laboriously collected.

"As long as you don't have an idea of how to light stones, I think we'll have to make do with it," Nikolas replied.

Pitt had snatched a handful of muddy apples and a hard bread crust from the trough of a pigsty, and Klaas had stolen two capes of coarse wool and a linen drapery from a farmer's clothesline.

After finishing their meagre meal, they wrapped themselves in the capes and drapery and fell into a dreamless sleep that left them to rest until the late hours of the morning. The fire had burned out a long time ago, for they had not replenished any wood, and so they used the remaining feeble supply to rekindle it.

"Do you know what I don't understand? Why did they destroy our ships?" asked Klaas, rubbing his stiff fingers over the more smoking than burning fire.

"Maybe the French have enough ships," Pitt said.

"I rather think they had no other way to destroy us if they didn't want to put up with big losses," Nikolas said.

"We're just too good," Pitt said.

"I wonder if anyone else has made it out of there," said Nikolas aloud.

"As far as we could see from the plateau, none," Klaas replied.

"Well, we didn't wait for them to shoot our ship in ruins. What was it, anyways? Cannons? Since when do they put cannons on ships?" asked Pitt.

"A few men on the *Victory* might have survived," Klaas said, more to himself than anyone else.

"But probably not for much longer. My impression is that they don't wait long here to let heads roll," Pitt continued grimly.

"Ben was on the *Victory*. Do you think he made it?" Nikolas looked at his comrades in doubt.

"Definitely. He's as tough as dog's leather, and he still has a few body parts to give away." They laughed despite the bitter taste.

"In any case, Ben would be the only one worth saving." They nodded in agreement.

Soon after, they set off. Although the hunger plagued them terribly and the night had brought them little rest, they decided to avoid the village and made their way to the riverbank. If Ben had been taken on board on one of the French caravels, the ships would call at a port and hand over the prisoners to the jurisdiction.

They had not come far when they reached the next village and couldn't go on without eating anything. As they approached, they saw that this village was under diligent construction. The whole place was humming like a beehive, and carts were constantly rolling along the already downtrodden and grooved path. The carts transported large bales of cloth in dark green, rich blue, or natural grey beige. Others brought finely tanned leather, furs, cords, and yarn to the village.

On the carts that left the village, they saw clothes. Capes and tunics, shirts and hoses, blouses and gugel hoods. But not just a few pieces, whole bundles of clothes. Astonished, they followed the road leading into the village and found that the settlement was not so small. On the contrary. The village seemed well on its way to becoming a thriving trading town. They arrived at the end of the road without even having had a chance to steal an apple, and there they also reached the oldest buildings of the village, which apparently harboured the secret of the successful trade. The coming and going of all the carts was concentrated in a courtyard that belonged to a building with a water mill. They entered the sprawling square with a large oak tree in the middle, which served as a turning circle for the arriving carriages. Buildings had been erected on all three sides of the courtyard, although the two outer ones had probably been added later. The left wing had been expanded at least once and the right wing housed a workshop, but the heart of the yard was the old middle part. As unobtrusive as possible, they looked around.

"*Eh, t'attends le dégel ou quoi? Allez, allez!*" Astonished, Nikolas looked at the little bearded man who had just addressed them. "*Quoi? Es-tu sourd?*"

With a questioning glance, Nikolas pointed to himself. Impatiently, the little man threw a large bale of cloth into Nikolas's arms, which made him almost fall backwards in his exhaustion. Without hesitation, he joined the queue of workers and carried the bale into the storehouse, where he was thrown another bale to carry into the middle section.

The large room was illuminated by many oil lamps hung over a row of tables. Women sat at the tables bent over fabrics concentratedly sewing. But they did not sew with needle and thread and each stitch individually, but they slowly pulled the fabric over the table, to which a monstrous tangle of gears, cranks, and shafts was attached, which moved in the rhythm of the mill wheel. The women made clothes at a speed that would have taken a simple seamstress ten times as long.

Nikolas had unloaded his bale of cloth and was about to take a closer look at the mechanism when the little bearded man appeared next to him and chased him out.

"Psst, over here." The heads of Klaas and Pitt protruded from a narrow passage between the storage and the central house. Nikolas strolled over and then disappeared with them in the shadow of the alley.

"Here around the corner is a window to the workshop. There are new trousers and shirts right under it," Klaas explained.

"We deserve some new clothes," Nikolas replied.

"The problem is that the window is high and narrow, and you are the only one of us who can get in there. Pitt is going to put his hands together and give you a boost, and I'm on guard."

"I have a better idea." With that, Nikolas left the two and went back into the yard.

He walked busily towards the main gate of the workshop, and moments later came back out with a bundle of clothes, marched across the yard, and threw the bundle unnoticed into the narrow passageway where Klaas and Pitt were waiting. He did another round before rejoining them. The other two had already changed clothes, and Nikolas quickly slipped into the new garments.

They had seized several sets of tights, shirts, jerkins, and tunics. And not only that, but the clothes also had ornaments, as only adorned the robes of rich gentlemen. They quickly washed their face and hands on an unattended water tub and tried to tame their hair as best they could before setting off again.

"Now we look like rich merchants, but we still can't afford to eat anything," Pitt complained.

"I already have a plan for this," Nikolas said, looking forward to a hill behind the village, where the walls of a monastery towered.

A few minutes later, they walked through the open gate into the courtyard of the monastery complex. Smoke rose from a building—which was apparently the kitchen, as it was the only stone-built house on the site—and the scent of fresh bread blew over to them. With the wind, a monk rushed towards them.

"*Que puis-je faire pour vous?*" he called out kindly.

"I'll take care of it," Nikolas whispered from the corner of his mouth before the monk came to a stop in front of them. "We're sorry, but we don't speak French," Nikolas said in perfect Latin. Klaas and Pitt looked at each other and followed the conversation silently without understanding a single word.

"My father is Mister Bartholomew from Hamburg, and he sent me and my two business partners to forge new trade relations here. Dreadfully, we were attacked yesterday and robbed of our money and our horses. We haven't eaten anything since, and the time is pressing for us to return to Hamburg."

"I understand. Follow me, I'll take you to Prior Jean, he'll know what we can do for you." With these words, the monk turned around and stepped ahead of them to a small house connected to the ambulatory of the monastery.

# 23

## To Live and Die Like Störtebeker

They didn't just get to eat and sleep at the monastery. The surprisingly young prior showered them with ideas to help them. He offered to take them the next day to Caen, where he had an audience with the bishop. He promised to ask the bishop to help them, as a man in his position had many more options. At the same time, the young prior was obsessed with hearing news from other countries, and Nikolas wondered if it was not a sin to indulge in gossip. He had no choice but to expand his story to withstand the onslaught of questions from the clergyman. Luckily, no one seemed to know anything about Hamburg's merchants, and so he put up one childhood story after another.

The next morning, after breakfast, Prior Jean set off with two of his brothers. A strong cart horse from the stable of the monastery pulled a carriage with the three monks, and the three pirates just about found space in it as well.

After a few hours of bumpy driving, they finally reached Caen. The prior dropped them off at the cathedral school, where they would find lodging for the night. Then he drove on to the bishop's residence.

Nikolas, Klaas, and Pitt strolled through the streets of the city, letting the mild spring sun warm their faces and bantering with the women on their way. Eventually, they came to a large square dominated by a massive church. Right in front of it, a scaffold was being erected. The three comrades stopped at the end of the road in the shade of the last buildings. The setup would certainly take until the next day, not because it was so laborious but because the workers moved in a leisurely manner and often passed a bottle of wine, bread, and cheese around.

Despite the work still on its way, a small crowd was already gathering. When the tower clock struck eleven, an official-looking man in strangely tight leg dresses and pointed shoes made his way onto the scaffolding, and the crowd of curious people grew even bigger. Without further ado, the herald unfurled a parchment roll and shouted out the announcement in Latin and then in French.

Nikolas translated to his friends: "Tomorrow, on the eighth day of the month of Julius at noon, seven men are sentenced to their righteous punishment in the church square in front of St. Etienne. They are guilty of piracy and multiple devious murders and will suffer death by beheading, as a reminder to all who walk the paths of sin."

"Only seven," Klaas said.

"Maybe we can find out where the convicts are being held," Nikolas replied.

"Over my dead body, we don't have to round up the number of executed to ten," Pitt said.

"Don't forget, we are now traders from Hamburg. We just want to look at the prisoners to send a message to our jurisdiction at home, as we have heard rumours that one or more of the men have also been doing their bit on our shores," Nikolas said with a glow in his eyes.

"Well, but how do you want to find them?" Pitt answered.

"If the execution takes place here tomorrow, then the convicts will be housed nearby. There would be no point in dragging them through half the city, because the gaffers will be waiting here on the square."

"Alright, we separate and look for a prison and meet again in an hour," Pitt suggested.

In the street from which they had come, they had only noticed crafts and street shops, and so they walked off into the other three streets leading to the square.

An hour later, it was Pitt who brought the news that there was a building with coats of arms and guards in a side street. Since the other two had found no further clues, all three set out to take a closer look at the building.

From the street corner, Pitt showed them the house. It was undoubtedly a prison.

"We are doing it the way we discussed earlier. We are traders and we want to see the prisoners to bring our city the happy news that these culprits have received their deserved punishment," Nikolas explained again. "I hope one of those guards understands Latin, otherwise we'll be in a fix." Then, he moved decisively towards the prison.

They did not for a second leave the guards out of sight to be able to flee at the slightest sign of danger. Nikolas addressed the guards in Latin, but the incomprehensible expression on their faces spoke volumes, and hand signals did not help in the communication either. But to their luck, the gate opened, and Prior Jean stepped out.

"What a coincidence to see you here," he said when he recognized them.

"We learned on our way through the city that there will be an execution of some pirates tomorrow," Nikolas said, noting how his face got hotter.

The prior explained to them that he was just with the prisoners to provide spiritual support on order of the bishop. At least one of the prisoners also came from the *Nationis Germanicae*. He looked as if the devil had personally thrown him out of hell. Covered with scars, his left eye missing, and a hand and a leg were also lost."

"Ben! The old dog actually made it," Pitt exclaimed.

It was fortunate that the prior did not understand him, so Nikolas explained that they would also like to see the prisoners and send a message home that they had been freed from a terrible plague.

The prior nodded sympathetically and translated their desire to the guards. The guards were sceptical, but they did not dare to contradict the clergyman. A short time later, they were led through a small courtyard to a barrack, whose windows were secured with grates and whose strong oak door was additionally covered with iron slabs. Inside were two cells, and in one of them they discovered Ben.

He truly was a frightening sight. He had his eye patch, hook, and wooden leg removed, and the ragged smock he had been given barely covered the deep scars he had always been so proud of. He was joined by six other men who had been with them since London. A security guard stayed with them while they stood in front of the cell. It was unnecessary, as neither he nor anyone else understood German, and so they could talk freely.

"Have you gone mad?" Ben barked with little joy. "If they identify you, the executioner will earn three more boots tomorrow!"

"Don't worry, our little one here has spun a sailor's yarn, old Christian would be proud," Klaas explained.

"Even if they don't understand you, those have already recognized you."

The other prisoners, who had been their companions in misfortune a few days ago, had gathered around them.

"They're not going to grass on us. They're hoping we'll get them out of here," Pitt replied, smiling cheerfully at the others to feed their hopes.

"You don't really want to get me out of here!" Ben said, aghast.

"Tomorrow on the way to the scaffold, when they lead you through the gapping crowd, we'll get you. Klaas and Pitt will put on a rumble, and you and I can slip away unnoticed. I think we can convince the prior to give us four horses, one for purported luggage. We'll be gone before anyone realizes what happened!" Nikolas whispered excitedly.

He knew that much of this plan could go wrong before they even got close to the prisoners, but they had to try.

"Stop it," Ben interrupted. They looked at him in surprise. "I have grappled for a long time with what leaving this world would mean for me. I have done all the things I have always dreamed of, and unfortunately, I have had to do a lot of things that give me nightmares. There is nothing here that holds me. You, Pitt, you have a family. Don't you think it's time for you to go back to her and be a good husband and father? And you, Nikolas, you're still young, you're smart, you can still make everything out of your life. And you, Klaas, well, you are no longer the youngest, but younger than me, and you still have all your extremities. And I'm sure good friends like you and Pitt will continue to go through thick and thin."

"But you, too, are our friend, and we will not let you down," Klaas said.

"Don't be stupid and don't put yourselves in danger for an old man," Ben argued.

"You haven't made all your dreams come true yet," Nikolas said. "The treasure of Störtebeker. I know where it's hidden." He fidgeted on the small leather bag under his shirt and pulled out the gold ring with the red ruby.

Klaas and Pitt looked at the jewel, holding their breaths.

"God's friend and the world's fiend. The motto of the Victual Brethren. I knew you were going to solve the puzzle at some point," Ben said, looking at Nikolas wistfully. "But now that the end is near, I realize that I never wanted to be the one to find the treasure. I wanted to be free and not have to follow the duties that my father had imposed on me. I wanted to live like Störtebeker. And you three helped me live this dream. Divide the treasure amongst you if you really find it. It should help you fulfil your dreams."

Nikolas couldn't come up with any more persuasions.

"I've lost an eye, a leg, and a hand, so it's only right if I lose my head at last," Ben joked.

The guards interrupted them in quick French and made a few gestures, and they understood that they were no longer welcome.

"Don't worry about me, and woe betide to you if I see even one of you on the square tomorrow to save me," Ben exclaimed.

Nikolas put the ring, which he had kept so carefully all these years, in Ben's right hand and closed it. With a last look at his captain, they left the barrack.

Silently, they went back to the cathedral school.

"We can't just let them execute this madman. If he's finished with life, he should at least die in battle, as it should be for a true pirate," Pitt said.

"But if he doesn't comply with our plan, we're only putting ourselves in more danger than we would be anyway," Klaas said.

"Well? Then we'll all go down with him! That's the fate of a pirate."

"Nonsense. You should hear yourself talk! And you are the one who has a family to return to and the chance to lead an honest life!"

"Pah, honest life! Out before sunrise to warp my back in the fields and to bed in the evening like a broken man."

"If you consider it, then you've done harder work over the years at sea...with much more deprivation and the daily risk of being stabbed, slain, or drowned," Klaas said.

"But I could do what I wanted, as Ben said. And I had women when I wanted."

"When it comes to women, you'd get a lot more if you returned to your wife. Think about it, you could sleep with her every day and not just every few months when we go ashore, and without paying anything for it," Nikolas said. "Moreover, we could take the treasure as a foundation, and if we use it wisely, it could set us up for a long time without having to slog away for the rest of our lives."

"But we've got to try it at least. We just have to be careful enough, and if Ben really doesn't play along, then we can still vamoose and I will return to Hamburg as a loyal family man and you will never hear another word of displeasure from me," Pitt said, trying to change his comrades' tune.

"That, I want to see," Klaas exclaimed incredulously.

"That I return to wife and child like a beaten dog? You will if we at least try."

Nikolas and Klaas looked at each other uncertainly.

"It can't hurt to ask for four horses. And it's also settled that we are going to the execution. Why not create a little distraction and see what happens? Because of a brawl, we won't follow Ben right away to the gallows," Nikolas said.

"But then we will get out of here at once, and we have to be careful that none of the other scallywags rats us out when they realize that we are there but won't liberate them," Klaas said.

It turned out that the prior had already arranged for four horses without needing prompting. Unfortunately, however, the bishop had not been able to provide any further assistance. Where would the church be if she trusted every word of an unfortunate and offered support free of charge? Prior Jean did not explicitly say so, but Nikolas suspected that the four horses were not intended for them either and that the young clergyman had acted on his own initiative.

"Take good care of the horses. When you arrive back in Hamburg, send them to the capitular of the cathedral with kind greetings to Bishop John," he instructed them.

They had taken a look at their horses in the stables of the cathedral school and said their farewells, feeling awkward to accept such a generous offer based on a grandiose lie. Before dark, they made their way again to the execution site to check out the area and possible escape routes. To their surprise, the scaffold was completely built, but instead of the usual executioner block or gallows, there was an apparatus that they had never seen before. It was a kind of vice where only the head was trapped. A blade hung on a rope at man's height and was guided on two vertical rails.

"They not only designed machines for sewing clothes, but they also invented a device for mass execution," Nikolas whispered with a shudder.

"And the basket for the heads is also ready, as peaceful as if it were to receive a few cabbage heads at the market tomorrow," Pitt added.

"Psst," Klaas whispered, nodding towards the street corner, where a bailiff had appeared. They bowed their heads in the evening greeting and disappeared in the twilight. On their way to their lodging for the night, they sought out the shortest route from the scaffold to the cathedral school and, from there, northwards out of the city.

None of them went to sleep easily that night, and each quietly hung on to their thoughts about the day ahead.

They got up at dawn. After breakfast with the novices and other guests, they set off again to the city centre, as they couldn't sit around idly and wait for noon.

The first traders had already erected their stalls on the square, where they offered pastries and other goodies to the waiting bystanders. A landlord was setting up bar tables and having a few barrels of beer fetched from his nearby storage. Small stalls popped up also in the streets and alleys around the square, which had not been there the day before. Everything seemed to be set for a big spectacle, but these new obstacles could be a disaster for them, as their escape route was severely restricted. But any other way would cost them even more time, and so they stuck to their initial plan. At least, there should be no problems getting from the cathedral school to the northern city gate, as the stream of people flowed in the opposite direction.

Time moved tenaciously, and although their feet began to hurt, their legs were too restless to stand still. Finally, the church clock sounded the eleventh hour, and they rushed back to the cathedral school to ready their horses for a fast departure. They had already packed their bundles of stolen clothes and provisions in the morning, and yet they checked again, uneasily, whether they had forgotten anything.

Eventually, they set out to take their positions around the market square. Klaas and Pitt would start a fight amongst the spectators at two points on the southern side, so that the guards, blinded by the sun, had to go to the place of the riot, while Nikolas would fight his way through to the prisoners and disappear with Ben northward into the shadow of the houses.

The people flooded past them laughing and chatting, without taking notice of the three darksome looking figures who kept peering up to the tower clock.

Finally, a quarter of an hour later than expected, a drumbeat commenced evenly, and Nikolas saw the crowd in the alley across the street parting. First the drummer appeared, followed by a flag bearer and a clergyman. Then came the executioner, masked with a black hood that only left space for his eyes, and then two guards holding a rope. The prisoners were tied to the rope and additionally bound with chains on their hands and feet, so that the drumbeat mixed with the rattle and sloshing of their feet to create an oppressive rhythm. When Nikolas saw this, the courage left him, as even if Ben agreed to attempt an escape, the only possible moment to free him would be on the scaffold when he was released from the line of delinquents.

But when Ben finally came into view, a load fell from Nikolas's mind. Their captain, marked by fights and captivity, was not chained to the other convicts, nor was he otherwise tied up. It seemed probably unnecessary to bind a one-legged and one-armed old man on the short distance to the square. Ben had even been given a stick to laboriously limp after his fellow sufferers. The guards had turned their attention to the six other prisoners, and it appeared an easy task to get away unnoticed with Ben—provided he played along.

As the drummer approached the scaffold after a large turn around the market, a loud ruckus started on the other side of the square, and the people dispersed to make way for two wrestling ruffians. At the same time, a similar spectacle started in another place, and more and more onlookers, who were still in good spirits, became involved in the fracas. Nikolas had to admit once again that Klaas and Pitt were almost too good at instigating trouble.

The line of prisoners was now so close that Ben was almost within reach, and Nikolas pushed his way through to him.

"We won't give you up, no matter what you say," Nikolas whispered.

"Be gone," Ben replied.

"We have four horses, the fastest way to them is just up this alley."

"Look at me. A snail is faster than me, and you ask me to take a flight through this crowd and put you in danger?"

"We thought everything through. We will reach the horses and have left the city before they even know in which direction we have disappeared."

"Have you ever sat on a horse?"

Time was running out, and Nikolas discovered Klaas and Pitt, who had worked their way through from the other side of the square, were now waiting for them at the next corner. Nikolas shook his head to let them know that Ben didn't want to come along. Just as Pitt was furiously pushing through the crowds in their direction, the guards came to force Ben along.

Ben shoved Nikolas back with his arm stump. "Living and dying like Störtebeker, that's only just!" he shouted to him as the guards dragged him to the other prisoners.

Nikolas held Pitt back, who trotted through the crowd like a wild bull.

"Leave him. It's too late," Nikolas said, and he strained to dissuade his friend from storming forward.

When they found Klaas, Pitt was a heap of misery and couldn't stop his tears. They took him in their midst, hardly feeling any better. They supported each other and anticipated with squirming stomachs what they could no longer change.

The first six heads rolled swiftly and under deafening jeers of the onlookers. And then it was Ben's turn. Everyone saw him arduously climb the platform. A roar went through the crowd as people saw the disfigured body. No one pitied him, but everyone was glad to be freed from such a monster.

Ben was supported by a guard as he knelt before the executioner's contraption. His head was fixed in the device without a blindfold, and the priest made the sign of the cross over him. One last time, the drummer intoned his sizzling rataplan, and then Ben's head, the head of their captain that was so familiar to them, fell into the ready basket.

The executioner held up the severed head by the hair to show the gaping crowd that even the last of the convicts was really and truly dead.

In the cool shade of the houses, Nikolas, Klaas, and Pitt had already reached the end of the alley as the clapping and cheering of the crowd slowly ebbed away. They had wiped off their tears and were compelled to leave this country and all the years of robbery and murder behind. Even Pitt was inspired solely by the idea of returning to his wife and embracing her and his children.

# 24

## Over Hill and Dale

*A*s they had not managed to free Ben, there was no need to leave in haste. They thanked Prior Jean for his help and promised to send him a message as soon as they returned safely.

They led their horses out to the city, with Pitt guiding the fourth horse now as a pack animal. When they finally mounted their horses outside the city walls on the side of the road, Nikolas found that horses did not always do what they were asked to do. Klaas and Pitt quickly sat in the saddle, as they had ridden farm horses in their youth. Now Nikolas tried his luck, but getting his foot in the stirrup alone seemed to be an insurmountable hurdle.

"Get on with it, you look like a woman in a skirt," Pitt called as he overtook Nikolas.

"God certainly didn't mean for me to lift my leg higher than it would take for a targeted kick in the ass," Nikolas said in a grump.

"If you want to get mine up here, you have to aim a little higher." Klaas had stopped and watched, laughing.

After another three rounds in a circle, Nikolas finally managed to jam his foot into the stirrup. But now he was stuck in the leather strap at an angle that made it impossible to pull his foot out while the other one was still on firm ground. Restless because of the load that was now hanging from its side, the horse pushed ahead, and Nikolas had to follow him jumping on one leg.

Klaas and Pitt enjoyed themselves deliciously.

"You have to pull evenly at both reins to keep it still," Klaas shouted, but that was easier said than done.

While trying to coordinate the reins, Nikolas stumbled and was dragged along the country lane by the frightened animal. A farmer approached them with his cart and tuned in to the laughter of Klaas and Pitt.

"Come here, I'll help you," Klaas finally said, waving to the dust-covered Nikolas.

He let his own mare go to graze on the side of the road and caught up with Nikolas's horse. "Angle your left leg, and at three, you push yourself off with the right. Be sure that you don't tumble down on the other side. Take both reins and kick the horse properly into the sides," Klaas explained as Nikolas followed his instructions.

But Nikolas's horse did not respond to his feeble nudges until Klaas gave the animal a smack on the backside, whereupon it reared up its head and returned with a few steps onto the lane.

"Are you ready now, or should we give our little one a few more riding lessons," Pitt shouted back to them, as he had already ridden ahead.

"I think he'd rather be ridden by a brunette than ride a bay," Klaas replied with a grin.

"How can you hold that against me?" snapped Nikolas, but fortunately his horse now followed Klaas's willingly and soon they had caught up.

On that first day, Nikolas's horse cantered several times due to its unsettled rider, and he fell off each time. Luckily, he only sustained a few bumps and bruises and the worst happened when he fell into a nettle field, which saw him covered in itching red pustules for more than an hour. Klaas and Pitt enjoyed themselves royally, but at least the involuntary dismounts gave Nikolas ample opportunity to learn how to mount his horse.

They spent the evening in the open, as they had not managed to get to the small forest monastery that Prior Jean had suggested as their first stopover. According to Klaas's estimate, they had only made it half the way.

It was not advisable to spend the night in the wilderness, for there were bandits and thieves everywhere, but they were three seasoned pirates who had faced battle and death for more than a decade. They hardly wasted any thought on the dangers that might lurk around them in the darkness. In a clearing a little off the road, they took off bridle and saddle and lit a small fire.

Nikolas was nodding off when shouting and cursing startled him. He jumped up and looked for attackers, ready to rush at anything that was moving in the shadows.

But in the glow of the fire, he could only identify the figures of Klaas and Pitt, who, like in a satanic dance, jumped around the flames.

"What's going on, why are you howling?" cried Nikolas.

"These cursed beasts," Pitt screamed, slapping his arms around himself.

"Where? I don't see anything." Nikolas had rushed around the fire to help his friends.

"Ants!" shouted Klaas, pulling down his pants.

Nikolas stood motionless for a moment, and then burst into resounding laughter. His revenge had come. All day long, he had been mocked, but now he had the last laugh. He sat comfortably on his blanket and watched his two friends, who stood completely naked in the middle of the clearing in no time.

Not far was a small stream, where the two battered and bitten pirates washed away the plaguing pest, while Nikolas laid wood and stoked the fire. Still smiling, he did not notice that the horses had pricked up their ears and were restlessly treading on the spot blowing their nostrils.

Five dark figures, attracted by the screams, had sneaked up between the trees, and when they were just a jump away, they struck. Two of them pulled Nikolas's arms behind his back and gagged him, while the other three searched the baggage.

Nikolas fought back with all his might, but he did not measure up against the two outlaws, who held his arms as if with iron clamps.

Klaas and Pitt were still ranting about their unpleasant encounter. Not only were they frozen after the involuntary bath, but they still felt hundreds of ants crawling on their skin.

Klaas bent down to pick up the second of his stockings, which he had thrown from him on the run, when Pitt tapped him on the shoulder.

"What?" rumbled Klaas.

"Something's wrong," Pitt whispered, sneaking behind the next tree trunk. Klaas followed him.

"Hey, find your own tree," Pitt hissed.

"Now, don't act like that," Klaas replied.

Grumbling, Pitt turned away and carefully stretched his head out behind the tree to have a better view of the clearing.

"They must be weary of their life," Pitt exclaimed excitedly, and before Klaas realized what was going on, Pitt stomped barefoot through the undergrowth towards the clearing and threw his bundle of clothes into the next bush.

In a dither, Klaas followed him and was astonished to see how good Pitt's eyes were in the dark, for he only grasped the situation when the naked Pitt punched a dark shadow.

Then Klaas also threw away his clothes and stormed with a roar into the clearing. Nikolas took advantage of the intermission and deftly freed his right arm. As in former times, he hit the first of his adversaries with a right-hander and then knocked the other to the ground with a headbutt. Swiftly, he tied their hands and feet with their own ropes and then turned to help his comrades, but they had the other three attackers well under control.

Klaas had thrown himself onto a thief who had tampered with their horses, and Pitt pranced between the other two, who were attacking him with knives. A trembling laugh broke out of Nikolas's throat as he watched Klaas and Pitt beat up the thieves in the moonlight, still butt naked. He sat down on a fallen tree trunk nearby and watched as, one by one, the other bandits joined the two already tied-up thieves. He took a deep and slow breath of the cool forest air and for the first time consciously noticed the woody and spicy scent of the pines around them.

"You should always fight naked. This sight alone had them almost taking flight," Nikolas jested as Klaas and Pitt tied up and gagged the last attacker.

"Better get our clothes," Klaas said. "It's freezing cold."

Nikolas rose cumbersomely and fished the discarded shirts and trousers out of the undergrowth.

"Tomorrow, we must reach the monastery. Honest people like us could be put to death in these woods." And with that, Pitt rolled back into his blanket, but this time on the other side of the fire.

Klaas and Pitt snored peacefully until dawn, but Nikolas was repeatedly woken up by the whimpering of the thieves whom they had left on top of the anthill.

They washed down the remnants of their dry bread with the clear water of the stream and then packed their belongings. The beaten and bitten scoundrels pleaded with them with begging eyes and muffled grunts, but none of them paid them any attention.

Sore muscles pained Nikolas in places he had never known before. The inside of his thighs burned at every step, and he could not see himself getting his legs far enough apart to sit on a horse again.

As they prepared to mount, the five thieves on the ground, with their gags still in their mouths, writhed in despair.

Klaas and Pitt were already sitting in their saddles—and by the torment on their faces, even their bodies had not survived the unfamiliar strains of horse riding without pain—when Nikolas showed a heart and cut the ankle ties, so that the bandits had at least some chance to move around before the ants could devour them.

The three friends let their horses trot comfortably along the forest path, and in the afternoon, they finally reached the monastery, hidden away between trees.

The monks there kept goats and tilled a few fields. They also cultivated some beehives and produced honey from the wildflowers in the forest. Most of their produce was sold at nearby markets, and they kept only the essentials for themselves. That also meant that their guests only got a meagre supper, after which they went to bed still hungry.

The next day, they set off early after attending the Mattins, which had been expected of them as God-fearing merchants. The early wake up was compensated with a few provisions, which were supposed to last until the next breakfast, but they were so starved that everything had disappeared by the afternoon. Although their bodies still hurt, they moved faster now. Nikolas found that it was much more comfortable when the horse galloped instead of trotted. As a result, they reached their next resting place in time.

So, they travelled for several weeks from monastery to monastery and from cathedral school to cathedral school, and whenever they had to spend the night in the open, they took turns taking over the night watch, just as they had done on the *Gundelinde*. At the cathedral schools, they were given richer meals, and they rushed their way between cities to reach them, but the cathedral schools allowed only one night to not have their charity taken advantage of.

It was the end of September when they heard familiar words for the first time in weeks. They didn't know that they had crossed the border to the Holy Roman Empire and were already in Lorraine. They would have liked to have gone into a tavern and played cards accompanied by a jug of beer, but they hadn't had any money for a long time.

They strolled through Trèves and flirted with the women on the streets when Pitt came up with an idea.

"We have to make money," he said. "It wrenches my heart to just walk by the displays without being allowed to touch any of it." He peered at the high-set breasts of a gold-haired woman with plenty of red applied to her cheeks.

"We are making good progress. But if we stop to work, we will not make it to Hamburg before winter," Klaas said.

"And you wanted to go back to your wife and start an honourable life," Nikolas added.

"That is still the plan and my honest intention." Pitt turned his gaze away from the maids. "But instead of living from the church's alms, we could also offer our services here and there against a few kreuzer and eat something other than thin porridge. The winter harvest is soon to start, and every farmer will be happy about some help. And my wife has been waiting for so many years now, she won't know if she has to wait a few weeks longer."

"And she will only be able to rip your head off once, whether you add one more whore to the hundreds or not," Klaas concluded his friend's argument.

Pitt only grinned, but they agreed, as the other two were also fed up with the meagre meals in the guest accommodations of the monasteries.

The next day, they headed for a large farmstead that was on their way and asked for work. As Pitt had predicted, they were welcomed with open arms. All day long, they stood with the servants on a golden wheat field and cut down the thin stalks crowned with heavy heads with the regular movements of their scythes. They stayed for three days and set up their camp in the barn. Their horses were put up with the two dray horses, who pulled the cart with the grain sheaves to the threshing floor. The three received less money than the servants, but Pitt had picked up one of the maids, who agreed to share her bed with him for the night.

So, they went from farm to farm, and lived from hand to mouth, and saved nothing. In between, they had a few beers in taverns, however, not drinking as much as they did during their heydays.

They had left Hamm behind and had already weathered the first autumn storms when work became scarce on farms. Fortuitously, they were all so gifted in craftsmanship that they found some work here and there with blacksmiths, carpenters, or coopers, even if it was just lugging coal or stacking wood for a day. They also used the hospitality of monasteries more often again to get accommodation and food if they were not lucky enough to find a job. But the shorter and less frequent interruptions also made them travel faster again.

At the beginning of December, when the first snow fell, they had reached their last stop in Ramelsloh. They handed over the horses of Prior Jean here, as they feared that they would attract too much attention if they had actually called on the bishop at St. Mary's Cathedral to deliver kind greetings from France. The next day they would set off on foot to Hamburg.

Nikolas sat in front of the small window of their monastery cell donated to the Benedictine monks by Bishop Ansgar almost six hundred years ago, staring out into the snowstorm through the pig's bladder that sealed the window. They had exchanged their last earnings for clothes, and now he was sitting in a thick wool shirt with only his nose frozen red. The candle on the table flickered in the draught, and on the paper, which he smoothed absentmindedly with his hand, were only a few sentences. He wrote to Prior Jean as he had promised months ago, but his thoughts kept trailing off.

He saw the streets and alleys of the city where he had grown up. Images of sunny days when he had played in the merchant's yards seemed as real as if he were the little seven-year-old boy of that time again. His father's face also kept popping up. He remembered the cathedral school, where he had learned so much, and for the first time, he felt gratitude towards the master. Had he not gone, he would never have come to know all the basic things that had seemed like a waste of time to a child but had helped him so often in difficult situations later. Master Deubel was certainly dead for years now, and it seemed there was nothing or no one worth returning for. But there was another face that was pushing itself more and more often in front of his mental eye. A face he thought forgotten, but now he had to admit that Mathi had accompanied him in his subconscious all these years.

Klaas and Pitt burst into the cell and brought in an icy wind.

"It's going to be a tough winter," Pitt said, patting the snow off his shoulders. "It's only right that we spent our money on these wonderfully warm coats."

"If you had your way, you would have wasted everything on whores," Klaas said, shaking out his sheepskin hat.

"That would have warmed us too... Do you think someone will recognize us in Hamburg?" asked Pitt.

They looked at each other, but no one answered.

"Well, I'll stop by the sailor's yard and see if Irma is still working there," Pitt said.

"You really have to enjoy yourself until the last minute," Klaas said.

Nikolas looked up from the piece of paper. "I think I'll stop by the Wild Boar."

Klaas and Pitt looked at each other tellingly.

"You're not still chasing that little bird that has knocked you of your socks?" Klaas asked, smiling.

"Be careful and don't get caught by a hussy, that's just more trouble than it's worth it. Look at me," Pitt muttered.

When they left the next day, everything around them was quiet, and the world seemed to have already retreated into its hibernation, but excitement tickled Nikolas's stomach.

Finally, the city walls of Hamburg came into view. They rose darkly in front of the leaden sky, which seemed to hold more snowfall. When they reached the Brook Gate, they were suspiciously eyed by the guards, but none of the soldiers refused them entry.

With great curiosity, they looked at all the new buildings and changed facades along the streets, but they also saw many familiar corners.

A poor fellow was trapped in the pillory, his dirty face and emaciated body indicating a street vagabond who might have tried to nick a loaf of bread. Perhaps, after the humiliation, his offending hand would also be cut off. The ugly laughter of the street boys brought Nikolas back to the present. He looked pityingly at the man as he was pummelled with snow-balls. He, too, had once been one of the boys.

There was the Eimbeck House, where they had enjoyed themselves years ago at the expense of the upper class. And there on the right stood the tower where the great Klaus Stör-tebeker had spent his last hours more than ten years ago. They crossed the Consolation Bridge and arrived at the Hop Market.

Nikolas's heart tightened, surrounded by all the memories. Where would he be if he hadn't run away on that foggy October night?

At St. Nikolai, they passed the wall that surrounded his old schoolyard. And there was also the small side gate where he had last seen the master. An oppressive feeling mixed with the urge to open the door and enter the courtyard, where the scholars spent their breaks in serene conversations or in silence. He was curious whether students were quietly doing their rounds and whether in the farthest corner there was still the old gnarled pear tree into which he had always climbed and eaten the juicy fruits.

"Are we getting older or has the city gotten younger?" asked Pitt, staring up at a three-storey building whose facade was decorated with fantastic carvings up to the gable.

"That's the way it is with cities, they get bigger and older, and yet they look younger and younger over time. Unlike you," Klaas joked.

A lad came around the corner and hit a pan with a wooden spoon, shouting: "Reopening! Half a litre of beer for half a penny!" He finished his round and returned to a tavern not far from the three friends.

"I think I could bear it here," Pitt said, referring to the newly opened inn.

"With the prices, you won't have much fun here," Klaas remarked, as two drunken fellows were kicked out of the business.

"Don't put in an appearance until you've paid your debts," the landlord thundered, cracking his knuckles. The two drunkards picked themselves up and staggered to the next drinking hole.

When the landlord saw the three travellers in their good clothes, his face changed. "Come closer, come in. You won't get a better barley juice at a cheaper price than here."

"Thank you very much, Mister Innkeeper, maybe we will take you up on your generous offer later," Nikolas replied and nodded his head.

The landlord bowed before retreating into his inn.

"Why that?" Pitt asked. "Why miss such an offer!"

"You can stay if you like, but I'm going to the Wild Boar," Nikolas replied.

"Oh my God, our laddie is serious about sticking a woman to his cheek. Klaas, help me to bring him to his senses so that he does not have to suffer the same fate as I will have to face in a few days. Isn't there a maid here who wants to warm her bed with this pretty young lad here for an hour or two? What about you, my two pretty birds?" He bowed to two girls who were carrying their foodstuffs home, but they only giggled and gave them a wide berth.

"Let it go. You behave like a lovestruck dog that smelled a bitch," Klaas shouted back over his shoulder.

# 25

## Surrounded by Water

*A*fter a short search and walkabout, they turned into the small alley where the Wild Boar lay. Already from a distance, Nikolas saw that the green sign with the boar's head did not hang over the door and only the empty iron frame protruded into the alley.

The door was locked, and some of the panes of the small windows were broken. Wooden boards had been nailed from the inside to stop anyone from entering.

"Heya! Is anyone there?" Nikolas knocked loudly on the door, but nothing moved inside.

"Come. There's no one left," Klaas said.

Resigned, Nikolas turned away. He had been so sure to see Mathi here again. One last time, he looked up at the wall of the house, but even on the first floor, the windows stared down at him gloomily and empty. She had probably married and had moved away. He brushed aside his disappointment.

"Come on, let's see where we can give Pitt one last beautiful time before we return him to marital serfdom." Klaas patted him on the shoulder.

"Have you finally realized what marriage is?" asked Pitt. "But I'd like to request that it's not you who gives me a good time but a voluptuous blonde."

"Two, if you can handle it."

"Well, that's a word. So, off to the Sailor's Yard!"

That evening, they spent all their money, and Pitt did disappear with two maids in his arms into a back chamber.

Klaas and Nikolas woke up early the next morning with their heads on the table when a servant noisily moved the chairs around to clean the floor. Soon after, Pitt stumbled back into the taproom.

"You were right. I'm getting too old," he groaned. His shirt still hung half out of his trousers and his second boot was in his hand. "You can't imagine how exhausting last night was. And I don't hold my liquor anymore. The last few months have made me an ascetic."

Pitt bent over to put the boot on and nearly tumbled over.

"Time to go home." The landlord had come out of the kitchen.

"Yes, master, we're finally going to go home," Pitt agreed.

The fresh morning air outside cleared their heads.

"What did you mean by that?" asked Klaas.

"We go home. My home, your home." Pitt didn't look his friends in the eye, but his voice told them he was serious.

"When shall we go?" asked Nikolas.

"Immediately. We don't have any money left to spend another joyous day here."

The sky had been overcast during the night, and so it hadn't cooled down much, but now the clouds parted, and it promised to be a sunny day. The streets and alleys were still empty, and only the rattling and splashing of the water mills at the Mill Gate behind St. Peter interrupted the soothing silence. Nikolas walked through the gate wistfully; he had no idea whether the travelled road had taught him anything that would be useful on his way ahead.

They walked all day. Under their winter coats, they warmed up quickly, and the sweat ran over their foreheads despite the cool temperatures. It started to darken when they finally reached Wandsbek. They knocked on the door of the farmhouse that Pitt's parents had once owned.

"Who's there?" asked a woman's voice.

"Open up, *snuutje*, it's me," Pitt replied.

They could hear a heavy wooden bar being pushed back on the inside, and then the door opened.

"I'd recognize that voice even after a dozen years. Oh wait, it's been a dozen years." The blond hair of Pitt's wife was streaked with grey, and the tough years as a farmer, who had to take care of the homestead and children alone, had hardened her face.

"And you still look like you did twelve years ago." Pitt laughed endearingly and spread his arms, but instead of a warm hug, a punch hit him right on the nose.

"What's that for?" he yelled. Tears shot out of his eyes and blood ran from his nose.

"What kind of welcome did you hope for?" she scoffed.

"You're right, I was a terrible husband, but I promise that I'll make up for it all. I came back to stay."

"That's an elaborate way to say that you have no money and would like to scrounge off of me."

"I promise that I will work twice as hard for all these years that have come and gone, and you can rest now for a while."

"Why should I believe you?"

"He is a repentant sinner. We vouch for him." Pitt looked gratefully at Klaas through his slowly swelling eyes.

"And who are you?"

"We are friends and we've travelled together for the last twelve years."

"Pah, what kind of friends are you to roam around with my husband all these years but can't or won't persuade him to come home and do his duty." She eyed Klaas and Nikolas.

"I'll tell you everything, but let's get in first. It's dreadfully cold and my nose is bleeding like a slaughtered pig."

Still dismissive and with her arms crossed, she stood in the doorway. "And, of course, you want to eat something, or what? Have you at least brought money from your adventures?"

"Unfortunately not. But I can assure you that Pitt will bring home so much money come springtime that you will be sleeping softly for many years," Nikolas said, and she looked at him and Klaas with astonished eyes.

"And why should I trust you? I see you for the first time today."

"If I am wrong, you can still send us to the devil in spring, but until then, we will help you. Three strong men for the price of one." Nikolas noticed how her face relaxed a little.

Over the years, a lot had accumulated on the farm that needed to be repaired urgently. A few extra hands could get the yard up to scratch before the fieldwork started again.

After another thoughtful pause, she stepped aside and let them in.

"This is your father," Pitt's wife told four girls who were busy preparing dinner or spinning wool. They looked silently from one to the other stranger in their home.

"I thought we only had three, who is the little one?" Pitt whispered through the side of his mouth.

"She's yours. Remember the last time you came across for a skip and a hop?" she replied bitingly.

Pitt looked surprised, but he couldn't deny a certain resemblance to his youngest daughter, and with a smile, he remembered that last night.

"There is a stack of wood behind the house. I assume you still know your way around? Not much has changed." She signalled to Pitt to stoke the fire as she fetched bread, cheese, and diluted wine from the pantry, which she warmed over the flames and seasoned with a few herbs.

As the fire blazed and spread a pleasant warmth around the room, she picked up a damp rag and wiped the blood from Pitt's face, not exactly tenderly but at least helpful.

"I'm called Ranghild, by the way," she said.

"My name is Nikolas."

"And I am Klaas. We've heard a lot about you."

"Is that so? Unfortunately, I have never heard of you."

They looked shamefully into their cups.

Pitt's children joined them, quietly ate their bread, and looked at them with interest.

"Let's see if I can still get this together: Elsbeth, Hilda, Barbara, and?" Pitt was eyeing his youngest daughter.

"Agnes," the twelve-year-old replied. "Mama said you went all the way to India where the pepper grows."

"Not that far, even if your mother would gladly sent me there."

"Oh." The little one was visibly disappointed, and so Pitt told them about the fantastic adventures of their travels, without admitting that they had robbed and murdered as pirates.

Ranghild listened to his stories as she cleared the remnants of dinner away and swept the room. It was a cosy evening, and the atmosphere became more relaxed the longer the family and the visitors got used to each other. Nikolas dozed away leaning against the wall and his head sank onto his shoulder.

"You can sleep in the barn," Ranghild said to Nikolas before he fell off his chair.

"It's warmer in the back," Pitt added.

"You too." Ranghild scolded him with her arms crossed.

Pitt wanted to protest, but when she raised her chin, he fell silent.

"Come, I'll show you where the barn is." And with that, he trotted ahead of them.

The hay harvest had been good, and the barn was full of dry grass, where they made their night camp. The smell of summer flowers and herbs lulled them all quickly into a peaceful slumber.

Pitt woke them up early the next morning by turning the barn upside down, full of energy to keep his promise. He collected the few tools lying about and sorted them near the door. Then he knocked on the panels of the walls, and every time he found a rotten board, he kicked it in.

Nikolas and Klaas were still watching him, sleep-drunk, when Ranghild came in with a breakfast basket.

"Have you been abandoned by all good spirits," she yelled at Pitt as she saw the holey walls of her barn.

"Don't get upset, Snuutje, the barn will soon be like new," he replied.

"And how do you want to fix that?"

"With new boards."

"And how do you want to pay for those?"

During the following week, they were busy chopping down trees, cutting boards, and repairing the barn.

They were about to hang the door back on its iron hinges when Ranghild walked across the yard with Elsbeth in tow.

"It looks pretty good," Ranghild said. "You're not going to freeze anymore at night."

Nikolas pushed the door shut and proudly used the new bar he had carved to lock it.

"There seems to be enough wood left to overhaul the barn and patch up the roof," suggested Ranghild.

"Already on the list and one step ahead of you," Pitt answered proudly.

Ranghild and Elsbeth still didn't move.

"Anything else?"

Ranghild looked at her eldest daughter. "Elsbeth will get married next Sunday."

"I want to see that fella first," Pitt protested.

"You forfeited the right to play patron and father long ago. I know the boy, he is well educated, hardworking, and will inherit his parents' farm. The complete opposite of you, you see. Without question, I'll take him with joy as my son-in-law."

Pitt snapped for air.

"But she's a good daughter and would like her father to be at the wedding."

Pitt looked at Elsbeth, still defiant, but then he spread his arms and gave her a kiss on the forehead. "If your mother agrees, then I follow with great pleasure. Although she doesn't have the best eye when it comes to husbands."

The wedding was a modest celebration, and after the ceremony in the church, the wedding feast took place at the house of the groom. As it was a family affair, Nikolas and Klaas went back to the farm and cut more roofing shingles in the meantime.

Over the winter, they gradually repaired all the buildings, and took care of the fifty sheep, dozen chickens, and two horses. Ranghild and her daughters spun and knitted so much wool that they had already used up all the fleece at the beginning of the lambing season in February.

With the melting of the snow, Pitt was even allowed to sleep in his marital bed again, and when he appeared contentedly whistling at work one morning, Klaas and Nikolas knew that the couple had found harmony once more.

But Nikolas had another problem to solve besides the farmwork, and Klaas and Pitt pestered him almost daily about his progress. After all, he had promised to fill their pockets with a small fortune come spring. But to do so, he had to come up with a way to retrieve Störtebeker's treasure from the bottom of the sea. When everyone was asleep, Nikolas was often still awake in the depth of the night, making sketches for the construction of strange devices that slowly took shape in the barn during the day.

He frequently had to change his designs during the construction phase, as he did not have all the right materials at hand and had to settle for scraps from the farm and the surrounding workshops. Nor did he know whether his invention would work at all, as he had no way of trying out his creation apart from the old bathtub that was being used to collect rainwater in the yard. In this very tub, he had noticed that air did not escape from underneath an inverted clay bowl that he had used to ladle water on his muddied boots, as long as it was calmly and evenly pushed underwater. He had taken advantage of this principle.

He had braided a sphere from old barrel hoops and filled the holes with chipped bullion glass, only leaving one opening large enough to put his head into the orb. The gaps between the metal and the glass were sealed with tar so that it was waterproof, like the planks on a ship, and finally he slapped leather belts around the orb to strap it to his shoulders and hold it securely on his head without having to use his hands. He looked like he had put a gigantic and deformed oil lamp over his head.

When the first buttercup anemone began to bloom under the still bare beech trees, Nikolas set off to a nearby lake for his first diving attempt. He pulled the diving bell along on a handcart, where he had placed it like a fragile egg in a nest of hay. Arriving at the lake, he sought a sheltered entrance and undressed down to his braies. The sun had already thawed the top layer of the ground, but it was still decidedly too cool to undress in good faith. Nonetheless, Nikolas clenched his teeth and submerged his feet in the even colder water.

Carefully, he waded farther into the lake, and if an unsuspecting person had seen him with this colourful assembly over his head, he would surely have thought of him as a sea monster and taken to his heels in terror.

As he stood up to his chest in the lake, he slowly bent his knees until the water closed over his head. The air-filled orb resisted being pulled underwater as if air and water were not meant to be mixed, and he made a mental note to attach some sort of weight to resist the urge of the air to escape upward. Cautious not to let any air leak from his orb, he sat down on the slushy ground.

Fascinated, he glimpsed into a secret world. The light broke underwater into a myriad of rays, and through the colourful glass discs of his diving bell, Nikolas saw the stalks of the bulrushes in fascinating new hues. A school of fish passed by, and above him paddled the feet of two ducks.

He became dizzy, and just in time, he realized that he was running out of air. Panicked, he jumped up, water poured into the orb, and he swallowed a good mouthful. Spluttering and coughing, he ripped the orb off his head and gasped for air.

His diving bell worked, but he had to be able to stay underwater for much longer to get to the bottom of the sea.

Back on the farm, he set about to improve his diving construction. He sewed a leather collar that connected to the orb and could be laced at the back of the neck, so that the opening through which water could still penetrate was much reduced. In addition, he attached small hessian bags on a belt filled with sand to counteract the buoyancy of the air-filled orb.

Finally, he tackled the problem of allowing a constant air supply. He first experimented with the reed stalks and tried to get air through the hollowed-out pipes in the bathtub, but he had to suck hard to get enough air through the thin stalk. Either the breathing tube had to be much thicker, or he had to actively pump air into the orb. He chose the latter. He found an old bellow while rummaging around the barn, which seemed suitable for this purpose.

Now a long work began. First, he spent days searching for thick and firm reeds. Then he sewed leather hoses to wrap the pipes and waterproof them with spruce gum.

Eventually, he made his way back to the lake, but this time, Klaas and Pitt came along, as one had to pump the air and the other had to hold a safety line that Nikolas had tied around his belly to be sure he could come back to the surface once he had reached a depth that was more than his own height.

Excited, Klaas and Pitt watched as their friend waded into the water and disappeared. Pitt pumped the bellow evenly while Klaas slowly let the safety line slide through his hands. Should Nikolas pull on the leash twice, Klaas would get him ashore as fast as possible. But everything went smoothly. After fifteen endless minutes, Nikolas reappeared and beamed with joy as he freed himself from his apparatus.

Two days later, they left the farm. Doubtful, Ranghild stood in the doorway and watched as they pulled out of the yard with a horse and cart.

It took them a few days to arrive at the coast. None of the fishermen, however, was willing to lend them their boat, so they had no choice but to hijack a vessel in good pirate manner. That night, they pulled a sloop into the water and hoisted the little sail.

As the morning dawned grey, they spotted the rock arch at Helgoland's tip rising red from the sea. A few hours later, they had reached the island. They had to be careful not to get smashed against the rocks with the sloop, as although the sea was calm in the open, the surf raged around the bluffs.

Another cliff edge, and they entered the bay, where Nikolas had found the ring many years ago. They dropped anchor, and Nikolas put on his diving bell. Gradually he let himself slide from the boat into the water. He was still holding on to the edge, but the sand belt already pulled him under. Pitt threw the pipe construction behind and began pumping. Although Nikolas knew he had enough air, he was panting. Klaas held the lifeline loosely in his hand and made an encouraging gesture. Then, finally, Nikolas signalled despite his sudden doubts that everything was fine, and slowly he sank into the depths.

It was strange. The deeper he dived, the more the weight of the water pressed on his body, and suddenly he feared that the water might crush him, and if not him, then the air-giving orb around his head. He closed his eyes and tried to dispel the horrible thoughts. Just as his searching fingers had found the knot on his belt to discharge the weights and swim back to the surface, his feet settled on the fine sandy ground.

Nikolas opened his eyes. White sand reflected faintly the dim sunlight. The water here was clearer than in the lake, and around him, he could see hundreds of fish that drew their circles like in a dance. A few steps away, strange-looking aquatic plants grew on red rocks that had once fallen from the cliffs into the sea, and a little farther stretched a forest of algae. Nikolas was glad he hadn't landed there; he probably would have died of panic.

But then he saw something that stopped his heart for two beats anyway. A face floated between the seaweed forest. Two large black eyes watched him, and slowly the rest of the body swam into view. It was a young cone seal that was now curiously swimming towards him. He had seen many seals lying lazily in the sun on sandbanks, waddling elaborately if at all, but here in the water, the animal moved as elegantly and playfully as if it were born for it. The seal came closer and turned loops around Nikolas. He stretched out his hand and spooked the seal away, only for it to come back after a cautious observation. Suspiciously, it eyed the outstretched arm until it was sure that there was no danger coming from the hand. It let Nikolas pet its stomach, then swam away blissfully, but appeared again and again near him to see what this unfamiliar being was up to in his underwater world.

Nikolas let his gaze wander and discovered a rusty chain that led to a ring on a boulder. The resistance of the water surprised him, and he strode laboriously towards the rock to lift the chain. It was longer than he had thought, and so he followed it away from the rock until he came across an old chest that was completely overgrown with seaweed.

His heart bounced. He had been right. Störtebeker had sunk his treasure off the coast of Helgoland and attached it to the cliffs with a chain to pull it up again when he needed it. The cliff must have eroded and the rock with the chain plunged into the sea. Therefore, no one had found the treasure, surrounded by water, until now.

He quickly discovered two more chests. One of them had burst open on one side, and as he scraped the sand with his feet, he uncovered trickles of coins. He placed the chest with the open side up and collected the scattered coins. Although relatively small, the chest was heavy once filled up again.

As he could not swim to the surface with the chest in tow, he untied the lifeline and secured it to the handle. Then he tugged twice on the rope, and Klaas reeled the line in right away, Nikolas pulling himself up alongside it.

When he reached the surface, Klaas was heaving heavily. Nikolas told him to keep pulling the line up until the chest finally hit the hull of the boat. With united forces, they pushed and pulled the first chest on board. Then Nikolas dived down again. The other two trunks were also quickly lifted. Nikolas was sure that more pieces were scattered across the seabed, but they would probably remain there for all eternity.

Before his final ascent, Nikolas looked around one last time. The seal was still there and observed him with its head slanted. He stretched out his hand, and it came and let him stroke its belly one more time. Then it looked directly at him, and it seemed like it was smiling before it disappeared into the seaweed forest. He then loosened the belt, dropped the weights to the ground, and set out to return to the surface.

# 26

## Destiny Takes its Course

$\mathcal{F}$ ive days after the departure from Pitt's farm and twelve years after they had set foot on the *Gundelinde* for the first time, the three pirates finally returned with real treasure.

Ranghild had just driven the sheep into the stable for their first shearing of the year when she recognized Pitt. Stupefied, she stopped in her tracks, and some sheep promptly broke out and ran loudly bleating across the yard. Pitt jumped off the cart and herded the runaways back.

"You look like you've seen a ghost." Pitt approached his wife smiling.

"I would have found that easier to believe. I didn't think you'd come back."

Nikolas and Klaas had steered the cart to the front of the house and unloaded the treasure chests which they had hidden under logs and branches. Still unable to move, Ranghild had forgotten her sheep, and Pitt closed the barn door behind the herd.

"Come." Pitt took his wife by the hand and guided her into the house. She was not going to be disappointed again. The chests were filled to the brim with gold coins interspersed with precious chains and rings, hair accessories, and bejewelled brooches.

"Not here, not now," Ranghild whispered when she found her voice again. "When night falls and the children are in bed, we can have a closer look. I don't dare ask where you got this from."

Pitt wanted to explain, but she hissed at him. "Don't say anything, I don't want to know. Quick, push the chests under here."

They hid the three boxes under a stack of freshly felted blankets and spent the rest of the day shearing the sheep as if nothing had happened.

It was only when the three girls had fallen asleep in their chamber, the shutters were closed and the door locked, that they retrieved the chests. They sat on the floor, marvelling at their sudden wealth.

First, they sorted out all the jewels and then counted fifty guilders at a time into leather bags. In the end, they had counted four hundred and sixty gold guilders, two hundred and thirty Florentine florins, eight hundred and ninety kreuzers, and sixty pennies. From the pile of jewellery, everyone took a piece in turn until there was nothing left. Nikolas wanted to divide the money equally amongst the three of them.

"Honest to the last breath. That you survived amongst pirates is still a mystery to me." Pitt shook his head in amusement.

"Even amongst pirates, things were always shared fair and square, and here I sit with friends," Nikolas said.

"That's why you should have a greater share." Pitt threw a bag of guilders into his lap.

"And you now have to look after your wife and children," Nikolas said, and the bag flew back.

"Without you, we wouldn't have anything." Now it was Klaas who shoved a bag into his arms.

Nikolas weighed the coins in his hand. "Give it to the orphanage where you grew up. The world doesn't need another scallywag like you." And with that, Nikolas also threw this bag back.

The next day, they built new chests to store the leather bags. Pitt and Ranghild buried most of their money in different places on their farm and would probably be able to live of it for the rest of their lives, but they were wary of telling anyone about their new prosperity. Not even their children learned about it for fear that a word might get out to the neighbours and lead to envy, causing resentment or worse.

Nikolas could hardly believe for a long time that they had found Störtebeker's treasure. It had taken so many years and so much work and even more luck to achieve this goal. And it had also cost many lives on their way. Again and again, he looked at the jewels and thought about who they might have belonged to and when they had been stolen. Had the former owners survived the robbery? No other gem had an engraving like the ruby ring he had given to Ben, which had probably put food on the table of a French gravedigger.

The sheep shearing was over, and the first delicate green of spring covered the pastures. Klaas had met a young widow during Sunday mass, with whom he got along exceptionally well. To everyone's surprise, Ranghild had fallen pregnant again, and Pitt announced that he hoped to have another daughter, as he would not be a good role model for a son.

Only Nikolas was eaten away by a growing unrest. He simply could not imagine squandering his life as a farmworker or giving himself up to idleness. So, he decided to go out again and challenge life once more.

It was a warm late-summer evening; family and friends had gathered in the farmyard to finish a long harvest day with a juicy roast of a suckling pig.

Without being fully aware of his own intentions, Nikolas raised his glass, and everyone looked at him expectantly. "I wanted to thank you for giving me a roof over my head and a home to rest. I don't know why Pitt stayed away for so long. Should he ever put his travelling boots on again, I will come back and beat him up until he sings praises in his sleep." Some laughter got stuck in throats as his words sunk in. "As hard as it is for me to say it, I can't stay."

"Why not?" Pitt blurted out.

"Where do you want to go?" asked Klaas.

"I don't know. But the sea hasn't let me go yet. I'm thinking about hiring on a merchant ship and seeing where it takes me. If I don't like it, this is the first place, though, I'll come back to... Promise."

Silence spread around the table, where a few minutes earlier exuberant cheerfulness had reigned.

The smell of the delicious roast pulled Pitt out of his melancholy. "I think the piglet is good now. Then let's make the most of this mellow evening and say goodbye to the best fighter, most loyal friend, and the smartest son of a damn bitch I've ever met." Pitt swallowed hard.

"For once, I agree with you, Pitt, and I am glad that you have finally realized for yourself all my favourable characteristics, but you won't get rid of me so easily," Klaas quipped loudly, making everyone laugh until they cried.

It was still a happy evening, and at some point, the three friends sat alone by the fire.

"Do you know when you want to leave?" Klaas stared into his mug of beer.

"I thought tomorrow morning."

"Tomorrow already? And what about the harvest?" Pitt was indignant.

"You have enough hands on deck here and the money to pay for them. The season is good and there will be many traders in the port now."

"He's right, Pitt. We knew he wasn't going to stay here forever."

"I didn't know that," Pitt protested.

The morning started bright and clear, and promised to make way for another warm day. A neighbour from the village, who went to the market in Hamburg, had agreed to give Nikolas a ride. Klaas and Pitt were standing by the side of the road when Nikolas loaded his chest onto the cart.

"I'm afraid you'll have to take care of yourself from now on," Pitt said theatrically. "Normally I would come along. But I'm not going to find anything better than I have here." He held Ranghild in his arms and pressed a kiss in her hair. "Though you made a quite decent maid in that dress back in Stockholm." Ranghild looked astonished.

"I'm glad you've come to your senses." Nikolas smiled.

"I'm doing the same, sticking around here. After all, I must prepare for a wedding," Klaas said.

"What?" They were all surprised.

"Still have to propose! You see, I have my hands full," Klaas admitted.

"I wish you all the happiness in the world." Nikolas jumped onto the cart next to the neighbour, who had waited patiently. "I will miss you!" he cried as the cart slowly rumbled into motion.

Klaas and Pitt were still standing by the road after the cart had long disappeared behind a small birch forest. Nikolas did not look back, as he feared that his heavy heart would convince him to turn back and abandon his plan. But the tingling in his belly reassured him that he'd made the right decision.

All the way, Nikolas was engulfed in thoughts and barely heard a word of the swell of speech with which the farmer showered him. From time to time, he gave a grunt of feigned attention, and the man continued contentedly.

In Hamburg, he already egressed at the water mills, even though he could have stayed on until the fish market. He shouldered his chest, and his feet carried him back to the wall and the small gate of the St. Nikolai School without meaning it. He tried the rusty iron lever and was surprised when the door opened.

The bell rang for class, and the scholars crowded in front of the back entrance. Only one little boy remained in the old gnarled pear tree. He held on to a branch with one hand and laid the other over his eyes and peered into the distance.

Nikolas walked across the yard to the pear tree. "Any enemy ships in sight, sailor?"

The boy looked quizzically down at Nikolas.

"No, not yet. But I think I've seen the coast of Africa."

"Good work, sailor!"

Fast like a squirrel, the lad climbed off the tree and jumped to the ground next to Nikolas.

"Are you a real captain?"

"I'm a real pirate," Nikolas replied.

"But you don't look like one. You are far too clean and well dressed."

"What? You don't believe me, you little landlubber? I even have my own treasure hidden on a deserted island." Nikolas pulled a small gold coin out of his pocket.

With wide eyes, the little boy turned the coin over, watching it sparkle in the sunlight.

"You can keep it, but now run. If you want to become a good mariner, you must be able to read and write. How else do you intend to interpret treasure maps?"

The laddie nodded excitedly but stopped in his tracks. "What's your name?"

"I can't tell you, otherwise I'd have to cut your throat."

The boy stared at Nikolas with big eyes and then ran away in horror. Nikolas chuckled and then reached for a low branch to swing himself up into the tree. To the south, with the sun approaching its zenith, he could see dozens of masts swaying on the river, and in the middle of them, he made out the top of the small crane that was used to unload the ships' cargo.

He rented a room at a hostel near the harbour. The midday break was long over, and the chains of the small crane rattled again constantly while the men in the pedal wheel sweated. The merchant ships lay sluggishly on the Elbe, and countless small barges were stalked through the canals to the warehouses.

Nikolas bought half a stockfish from a street vendor and strolled along the moorings. He observed which ships were loaded, and by their names, he tried to guess where they would sail to. The coast of Africa was still playing on his mind when a name caught his eye.

Nikolas asked around the dockworkers until he found the captain of the ship.

"Are you the captain of the *Santa Isabella*?"

"So I am. What can I do for you?"

The slender and weather-tanned man spoke with an accent that Nikolas had never heard before. It resonated with both serenity and strength, which were rarely found together. Finally, the captain looked up from his list.

"Where are you going, if I may ask?"

"To Portugal. Lisbon."

"And when do you depart?"

"Tomorrow morning, if we've loaded everything by then."

"This sounds like you're lagging a little behind your schedule. I would like to sign on."

The captain scrutinized Nikolas from top to bottom.

"You look strong. Any sailing experience?"

"Twelve years on a cog and a holk," Nikolas responded with pride.

The captain nodded favourably. "There, these bags of pepper must be put in the barge and then on to the ship. Ask for Antonio, he will show you where everything should be stored. Tell him I hired you."

"And what is your name, captain?"

"José Lopes."

Nikolas worked all day. He towed sacks of spices from faraway lands, rolled barrels of domestically brewed beer, and shouldered bales of wool cloth made in the rainy lands of England, and by the time the sun was setting, they had made it. Through his diligence and good ideas for space-saving storage, Nikolas quickly gained the respect of the captain, and he felt that his fate had already begun to take a good turn.

Tired and happy, he strolled back to the hostel through the dark alleys.

Suddenly a figure, wrapped from head to toe in a dark cape, came out of a hidden lane and bumped into him. Both were surprised and terrified, but when the hood of the cape slipped a bit, Nikolas recognized the dark flashing eyes and long brown hair.

"Wait!" he shouted, holding the woman by the arm. But he shouldn't have done that. Like a lightning bolt, a right-hander hit him on the chin and sent him to the ground. "I should have expected that. Don't you recognize me?"

"Nikolas? Where have you come from?"

"From there." Nikolas pointed with his head. "And where are you going?"

"As far away as possible." Mathi looked around like an anxious deer, but no one could be seen far and wide.

"What happened?" Nikolas picked himself up.

"It'd take too long to explain. Can you help me disappear from here?"

"I will sail to Portugal tomorrow morning."

"Portugal. Is that far away?"

"If the wind is favourable, you can make it in two months, I'd say."

"That sounds far enough. And you're saying tomorrow?"

"Yes. You don't want to hire on a ship, though."

"Why not?"

"You're a woman."

"And?" Her eyes sparkled, wildly determined.

The lantern of a bailiff danced along the harbour, and Mathi ducked further into the shadows of the houses.

"I have a bed at an inn around the corner. If you want, you can come with me, at least for tonight."

Mathi nodded eagerly. They quickly reached the hostel and slipped up the stairs to the bedrooms. Luckily, the chamber was not shared with other guests, and they had the room to themselves.

"What happened?" asked Nikolas, as Mathi shut the moth-eaten curtains.

"Eberhart died last fall. It came completely unexpectedly. The tavern was full, everyone wanted to be served at once, and then he just collapsed and was dead. I tried to keep everything going, but many customers don't seem to like a woman as the landlady. The long and short of it, I had to shut shop."

"Couldn't you find work elsewhere?"

"With a brothel, or what?" she scoffed.

"Or you could get married." Embarrassed, Nikolas tried to save the situation.

"Either you become a whore and must serve all men, or you marry and serve but one. But serve you must." Mathi had sat down on the bed and pulled her knees to her chest. "I stayed in the Wild Boar all winter, but I had to hide, otherwise I would have been considered fair game." Her gaze was fixed on a fraying patch on the curtains. "The reeve of Ritzebüttel had been keeping an eye on me for a long time and finally ferreted me out. He offered to support me, be my guardian, if I wanted to reopen the tavern. But, of course, only if I provided certain repayments."

"I remember the man. And? What did you do?" Anger rose in Nikolas.

"I threw him out, as concisely as you can dare to be with such a person. But he kept coming back and even increased his offer." She snorted contemptuously. "The last time he came was a week ago. He tried to take what he wanted by force. I think I broke his nose and a few ribs." She wrinkled her nose and small lines formed on her forehead. "He threatened to have me hanged. This morning, his henchmen showed up. They kicked the door in and turned everything upside down. I hid on the roof of the stable until dark and then grabbed some things and got away."

"That's quite a pickle you're in. And I can see why nothing holds you here anymore."

"And if they have seen us together, you might not be safe either. But we just have to last until dawn, and then we're gone forever," she said with a pleading look.

Nikolas doubted whether it would be so easy but didn't want to upset her more for the night.

# 27

## Happiness on Foreign Shores

Mathi had fallen asleep in bed, and Nikolas had set up camp on the hard floorboards. They woke up fit for the knacker's yard after only a few hours of sleep.

Some minutes later, they stood in front of the inn on the street. No one had seen them go, and they didn't meet anyone as they went to the port. Nikolas made his way through the piles of goods, and Mathi followed him like a shadow.

"You're on time, I like that." Nikolas had found José, who was standing on the quayside.

Most of the crew members were already on board.

"I hope I don't lose your favour if I ask you to take another passenger on board."

Mathi slipped her hood back.

"A woman?" The captain seemed uninterested, as Nikolas had guessed.

"She has to leave the city."

"There are certainly other ways. What am I supposed to do with a woman on board and one who has dirt under her carpet?"

"I assure you that you have nothing to fear from me." Mathi's voice trembled. "I have nothing left that allows me to live an honourable life."

"Suppose I believe you... I still can't afford an extra mouth to feed who can't work."

"Why shouldn't I be able to work?" Nikolas saw the rage in her eyes, even though her voice sounded calm and measured.

"May I speak to you briefly alone?" Nikolas put a hand on the captain's shoulder, and they took a few steps away from Mathi.

"Here, that should cover your costs for the whole crossing if you take her with you. And the scouring of the planks and patching of sails can also be done by a woman." Not so much the last words as the coins that Nikolas had placed in his hand made José change his mind.

"But I don't take any responsibility for what might or might not happen to her on the ship. A woman alone amongst men can lead to all sorts of unpleasant situations."

"I would be less worried about her than I'd be about your men."

The sailors were flabbergasted when Mathi climbed on board, but the captain quickly dissolved the gaffing crowd and gave orders to hoist the anchor.

They brought their few belongings belowdecks and found a small space out of the general sight where another hammock could be attached for Mathi. Not long after, Nikolas was busy with the running rigging to allow for a steady but controlled departure from the port and down the river. Mathi stood lost on deck, trying to stay out of the way. Eventually, she found a corner by the steps to the afterdeck and watched as they slowly left the city behind. The sun rose and covered the walls and roofs with a golden shimmer. Then the river snaked through green pastures and between raised dams and guided them towards an unknown future.

Nikolas watched her and remembered when he had boarded a ship for the first time and sailed down this very river. He knew all too well what she was feeling, but he had no time to sit down with her. When he looked at her again, she had fallen asleep, curled up with her back to the railing.

For breakfast, he wakened Mathi, as Nikolas knew that the usually light meal could keep seasickness at bay. The oatmeal, though, tasted horrible, and Mathi watched suspiciously over the ship's cook, Antonio, as he prepared lunch. He was making lobscouse, which could be served for the next few days. She helped peel turnips and suggested adding onions. She also saved the water of some gherkins and added it to the pot. The cook was annoyed about the meddling in his galley, but when the sailors patted him appreciatively on the shoulder and even the captain praised the tasty meal, Antonio gladly accepted her help.

Over the next few days, Mathi found more work to do. As she was able to write, she took stock of supplies and planned meals in advance until they could buy new resources at the next stopover. The captain was impressed when she presented him with her list and more so when her calculation came out even to the day. She knotted strings and ropes, patched clothes and sails, and soon worked as much as the men on board. But when she scrubbed the deck, the first sailor couldn't hold back voicing his thoughts and desires.

Mathi had tied up her skirt and knelt on all fours as a rough hand patted her buttock.

"How about you wipe me down afterwards, but nice and wet?"

The ensuing laughter attracted the attention of the captain. Nikolas stood next to him on the afterdeck, and they had a clear view of what was happening.

Mathi rose slowly, and when she turned to her assaulter, she smiled at him sweetly. But suddenly she pulled up her arm and hit him with the heel of her hand up his nose. Dazed, the man, who was well more than a head taller and broader than her, went down with a thud. The laughter fell silent, and a murmur went through the ranks of the gaffers.

"This is what I meant, I would worry more about your men," Nikolas said casually. "I speak from experience."

José had to laugh out loud and then asked his sailor why he was lying around so lazily.

A few days later, the next one tried to take on Mathi. She was handing out food when two hands grabbed her bosom from behind.

"May I have a second helping afterwards?" a voice murmured into her ear.

Nikolas was surprised to see a slightly panicked expression on her face, and for a moment, he thought about intervening. But like an irritated cat, Mathi wound out of the grasp and returned the advance with sharp claws. The man's face went white, then red, as his genitals were painfully squeezed.

"Do it again, and you'll only piss points into the snow. Do we understand each other?" The man nodded and swallowed heavily. "Good. And that applies to all of you. Is that clear to everyone now?" The men grumbled, conceding, as they stared down their plates and mugs. Finally, she let go of the sailor and picked up the soup pot again. "Do you want the second helping now?" The sailor sat down, shaking his head and holding his best piece in silence. For the rest of their journey, no one dared to get into Mathi's way, but behind her back, they boasted about what they would like to do with her.

Nikolas did not participate in these conversations, but he could not help having his own secret fantasies.

In Calais, they picked up more goods. The additional load slowed them down despite a strong breeze. Shortly thereafter, they became the target of a raid.

"All men on deck!" came the order when the lookout reported the nearing danger.

Nikolas knew they stood no chance. The pirate ship was smaller and more agile. It cut through the water quickly, and soon they could recognize the well-equipped men on board.

"Arm yourselves and prepare for battle." José, too, knew that they could not escape fight, and like Nikolas, he knew that this would be an unequal battle to their detriment unless a miracle happened.

They watched the pirates crossing their way and had no choice but to slow down.

"I have an idea." Nikolas jumped onto the deck and ordered a few men to follow him.

"Where are the bags of pepper?" he shouted to Mathi, who was hiding belowdecks.

"Behind those boxes."

Normally, pepper was transported in whole corns. But he recalled seeing some bags of pepper already ground when he had loaded them in Hamburg. Quickly, everyone grabbed a bag and brought it to the deck.

"Make everything ready to change course! If I give the signal, we must all work together," he screamed eagerly.

The sailors looked at him, aghast.

"Everyone, ready to change course," José repeated the order.

The pirate ship was keeping right ahead of them, forcing them to slow down as the gap between the two ships had already narrowed to twenty steps, and they could hear their chanting and sabre rattling at full volume. Nikolas and his helpers dragged the bags to the foredeck.

"Scatter the pepper in the wind!"

They did as they were told and threw handfuls of ground pepper overboard. The wind blew the spice over the sea and towards their attackers, who were quickly engulfed by a cloud of pepper.

"Ready about!" sounded Nikolas's voice over the deck, and this time, they all complied with his command.

There was no manoeuvre from the other ship to block their path any longer. The pirates stumbled about with tearful eyes and burning noses as they tried to rid themselves of the burning spice.

Loud cheers erupted when they finally got a good nautical mile between themselves and the pirate ship. José shook Nikolas's hand and invited him to become a permanent crew member, which Nikolas promised to think about. For the evening, the captain ordered unrestricted access to thin beer, which again triggered a storm of enthusiasm amongst the men.

They anchored off the coast and a raucous feast began. Music and singing echoed over the mirroring surface of the sea, and Nikolas danced exuberantly with Mathi. Everyone talked giddily, and the conversations soon turned from skilled jokes to embellished anecdotes to moral-free ribaldry with the rising alcohol levels. It was already after midnight when the last of the sailors staggered to their sleeping quarters. Only the guards and José had enjoyed the alcohol only in moderation and were happily continuing their work.

Nikolas and Mathi sat next to each other on a box and let their legs dangle.

"Thank you for paying José to take me on board," she began.

"You knew that?"

"What did you think?" She leaned against his shoulder.

"I'll pay it back as soon as I can."

"Forget about it. I'm rich."

"Sure, and related to the Danish queen." They laughed.

Like a shy boy, he pushed his leg closer until it touched hers.

"I'm glad we met again," he said.

She smiled. "Me too... What kind of language do they speak in Portugal?"

"Portuguese."

"Do you speak Portuguese?"

"José taught me a little. It's not that hard when you can speak Latin."

"Ha ha, and if you can't?"

"Then it's harder." Nikolas laughed. "If you want, I can teach you. I took some notes that I can show you tomorrow."

Mathi took a deep breath. "Do you want some more beer?" She got up and filled their pitchers. "And what kind of notes are they?"

"Some vocabularies and common phrases."

"You could show them to me now."

"If you'd like," Nikolas said.

He rolled the jug between his hands, and then she turned to him and kissed him right on his mouth. Nikolas reluctantly reciprocated the advance, unsure about the situation and where it could lead. Tenderly, she opened her mouth and pushed her tongue between his lips. Nikolas felt the warmth, tasted the beer on her tongue, and answered her teasing with the tip of his tongue.

Then she withdrew. "Show me what you have."

Without another word, they got up and Nikolas followed her belowdecks. They both headed for the piles of goods and the stack of empty bags behind them. No one could see them here from the common area, and they had as much privacy as they could hope for in the confines of a merchant ship.

Mathi kissed him again, and it was as if a floodgate had opened. In the dark, Nikolas unlaced his pants and her hands felt their way between his legs. His hands, in turn, gathered her dress and grabbed her soft butt cheeks. Without parting their lips once, they sank to the ground. Mathi was lying on her back and Nikolas leaned over her. Slowly he penetrated her, and just as slowly, they moved their hips until they found a common rhythm. Unexpectedly, Mathi rolled around and sat astride on top of him. She moved smoothly and determined how deep and fast she wanted to feel him. He glided his hands under her dress and cupped her breasts. Nikolas watched, mesmerized, as she threw her head back in ecstasy and fully settled down on him, which also drove him to the climax. Exhausted, she sank to his chest, and barely a second later, she was slumbering in his arm.

They woke up as they had fallen asleep, nestled close together. He had put an arm around her, and when he noticed that she was stirring, he gently stroked the bow of her waist. Their fingers found each other, and still sleep-drunk, they caressed one another.

With the first noises on the other side of their little hideout, they, too, got up and straightened their clothes.

The next few days, the daily grind occupied both, and neither Nikolas nor Mathi showed any sign that something had changed between them that night. And so, they worked side by side as before, while Portugal was getting closer and closer.

A lull in the wind forced them into inaction for two days just before reaching their destination. On the second day, Nikolas and Mathi sat down after breakfast for some Portuguese lessons, but Mathi seemed inattentive.

"How many women have you slept with?" asked Mathi out of the blue.

"I stopped counting at a hundred," Nikolas replied with a smile.

"In each country one, or what?"

"Something like that."

"And you never met someone you wanted to spend more than one night with?"

Nikolas remained silent. He was torn between telling the truth and bragging.

"I met someone I've had a lot of fun with over the last few weeks," she said challengingly.

"Do I know him?" Nikolas joined in the banter.

"He came on board with us in Hamburg," Mathi continued.

"Where does he come from?"

"Everywhere. I think he was once a pirate."

"I think I know him. What a small world."

Mathi had to laugh. "And he was the only one on board who didn't make a pass at me."

"Maybe he knew that we would arrive soon, and your paths would part." He had to swallow hard as he spoke this truth, and if he had looked at Mathi, he would have noticed that she was fighting back her tears.

They sat in silence next to each other and looked over the sea. At first barely noticeable but then stronger and stronger, the wind finally rose as if it had rested until they had talked to each other.

Two days later, they arrived at the port of Lisbon, and in the evening, they got their payout. Most of them would be back on board in the next few days, back to Hamburg.

Nikolas had decided not to accept José's offer to work steadily on his ship. He wanted to see foreign places and visit other countries. José understood him and advised he audition with the royal court. The younger prince was supposedly infatuated with seafaring and spent a lot of money to equip expeditions. A sailor as capable as Nikolas would certainly be welcomed with open arms. Nikolas thanked the captain warmly.

Mathi also received promising help, as Antonio offered to introduce her to his wife, who could help her find work. Once again, their farewell came far too quickly, as Mathi had to go with Antonio if she wanted to take advantage of this opportunity.

# 28

## The Mariner's Legacy

The next morning, Nikolas walked up to the Castelo de São Jorge, the royal castle. He soon began to sweat. The sun shone early from the sky, and the fortress stood at the highest point of the surrounding mountain chain, towering over the city. In the shadow of the Cathedral of Sé Sedes Episcopalis, he took a break. From here, he had a good view and his gaze wandered over hills dotted with white flat houses with laundry hanging on the roofs to dry, painting colourful specks into the landscape. Down at the harbour, he saw the ships, some with one, others with two or even three, masts. His view followed the Tagus River, whose shore was lined with palm trees. Outside the city, he spotted herds of goats grazing on the dried-up slopes.

A caravan of packed donkeys made its way through the winding streets of Lisbon up to the royal residence.

Somewhere down there was Mathi, but he chased the thought of her away and got up, determined to continue his path to the castle.

He waited half the day before being admitted to an audience. He then submitted his request to the king to be allowed to take part in the royal expeditions as a sailor. John I seemed unimpressed, even dismissive. He was unreceptive to a man who didn't speak fluent Portuguese. Nikolas noticed his disinterest and tried to change the king's mind by telling him about his inventions. He explained how a compass had to be constructed to fulfil its purpose even in heavy seas. But when he also wanted to describe how to determine the position of ships without sea signs but simply with a compass and a measure of a ship's speed, the king interrupted him with a hand movement.

John I had understood everything Nikolas had told him in Latin, but he didn't bother himself to respond in this ecclesiastical language but passed on his decision to a translator. That translator told Nikolas to contact the armada, where a general would decide whether there was still a need for a common sailor.

As he left the reception room disappointed, he heard quick steps behind him. Nikolas turned around and saw a young man rushing towards him, who had stood next to the throne during the audience. He addressed him in Latin.

"I want to talk to you."

"What about?"

"I followed with interest your remarks about the sightless navigation and would like to know more about it."

"Of course, but first I want to see if I have a chance to sign on with a ship down at the port."

"I am Prince Henry, the king's fourth son. I guarantee you a place on an expedition ship that will sail to Africa if you are at my service."

Nikolas listened attentively. So, this was the prince who was interested in seafaring. He was a few years younger than Nikolas, but with his bright character and apparently great understanding of navigation, he immediately gained Nikolas's sympathy.

The two young men went to the castle garden. Nikolas explained his theories about navigation and what he had already undertaken to prove them. The young prince listened intently and then convey his own ideas. Nikolas was delighted. He had never found anyone with the same interests. Until the sun set, they were immersed in discussion, and Nikolas listened enthusiastically to the construction of a triangular lateen sail that allowed crossing in front of the wind. When Nikolas explained his efforts for a smooth compass suspension, the prince described to him the magnetic properties of metals and that this was the secret behind the compass needle. Copper and lead were not magnetic and should therefore be suitable as a material for the suspension of the compass rose.

"I want to establish a school for seafarers. My father's only concern is to expand the empire, and his captains are there to take soldiers to the battleground the fastest way. I want to find a sea route to India and the Far East, but for that, I need well-trained sailors. I learned more from you in one evening than I have heard from my scholars in ten years. Would you like to teach at my Academia Nautica?"

Nikolas was deeply moved by the faith and recognition of his abilities that was shown to him, especially since it came from someone who had accumulated great knowledge in this field.

"Of course, you will also get the opportunity to go on expeditions yourself," the prince added when Nikolas did not immediately agree.

From then on, Nikolas went up to the castle every day. Together, they made plans for the subjects they wanted to teach at the school. Nikolas wrote lists of equipment that needed to be purchased, and Prince Henry wrote letters to scholars whom he wanted to teach at the academy. Soon Henry invited him to move into a guest chamber in the castle to spare him the long walk up the hills every day.

The friendship between the two men was suspiciously eyed at the court, but in addition to their technical discussions about seafaring and the deliberations about starting a school, Nikolas also learned Portuguese, and soon he was able to speak fluently, which earned him the respect of the other inhabitants of the castle.

He even took part in royal hunts and was always happy when he could dismount the horse again.

At the beginning of the next year, the prince had a lot to do, as the king was planning an attack on Morocco and Henry was to lead some of the ships. On those days, Nikolas went into the city, where he worked his way through the scrolls and folios of the university. In particular, he was attracted to the records of Greek antiquity. He devoured the works of Seneca, buried himself in Strabo's writings, and became deeply engrossed in Aristotle's theories.

He would have liked to have shown his old helmsman Hein the proofs of the ancient Greeks that the earth was a sphere after all, and at this thought, he had an idea. If one were to simply sail farther west, they would eventually have to hit land again, for example, India. But no one knew how far it was. He studied all the maps the library had to offer and arranged for Henry to buy up a variety of nautical charts, as Ben had done years ago, and personally oversaw their matching and updating.

Often, he ventured out of the city early in the morning to a nearby mountain, from where he saw the ships arriving over the sea and entering the port of Lisbon on the Tagus. He watched as first the masts of a ship appeared on the horizon before the body of the ship slowly came into view. There could only be one explanation for this phenomenon: the Earth was a sphere. If there was a sea route to the west, then one would have to sail for a long time without a view to the coast, and sightless navigation would be inevitable.

He went back to town humming happily. He walked through the port and watched the king's assembling troops. In a few days, the journey to the Moroccan city Ceuta would start.

From the harbour, he wanted to go back to the library, but he was stopped at the next street corner as he bumped into Mathi.

He hadn't seen her since they had left the Santa Isabella upon their arrival in Lisbon. Twice, Mathi had written to him and told him how she was doing. Everything seemed to be going well, and Antonio had kept his promise to help her find work. He had always wanted to write an answer, but his new life and work had completely taken over his every thought. And at some point, it was simply too late to write back without losing face. Nor had he tried to find her for fear of stirring up old feelings. But now, after all these months, he was glad to see her.

"What are you doing here?" he exclaimed in surprise.

"I live here, if you haven't forgotten it."

She had answered him with a laugh and covered her disappointment over the loss of contact so well that Nikolas didn't notice it. She had become a little fuller, which looked good on her, and Nikolas avoided staring at her plumper bosom. Her skin was suntanned, and with her dark hair, she looked almost like a local. They hugged like old friends.

"I heard that a Northman was turning the royal court upside down."

"Really? I haven't met any Northman yet." Both laughed. "How are you?"

"I'm still working at Antonio's. He has now opened his own inn and it is going pretty well. Before, they had a small shop where I helped his wife. But I told you about it all in my last letter."

It was only now that Nikolas realized that she was disappointed, and he was sorry that he had never answered.

"I get free food and lodging and a small wage. I try to save most of it so I can buy a few goats and a small hut on the outskirts of town when I'm old," she explained to cover the silence.

"That sounds good. I'll make sure to come and visit you."

"If you'll ever find the time."

"And what about the men? Are you still beating them up or has someone finally caught you?" He tried to cheer up the mood a little.

"Nothing new. Those I want do not want me, and those I do not want run after me like foolish dogs... If you want, you can come by some time, and we can talk a little longer. I must run now."

"I'll do that."

"Yes please, you'd be very welcome." Mathi looked at him seriously, and he nodded in honesty. They said goodbye and went their separate ways again.

Nikolas had genuinely planned to visit her. But two days later, Henry called upon him and told him that he would also sail to Ceuta. Nikolas packed his belongings, many of which contained maps and measuring instruments, and the next day, he finally stepped on the planks of a ship again.

They conquered Ceuta, and Portugal was able to extend its realm to the African continent. Henry took over the administration and defence of the city, so they had to stay there for a few months.

After the city was secured and the troops positioned to maintain peace even without the presence of their supreme commander, Nikolas and Henry took the next ship back to Portugal. They did not land in Lisbon but instead went ashore at cape São Vicente. Here, Henry had chosen the small town of Sagres to finally establish his academy.

The two men worked tirelessly. Nikolas was particularly concerned with collecting books and making his first transcripts as more and more scholars came from all over the world, attracted by the knowledge that was now concentrated in Sagres. Nikolas loved to talk to all the newcomers and learn new things and hear about different ideas. He often sat in the great hall for nights on end and listened to the lectures and ensuing dialogues. His eloquence in many languages was one of his greatest treasures, and he received many requests to translate foreign texts.

Two years after the conquest of Ceuta, they discovered the island of Madeira, later the Azores and the Cape Verde islands. Nikolas perfected his ideas about sightless navigation and developed the method of dead reckoning, which allowed one to determine the position of a moving ship by using a previously determined fix point, direction, speed, and time, but for now, there was still no need for his discoveries, as the expeditions continued to focus on the coast of Africa.

It had been six years when he returned to Lisbon to bring books from the library to Sagres. With two scholars, he scoured the shelves and chests, and since little had changed since his last visit, they quickly collected the writings that were deemed to be useful to the academy.

The morning before they left for Sagres, Nikolas finally honoured his promise and went to Antonio's inn. He ordered queijo cheese with bread as a starter and a cooling gaspacho soup. A ten-year-old boy brought him the goat's cheese, and he asked him where Antonio was. Shortly after, the man himself came out of the kitchen.

"Is there anything wrong with your food, sir?" asked Antonio.

"On the contrary. This cheese reminds me of my homeland. Don't you recognize me?"

"Pepper! Nikolas!" Antonio laughed, pressed Nikolas to his chest, and sat down with him. "I have heard that you are in the service of the royal court?"

"Not directly. Prince Henry brought me to his Academia Nautica."

"In Sagres?"

"Yes, I will return tomorrow morning."

"Have you visited Mathi?" asked Antonio.

"I had hoped to meet her here. Is she no longer working for you?"

"Sure, she is, but only now and then. She makes the goat's cheese that reminded you of your homeland."

Nikolas looked at the creamy white pieces on his plate and thought back to the Wild Boar in Hamburg. "Is she coming in today?"

"No, but she doesn't live far. If you follow the road up the hill, you will come to a small house with a few olive trees in front of it."

Nikolas smiled. "She's not old enough to retire yet."

"Oh no. She is a woman in her best years. You really should visit her. She never married; you know?" Antonio had the same serious expression on his face as Mathi when she last asked him to visit her.

After finishing his meal and begging Antonio to let him pay for it, which he declined as an insult, Nikolas made his way to Mathi's house. The road was stony and wound uphill. Almost all the houses had olive trees in the garden, but only the last one had five brown goats resting in their shade. He opened a small gate and the goats slowly rose to greet the visitor. He knocked on the door and his stomach tingled in excitement.

A blond boy, about seven years old, opened the door. Nikolas's eyes seemed to play a trick on him as he looked into his own image, only twenty-five years younger. At that moment, Mathi came in through the back door and dropped the wooden cheese forms she was holding in her hands when she saw him. The boy and Nikolas came to her aid.

"What are you doing here?" she asked.

"I thought I would come to visit you as promised."

"Jasper, please go and bring the goats into the stable."

"Yes, Mama."

Nikolas didn't know what to say. He looked at the boy, then at Mathi, who dodged his gaze as she hung the wooden rings on hooks from the ceiling to let them dry. Finally, she turned around.

"Is that...?" Nikolas began hesitantly.

"Yes."

"Why did you never say anything?"

"I wanted to. I didn't know how. What would it have changed?" she asked him almost reproachfully.

Nikolas remained silent. He was happy with his life, but could he have been so happy if he lived here with Mathi and his son? He looked around the little house.

"Does he know who his father is?" he finally asked.

"Yes, but he doesn't know it's you."

"May I..." Nikolas could hardly arrange his thoughts. "Can I talk to him?"

"Of course."

Nikolas went outside, but Jasper had disappeared with the goats. He walked around the house and found the boy in the stable. Jasper had tied the animals up, given each one a handful of oats, and was milking them.

Nikolas took another bucket and a stool leaning against a wall and sat next to the boy.

"May I help you?" asked Nikolas.

Jasper looked over his shoulder at his mother, who nodded encouragingly.

"But be careful. Don't pull, just press," Jasper said, worried.

"I'll give it a try and you can tell me if I'm doing it right."

The boy nodded and watched Nikolas's efforts closely.

"Not bad," Jasper finally said. "Why can you speak German?"

"I come from Hamburg, like your mother," Nikolas explained.

"That's up in the north. There's snow in winter, and it takes two months with a ship to get there."

"That's true."

"A bird would be faster."

Nikolas was surprised, as he had never thought about how a bird could simply fly a straight distance from one place to another and did not have to make longer detours along a coast.

"The sails of a ship are similar to the wings of a bird, both use the wind to move forward," Nikolas explained.

"Do you think a ship could fly if it had wings?" Jasper had stopped milking and stared into the blue sky outside the stable, lost in thought.

They talked about the most fantastic things until all the goats were milked, and then carried the milk to a small, cool stone building, where shelves were full of cheese wheels at all stages of maturation.

Mathi invited Nikolas to dinner, which he gladly accepted. They took turns telling stories about Hamburg until Jasper fell asleep with his head on the table. After Mathi had carried the boy to bed, she accompanied Nikolas to the garden gate.

"I have to go back to Sagres tomorrow," Nikolas said.

"I wish you a good journey."

Nikolas saw her smile in the moonlight. He turned around and opened the small gate, but then paused.

"Do you want to marry me?" he asked abruptly.

She smiled still. "No."

Nikolas was confused. The evening had been harmonious, and he quietly begun to entertain the idea of staying with her.

"But it would be nice if you could visit more often. And Jasper has told me that he finds you rather nice." She still looked at him smiling.

"I promise." Nikolas's heart was heavy. He had a son. Although he had seen him for the first time today, he was already falling in love with this child and the idea of family life, which did not make it easy for him to say goodbye.

"I'll be back next month."

"We're looking forward to it."

And with that, he broke off and marched down the hill to the harbour without turning back.

This time, though, he kept his promise and came back the next month, and the following month, and every month after that during which he was not on a voyage with Prince Henry.

He supported Mathi financially, and after a year, they lived together like a family in the few days he spent in Lisbon. But they never got married, as Mathi insisted on keeping her freedom and leaving him his own.

Over the years, Nikolas went to sea less and less often. He had been able to preserve the treasure of Störtebeker almost completely, and on one of his last voyages, he brought it to a place that even the notorious pirate could not have chosen better.

Instead, he had discovered a new passion. Teaching. He smiled, reminiscing about Magister Deubel, who had planned for him a future as a lecturer at a cathedral school, and how he had run away at the very thought of it. But now that his hair had turned grey, Nikolas found it an honour to pass on his knowledge to the next generations.

Jasper had also come to the Academia Nautica, but he was less interested in seafaring than flying. He travelled a lot to study at other academies, but he found no one who thought it possible for a ship, or even a human, to fly like a bird. In Florence, at long last, he met a young student named Leonardo in the studio of the sculptor Verrocchio, who listened, fascinated to his theories and presented a sketch for a flying apparatus the next day. From then on, Jasper travelled to Italy again and again to share his knowledge that he had accumulated on his travels with Leonardo and to use his infinite talent to record his ideas on paper.

Nikolas returned to Lisbon every month, as Mathi stubbornly refused to give up her independence and move with him to Sagres. But when it became clear that she could not cope without help, he stayed with her until the morning that she did not wake up next to him.

* * *

It was a stormy night. Nikolas had long retired to bed. His little house was not far from the academy, so as often as his old bones allowed, he could go over and participate in the latest developments.

He had made himself comfortable before the open fire and was reading the work of Aristotle again, bent close over the pages, when someone knocked on the door.

The knocking didn't stop, so he finally shuffled to the door and opened it. A young man stood in front of him. He wore the clothes of a trader and an old leather hat on his head, under which brown curls fell over his ears.

"Are you the scholar of the mariners, about whom all the world is talking?" the stranger asked in Italian.

"All the world? The wind seems to be blowing strongly tonight and exaggerated many things you might have heard," Nikolas muttered.

"I want you to teach me."

"The wind not only exaggerated, but also seems to have lost half the message. I don't teach anymore."

"But you are still often seen in the observatory, and not just as a listener."

"So, you heard this little breeze."

The young man was not easy to get rid of, and even the rain that had now started didn't seem to move him from this porch, so Nikolas finally asked him in.

They warmed up with a hot cup of tea, and the conversation started to flow. Nikolas was pleasantly surprised by the young man. What ultimately changed his mind, though, was the fact that this greenhorn proposed to sail west to reach China and India.

"I'm too old to keep teaching, but if you want to have a chat with an old man tomorrow, I'll be happy to invite you for a cup of tea again."

The young man beamed with joy. "Maybe two or three cups?"

"Maybe that too. But tell me your name so I know to whom I pass on my most precious treasure."

"Christopher Columbus."

# Glossary

*Aftercastle:* Castle or raised defensive fortification on the stern of a ship

*Afterdeck:* The open deck area towards the stern of a ship

*Barge:* Type of ship that transports goods

*Beam reach:* Course with the wind, where the wind comes sideways from the back

*To bear away:* Change of direction of a sailing ship towards lee (averted wind side), so that the wind comes sideways from the back. Opposite of "to head up".

*Bilge:* Lowest level on a ship directly above the keel. Water often penetrates in wooden ships, and the bilge has to be regularly emptied.

*Bow/Nose:* Front of a ship

*Bowline hitch:* Knot for a fixed loop

*Braies:* Type of trouser, In the later Middle Ages used exclusively as undergarments.

*Canonicus scholasticus:* Ecclesial schoolmaster

*Capstan:* A vertical-axled rotating machine developed for use on sailing ships to multiply the pulling force of seamen when hauling ropes

*Caravel:* Ship type of the fourteenth to sixteenth century with two to four masts. Portuguese and Spanish caravels were crucial for the expeditions along Africa's coasts. Columbus's *Niña* and *Pinta* were caravels.

*Cog:* Ship type with one mast mainly used by the Hanseatic League as a trading ship, but sometimes equipped as a warship.

*Crow's nest:* Secured lookout at the top of a mast

*Cutter:* Smaller sailing boat

*Forecastle:* Castle or raised defensive fortification on the bow of a ship

*Foredeck:* The deck at the forward part of a ship

*Galley:* Ship's kitchen

*Halliard:* Ropes used to hoist or strike a sail; part of the running rigging

*To head up:* Change of direction of a sailing ship windward, so that the wind is coming from the front. Opposite of "to bear away".

*Heeling:* Tilt of a ship to one side

*Helm:* The steering gear of a ship, especially the tiller or wheel

*Helmsman:* Member of the ship's crew responsible for steering the ship

*To hoist:* Raising or pulling up of a rope, opposite of "slack off"

*Holk:* A type of medieval sea craft, a technological predecessor of the carrack and caravel

*In irons:* The "trapped" condition a sailing ship finds itself in when the bow of the ship is headed into the wind and the ship has stalled and is unable to manoeuvre

*Keelhauling:* A form of punishment and potential execution once meted out to sailors at sea

*Likedeeler:* Archaic/Nordic term for someone who divides something (goods or loot) evenly

*Lobscouse:* Lobscouse (or lapskaus) is a thick Norwegian stew made of meat and potatoes

*Main yard:* The yard is a log that holds the sail. The main yard is fastened to the very back mast

*Nock:* The upper fore corner of a log where the sail is fastened; related to nook ("corner, recess")

*Portside:* Left side (as seen from the stern to the bow)

*Railing:* Some form of banister surrounding the open deck

*Rigging:* Ropes on a ship made up of standing and parts of the running rigging

*Running rigging:* Ropes used to move the sails

*Scholaris major:* Older scholars of a monastery/ecclesial school who were prepared for clerical duties (scholares majoris, Pl.)

*Scholaris sub jugo:* Literally "scholar under the yoke", meaning under guardianship (usually clergy)

*Sheet/ sheet* Rope to manoeuvre the sail, part of the running

| | |
|---|---|
| *rope:* | rigging |
| *Ship's kobold:* | A goblin specific to ships; in German "Klabautermann", derived from the lower German klabastern: "to bluster". It's a bad omen if the ship's kobold shows itself. |
| *Shrouds:* | Traction that supports a mast on both sides towards the back, part of the standing rigging |
| *Sloop:* | Small sailing boat similar to a cutter |
| *Snuutje:* | Snout, term of endearment in the sense of darling |
| *Standing rigging:* | Ropes that brace and reinforce the masts, part of the standing rigging |
| *Starboard:* | Right side (as seen from the stern to the bow) |
| *Stern:* | Back of a ship |
| *The Hanseatic League* | A medieval commercial and defensive confederation of merchant guilds and market towns in Central and Northern Europe. |
| *To sound:* | To measure the depth of the water |
| *Topmast:* | Extension of a mast |
| *Victual Brethren:* | Likely derived from the French "vitailleurs" for army supply and "viktualien" (lat.), which means foodstuffs. Störtebeker's Victual Brethren originally provisioned blockaded locations, such as during the siege of Stockholm by Danish troupes, before turning to piracy. |

# A Final Note

I hope you liked my story, and the fifteenth century has come a little closer. *The Mariner's Legacy* guided you to historical places, introduced you to some characters, who actually lived, and let you take part in nautical developments of the Middle Ages. But I allowed myself some poetic licences. As such, the crew of the Gundelinde is completely made up, and whether sewing machines were invented as described is not verified. By now, historians dispute the existence of the Academia Nautica (*escola náutica*), founded by Henry the Seafarer to grow his expeditions, and it was most likely a story made up in later centuries.

I would like to thank my editor Michelle Hope for correcting my translation and putting everything into fluent English.

If you liked *The Mariner's Legacy*, please recommend it to fellow readers and take a minute to leave a short review on Amazon or another platform of your trusting.

Eva Laurenson

A message from your book

I hope you have arrived safely after your travels. Should you need to make space in your bookshelf, please give me to a library, a book café, or a bookish friend. I would love to be read more.

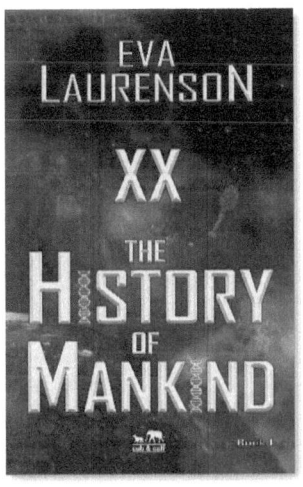